DISAPPEARED

FRANCISCO X. STORK

ARTHUR A. LEVINE BOOKS
AN IMPRINT OF SCHOLASTIC INC.

Library of Congress Cataloging-in-Publication Data

Names: Stork, Francisco X., author.
Title: Disappeared / Francisco X. Stork.
Description: First edition. | New York, NY : Arthur A. LevineBooks, an
imprint of Scholastic Inc., 2017. | Summary: Four months ago Sara Zapata's
best friend, Linda, disappeared from the streets of Juarez, and ever since
Sara has been using her job as a reporter to draw attention to the girls
who have been kidnapped by the criminals who control the city, but now she
and her family are being threatened—meanwhile her younger brother,
Emiliano, is being lured into the narcotics business by the promise of big
money, and soon the only way for both of them to escape is to risk the
dangerous trek across the desert to the United States border.
Identifiers: LCCN 2017017320 | ISBN 9780545944472 (hardcover : alk. paper)
Subjects: LCSH: Brothers and sisters—Mexico—Ciudad Juárez—Juvenile
fiction. | Women—Violence against—Mexico—Ciudad Juarez—Juvenile
fiction. | Crime—Mexico—Ciudad Juárez—Juvenile fiction. |
Kidnapping—Mexico—Ciudad Juarez—Juvenile fiction. | Reporters and
reporting—Mexico—Ciudad Juárez—Juvenile fiction. | Ciudad Juárez
(Mexico)—Fiction. | CYAC: Brothers and sisters—Fiction. |
Kidnapping—Fiction. | Reporters and reporting—Fiction. | Ciudad Juárez
(Mexico)—Fiction. | Mexico—Fiction.
Classification: LCC PZ7.S88442 Di 2017 | DDC [Fic]—dc23 LC record
available at https://lccn.loc.gov/2017017320

ISBN 978-0-545-94447-2

10 9 8 7 6 5 4 3 2 1   17 18 19 20 21

Printed in the U.S.A.   23
First edition, October 2017

Book design by Christopher Stengel

FOR JOHN A. SYVERSON

One Hour Late

By Sara Zapata

On the morning of November 14, the day she was kidnapped, Linda Fuentes opened the door to my house and walked into the kitchen, where my family was having breakfast. As usual, I wasn't ready. Linda and I had an ongoing argument: She said I was always late, and I said she got to my house early to bask in the adoration of my younger brother, Emiliano. But we had been best friends for fourteen years, so we could forgive each other anything. I heard her laughing and chatting with my mother and Emiliano until I was ready to go.

Our routine had been the same every morning for the past two years. We walked the six blocks from my house to Boulevard Pablo II, where we caught a bus that would take us to the Cathedral. From there I would catch another bus to the offices of this newspaper, and Linda walked three blocks to her job at a shoe store on Francisco Villa Avenue. Linda had dropped out of school and taken the job at the shoe store when her father was paralyzed in a construction accident. Her salary, along with a small income that her mother made from sewing, supported her parents and two younger sisters.

Linda always waited with me until my bus arrived. We stayed together as much as possible, partly because most abductions of women in Juárez occur downtown, and partly as protection against the comments of men driving or walking by. Every time a man said something offensive, Linda and I would whisper "puchi" to each other and laugh. I found an empty bus seat that morning—a small miracle—and when I looked out the window, I saw Linda jump up and down in excitement over my good luck. As the bus pulled away, she stuck her tongue out at me.

That was the last time I saw my best friend.

I worked all day at this newspaper. At seven p.m. I got a phone call from Linda's mother. I knew as soon as I heard Mrs. Fuentes's shaky voice that something terrible had happened. Linda got off work at four, and she had never been home later than six. If you are a daughter or a sister or a wife in Juárez, the one thing you always do if you are going to be late is call. And if your friend is one hour late and she hasn't called home, your heart begins to break.

Mrs. Fuentes was hoping against hope that Linda and I had decided to go to the movies after I finished work. She knew we would never do that without calling our families first, but when you are worried, you grasp at straws. Mrs. Fuentes had already called the shoe store where Linda worked, and the owner told her that Linda left a few minutes after four that afternoon. She walked toward the bus station with plenty of time to catch the 4:30 bus that would get her home by six at the latest. Linda usually left with another employee from the store, but that day, she traveled those three blocks alone.

What do you do? Where do you go when your best friend

has disappeared, and you know deep inside that the worst has happened? You pray for a miracle, but you act like a detective. I called the bus company and was assured that there were no accidents or other unusual occurrences on Linda's route. When I got home, I asked a neighbor with a car to drive me downtown on the same streets the bus takes. We parked the car near the Cathedral and walked the blocks that Linda walked every day to her job. We showed Linda's picture to store owners, to bus drivers, to street vendors. We drove to municipal police headquarters and were told that they had no jurisdiction to investigate missing girls. Later that night, I took Mrs. Fuentes to the State Police, and we were told to go home and wait. "Your daughter's probably having a drink with a boy," the officer in charge said, a smirk on his face. We drove to the General Hospital. She wasn't there. A kind nurse checked with the other hospitals. Nothing.

That night, everyone who knew Linda gathered at her house. Everyone offered Linda's parents and her sisters hope. We tried to be positive, but we couldn't shake off what we knew: In ninety percent of Juárez's missing-girl cases, their bodies are found a month or two later. We agreed to make flyers with Linda's picture and personal details and decided where to post them. We made a list of all the government authorities, all the groups of mothers of missing daughters who we would contact. We went on Facebook and Twitter and asked for help. Mrs. Fuentes finally cried herself to sleep around six that morning.

It has been almost two months since Linda disappeared. Every week I accompany Mrs. Fuentes to the State Police headquarters and we inquire about Linda. We know what the answer to our questions will be, but we want to keep putting pressure on the police. We want them to know that someone cares. Mr. and Mrs. Fuentes have been called twice to the forensic offices to identify pieces of clothing found on the bodies of young women. I have seen their relief when the clothing is not Linda's, and then, immediately, the return of the restless, gnawing grief that comes from not knowing what happened to your daughter.

I wake up each morning thinking that I hear Linda's laughter in the kitchen. When I step into the bus that took us downtown every morning, I look for two seats. Sometimes I think I see her waiting for me with the ice-cream cones we treated ourselves with at the end of the day. But those brief moments of hope quickly disappear, and I feel even more alone, with a sense of her absence so real I can almost touch it.

Maybe in other cities in the world, a young woman can be one hour late and it isn't a cause for worry. In Juárez, that is simply not possible. It is true that the number of Desaparecidas has greatly diminished over the years, so the number of killings and disappearances is now, as our public officials like to tell us, "comparable to other cities of similar size." By "comparable" they mean, for example, that the number of disappearances last year was *only* sixty-four. And by November, when Linda disappeared, there had been *only* forty-six reported cases of missing girls.

But optimism at the "normal" number of disappearances will never comfort a best friend's grief. The emptiness I feel can't be filled with comparisons to other cities or with statistics. Linda, the friend who entered my house every morning without knocking, is missing. And the only way to lessen the pain is to look for her. To keep looking for her for as long as we promised our friendship would last.

I will keep looking for you, my dear friend, forever and ever.

Part I

Mexico

CHAPTER 1
SARA

"You need to give up on the missing girls," Felipe says.

Sara isn't sure she heard him correctly. Although Felipe's tone is not harsh, the index finger he points at her makes his words sound like a reprimand. He's sitting behind his desk, covered in a disordered mess of envelopes and paper. Sara looks at her editor, Juana, who stands up and closes the glass door to the office.

"Look, Sara," Felipe continues when Juana sits down. "You've done a great job with your column, but now it's time to focus on the good stuff. This is not 2010, when twenty girls went missing every month. Juárez is prospering. Tourists are coming back to the shops, nightclubs are hopping again, Honeywell just opened a new assembly plant. We need to get on board and contribute to creating a positive image. Why don't you write a weekly column on the new schools opening? The slums getting cleaned up?"

Sara feels Juana's hand on her arm. Ever since her article on Linda's disappearance, she's written a weekly profile of one of the hundreds of girls who have gone missing. That column has been her fight and her comfort, the fulfillment of the promise she made to Linda to never stop looking for her. It cannot be taken away. Juana has always been Sara's close friend and staunchest advocate, and her touch gives her strength.

Sara speaks as calmly as she can. "You're right that there aren't as many girls disappearing as a few years ago, or even a year ago," she says. "But there are still so many girls who go missing, like Susana Navarro last week. And what about the dozens still unaccounted for? Where are they? Maybe some of them are still alive. The fact that we're still getting threats is proof that our articles hit a nerve. We're the only ones keeping the pressure on the government. They'd give up if it wasn't for us."

Felipe rubs the back of his head. Sara knows he always has trouble responding to logical arguments. "Bad news doesn't sell anymore. The newspaper is finally beginning to do well. We went from daily to almost dead to weekly and now we're biweekly. I don't want to take a step backwards here. No one wants to buy ads next to pictures of missing girls."

"But that's been true for a while now," Sara says. "Has there been a specific threat?"

Felipe and Juana look at each other. Then he sighs and pushes a single sheet of paper across his desk. It's a printout of an e-mail.

If you publish anything of Linda Fuentes we will kill your reporter and her family.

Sara reads the e-mail once, then again, pausing on the words *kill, reporter, family.*

"It was sent to me around six this morning. I forwarded it to you," Felipe says to Juana. Then, fixing his eyes on Sara:

"Are you doing anything with Linda Fuentes? Research, interviews, calling people?"

"No," Sara says. She's received threats before, but this is the first time her family has been mentioned. The thought of anyone coming after Emiliano or her mother makes her shudder. But alongside fear, something like hope blooms in her chest. If someone needs to threaten her about Linda, does that mean she's still alive? She places the sheet of paper on the desk. "I mean, Linda was . . . *is* my best friend. I'm still close to her family. They live in my neighborhood, and I go with Mrs. Fuentes to the State Police headquarters every couple of weeks. But I'm not doing anything about Linda that's related to my job."

"Well, someone thinks you're investigating or writing about her." Felipe leans back in his chair and touches the pocket of his shirt, searching for the cigarettes he gave up smoking a month before. "There's something weird about this threat. It's like they know it's you who's been writing the column."

"There hasn't been a byline on the column since Sara's article on Linda," Juana says. "No one knows it's her."

"You think those people can keep a secret?" Felipe points with his hand to the room full of cubicles outside his glass wall. "And what is this about family? Since when do families of reporters get threatened? No more articles on missing girls. That's it."

"Someone has to keep the memory of these girls alive," Sara blurts out louder than she intends. She takes a deep breath and looks into Felipe's eyes. "If we don't care about them, then who will?"

"Sara," Juana says softly, "I'm with Felipe on this one. We lost two reporters during the cartel wars. They were both young and enthusiastic like you." She takes a deep breath. "If our articles were doing any good, maybe it would be worth the risk. But has a single girl turned up since we've published these profiles?"

"No," Sara says. "But if nothing else, the families know their daughters and sisters are not forgotten. That makes a difference."

"I don't want to be responsible for another dead reporter," Felipe says with finality. "No more articles on the Desaparecidas. There's more to life than just evil and pain, no? Think of something happy for a change. I want a proposal for a positive story on my desk by the end of the day." To Juana he says, "You better clear your day tomorrow so we can finish that damn budget. That's all. Let's get to work."

Sara stands and walks out of the office. She needs to do something before she speaks—or worse, shouts—the words on the tip of her tongue. She heads for the stairs that connect *El Sol*'s IT room to the main floor. They are dark and cool, as expected.

She sits on one of the steps and grabs her head. Is it true that all she can see is the suffering and injustice that need fixing? She remembers her first column about Linda, the most personal article she's ever written. It was a miracle that Juana convinced Felipe to allow one of his reporters to write about something that affected them. In the days that followed the publication of the article, *El Sol* received dozens of letters from families of missing girls. The article provided hope and comfort to many, and the positive response convinced Juana and Felipe that a regular column on the Desaparecidas was worthwhile. The column has been Sara's way of keeping Linda alive in her heart—and Felipe just killed it.

Think of something happy for a change. There's more to life than just evil and pain, no?

She gets up and stands by the steel door that leads back to the newsroom. After a few seconds, she takes a deep breath and opens it.

Think of something happy for a change.

Yes, she can do that. Of course she can do that. Can't she? She thinks of Mami, getting on with life after Papá left her, making delicious cakes for a bakery. Or her brother, Emiliano, falling in love for the first time, and how he squirmed and blushed when Sara finally got him to tell her the name of the girl he's smitten with. Just thinking about Emiliano makes Sara happy. He was going down a bad path after Papá left, and now look at him, helping other at-risk kids with his folk art business. Thank God for Brother Patricio and the Jiparis.

The Jiparis, Sara thinks. They're like the Boy Scouts, holding long hikes out in the desert that save boys from delinquency. That's a feel-good story if there ever was one. She goes back to her desk and types out a brief proposal; then she attaches it to an e-mail and sends it to Felipe. A message from Juana appears on her screen.

Let's talk. Can you come over now?

In her office, Juana gestures for Sara to close the door. Sara sits down in one of the yellow plastic chairs in front of the desk.

Juana's voice is businesslike. "I'm sorry I didn't support you in there. But this one scares me more than the other e-mails. It mentions a specific girl, and it does seem to be directed at you and . . . your family."

"I agree with you that it's written in a peculiar way," Sara says. She doesn't tell Juana that the e-mail scared her too. "It's the first threat that uses *we* instead of *I*. It's as if it came from a group or an organization of some sort."

Juana knits her eyebrows the way she does when she's trying to read someone. "Look, I know you, Sara, and I know that regardless of Felipe's orders—or mine, for that matter—you're going to try to find out who and what's behind this. *Don't.* I agree with Felipe. From all kinds of angles, this is not a good idea. You are in danger, and I don't want anything to happen to you. But also, Felipe is right. It's not good for business to be pushing negative news right now. We're finally doing well enough to hire a few more people. We're working six days a week again. I want you to stand down, as they say in the armed forces. Stand down completely."

"You don't really mean that," Sara says. "That's not the Juana Martínez I know, who always says where there's a bad smell, there's a skunk, and it's our job to find the skunks. There's a skunk behind this e-mail. I want to find it."

"This time I think we need to live with the smell," Juana says, looking away.

"Juana." Sara leans forward, waits for Juana to look at her. "When the cartel wars were raging and every newspaper reporter had been threatened, you were one of the few who kept on. Even after *El Sol* lost two reporters, you continued writing the truth. I remember reading your articles when I was in grade school. You're the reason I decided to be a reporter. Your courage is why I'm here. You can't want me to stop looking."

"It's different now," Juana says quietly.

"How?"

"I told you already. This newspaper has to survive." Then, as if regretting the tone of her words, Juana shakes her head. "Nothing I say is going to stop you, is it?"

"I can't give up," Sara says, thinking of Linda.

For a moment, Juana looks almost angry, but she says, "Keep me informed of everything. I mean *everything*." She waits for Sara's nod. "This is not a request. It is an order from your boss."

"I will. I promise."

"Here." Juana picks up a business card and hands it to Sara. "Call this guy. He's constructing a new mall near Zaragoza. I want you to do an article about why he's doing it now—what signs he sees in the city and the economy that make him think a new mall will succeed. Go to the site where he plans to build it. Get some pictures."

Sara holds the card in front of her for a few seconds. "Is this for the happy article Felipe wants me to do? I sent an idea to him a little while ago."

"No, it's a favor to someone who's willing to spend a lot on advertising. This is a business, remember? We can't do any good if we're not in business. Do this one after you write the one for Felipe."

"Okay." Sara stands. "Juana, can you forward the e-mail with the threat to me? I want to study it a little more."

Juana reluctantly hits a few keys on her computer. As Sara

is leaving, she reminds her, "Sara, the e-mail mentions the reporter's family. Your family."

Sara swallows and says softly, "I know."

Back at her desk, Sara thinks for a long time. Does she really want to pursue something that could affect Mami and Emiliano, the two people she loves the most? They took so many precautions after Sara received her first threat. Their address is not in any public records. All the bills go to Sara at work. Juana is the only person at *El Sol* who knows where she lives, and most nights, Emiliano walks to her office after school and they take a bus home together. She's done all she can to protect herself and her family. She did all that so she could continue to investigate the disappearance of Linda and so many other girls. She owes it to them not to give up now. She will go slowly and carefully and stop if she senses any real danger. How can she "stand down," as Juana says, when Linda may be alive?

She forwards the threatening e-mail to Ernesto, the head of *El Sol*'s two-person IT department, and asks him if there's any way to figure out the identity of the sender. An hour later, Ernesto calls. "Just from a quick look, this e-mail was sent by someone who knows a lot about encryption. The server bounced the message around so no one can locate the sender. If it's okay with you, I'll send it to my friends." His friends are the Jaqueros, a group of technology and computer experts he knows. The Jaqueros helped her with an article she did on a joint investigation between the FBI and the Mexican Attorney General's Office. They had access to e-mails and texts betweeen cartel members and government officials that no one else could get.

Sara says what she always says when he offers to send something to the Jaqueros: "Okay, but don't break any laws."

He responds like he always does: "Who do you think we are?"

After Ernesto hangs up, Sara answers his question silently: *You're the people who will help me find my best friend.*

CHAPTER 2
EMILIANO

FRIDAY, MARCH 24
10:24 A.M.

Emiliano, in the front seat of the van, glances at Brother Patricio, who is driving and talking. He tries to think of something that will make the brother go a little faster. Emiliano wants to see Perla Rubi before she goes to volleyball practice at eleven, and he has a lot to do today. But Brother Patricio drives the way he hikes: slow and steady.

"I have to head over to El Paso and get Memo's new boots," Brother Patricio says. "I tell you, we are fortunate there was no school today. I'd never be able to do all that needs to be done before the trip next week."

"Yeah, it's too bad we had to get up at five a.m. on our day off," Paco says from the backseat.

"I'm sorry, but seven in the morning was the only time the Aguilas could play. They're a public school, remember. They aren't lucky enough to have the day off like us. Besides, we need all the exhibition games we can get."

"You got us playing again at nine tomorrow," Paco continues.

"Well, tomorrow's game is in El Paso," Brother Patricio explains. "The Conquistadors were the best team in El Paso last year. It will be a good tune-up game."

"The only tune-up I need is sleep," Paco says, yawning. "I'm burned out and the season hasn't even started."

"What are you complaining about? You barely moved all game," Pepe says.

"Hey, who scored the winning goal?"

"That was all Emiliano. You were just standing there picking your nose when the ball hit your head and bounced into the goal."

"Brother, take the other lane. It's faster," Emiliano says.

But Brother Patricio is not listening. "I wish I could take Memo to El Paso so he could try the boots on himself. It's chancy to buy boots with only a measurement."

"Why do you have to get Memo boots?" Paco asks.

Emiliano turns around and grimaces at him. That kind of question will only make Brother Patricio slow down even more.

Brother Patricio searches for Paco's face in the rearview mirror. "It's a tradition of the Jiparis Explorers Club. A Jipari gets new hiking boots at the end of his first year."

"Why do you call it an explorers' club?" Paco says. "You guys don't explore anything. All you do is get your brains fried in the desert."

Brother Patricio stops to let a car get in their lane. Emiliano throws his hands up in desperation.

"When are you going to join?" Brother Patricio asks Paco.

"When am I going to join? What's that pledge you have to take to be a Jipari?"

"You want to tell him?" Brother Patricio nudges Emiliano.

Emiliano recites impatiently, "'I will abstain from all

intoxicants. I will be honest with myself and others. I will use the knowledge and strength the desert gives me for the benefit of others.' "

"Hear that?" Paco says, animated. "That first one would kill me. While you guys are out chasing lizards, I'll be in the shade of my porch, having a cold one. If you get rid of that pledge and you let girls in, I'll sign up."

"Brother, watch it!" Emiliano shouts.

Brother Patricio slams on the brakes, just in time to avoid crashing into a truck ahead of them.

"Man, that would have been the end of all our seasons right there," Pepe says.

"I just saw my life flash before my eyes," Paco agrees, "and there were some very important things I didn't get to do."

Brother Patricio lets the truck gain some distance before he accelerates ever so slowly. "In response to your objections," he says calmly, as if they hadn't just barely escaped with their lives, "the first part of the pledge is important because so many of the kids we recruit have addiction problems. As to your second concern, we remain open to the possibility that girls will, at some point, want to be a part of the Jiparis. Women, after all, have as good or better capacity for enduring hardships, in the desert and elsewhere."

"You have a lot of experience with women?" Paco quips.

"Laugh if you will," Brother Patricio says with a mysterious grin.

Emiliano digs his cell phone out of his backpack and checks his messages. Perla Rubi's texts are always short and sweet. The last one reads:

At library. Come by.

Then there are three messages from Sara.

Can you pick up eggs and milk on the way home?
No need to come by work today. I'll take a bus.
Do you have money? I'll pay you back tomorrow. Be good.

Emiliano smiles. Sara always tells him to be good. She knows he'll have some money by the end of the day—assuming he can get to his bike while there's still daylight. Once they get to school, he'll head over to Javier's house to pick up the piñatas the younger boy made. Then he'll go to Taurus, where Memo's grandmother sewed some kind of purse. Armando, the owner of the club, is usually there till noon, and it's incredibly important that Emiliano talks to him. The kind of moneymaking opportunity he has in mind may not be around for long. But he'll never make it to Taurus by noon the way Brother Patricio is driving, or crawling. Maybe Armando will wait for him. Emiliano looks up Armando's number in his contacts and texts him:

Need to talk to you today. Got an idea that will be good for both
of us. Be there a little after 12:00. Will you be there?

Afterward, he'll take the piñatas and the purse over to Avenida Juárez and sell them to Lalo Torres, who will resell them to American tourists. All that will take Emiliano at least four hours, and then he needs to get home in time to shower and find a ride to Perla Rubi's house for her mother's birthday party. Oh, no. What about a present for Perla Rubi's mother? Maybe he can stop by one of the jewelry stores on Insurgentes after Lalo pays him. There's a ping on his phone. It is Armando's response.

I was just thinking about you. I need to talk to you too. I'll be here. But don't be too much later than 12:00.

Emiliano smiles again. If Armando wants to talk to him, that means he has some kind of business proposition in mind. Perfect. They're operating on the same wavelength. "Go, go, go," he tells Brother Patricio, who is slowing down for another yellow light. "In Mexico, yellow means step on it, Brother!"

Brother Patricio stops. The car behind him honks. "We are in a big rush, are we?" he says with a knowing grin.

"His rush is waiting for him at school," Paco says. "I keep telling him that he's barking up the wrong tree. He doesn't have a long-term chance with that kind of girl. She's too rich for him. But he doesn't listen."

It takes a few moments for Emiliano to realize that Paco is talking about Perla Rubi.

"Why doesn't Emiliano have a 'long-term chance,' as you say?" Brother Patricio asks. "She could do much worse than an honest, hardworking, law-abiding man like Emiliano."

"Hardworking, maybe," Paco says. "But honest and law-abiding? Just barely."

Emiliano sees Brother Patricio smile at Paco's words. Paco, Brother Patricio, and Emiliano all know about the time when Emiliano was not all that law-abiding. It's okay. Paco is Emiliano's best friend, and he's allowed to allude to his shady past. And he's used to Paco and Brother Patricio debating the "long-term" possibilities of his relationship with Perla Rubi. Paco's wrong, but that's okay too. Though they haven't talked about it, Emiliano knows that Perla Rubi likes him just as much as he likes her.

Finally they turn onto the tree-lined street in front of the school. Brother Patricio honks twice, and Cristobal opens the iron gates of Colegio México. Cristobal has been the security guard since before the time when schools in Ciudad Juárez needed security guards. Emiliano sticks his hand out the window and slaps him a high five as they drive by. "Perla Rubi's in the library," Cristobal tells him with a wink.

"You're living in la-la land," Paco says. "It's going to be painful to watch you crash."

"You're just jealous," Emiliano says, clicking off his seat belt, getting ready to bolt out of the van.

"Would you mind waiting until I properly park this vehicle?" Brother Patricio says. "I'll see you all here tomorrow at seven for the game against the Conquistadors. It's in El Paso, remember, so we need to give ourselves enough time to get across the border."

There's a collective groan from every single boy in the van except Emiliano. He's already sprinting to the library.

Emiliano knocks gently on the glass door of the library, and Chela, the cleaning lady, opens it for him. With a nod of her head and a smile, she points to where Perla Rubi is sitting.

"Thank you," Emiliano whispers. He looks at the round clock behind the librarian's desk as he enters. Ten forty-five. *You can't take too long talking to Perla Rubi, otherwise you'll miss Armando*, he reminds himself. He finds her at their usual table, tapping away on her laptop. She's facing away from the door, so she didn't see him walk in.

"Hello, Perla Rubi Esmeralda," he says, trying not to sound out of breath. They like using their full names with each other because the names are both so ridiculous.

"Emiliano Zapata," she says, suddenly beaming. "How was the game?"

"Okay. It was a practice game. No big deal."

"Did you win?"

"Of course. Too bad you had to come in today. Volleyball practice again?"

"Yeah, in fifteen minutes. We need all the workouts we can get. No one really minds. I got here early to study for a physics test and . . . see you."

Emiliano swallows. He tries to speak but he can't. When he looks into Perla Rubi's eyes, he is sometimes momentarily stunned. It's as if he remembers how beautiful she is and how fortunate he is and both things happen all at once.

"Are you okay?" Perla Rubi asks, more amused than concerned.

"Yes, why?"

"You seem, I don't know, strange, but in a good way."

Emiliano takes a deep breath. "I have tons to do before the party tonight, and we play again tomorrow. Brother Patricio's going a little overboard with the exhibition games."

She smiles. "How else are you going to win the state championship again?"

"We'll be exhausted by the time the real competition starts."

"Do you have time to go over your trigonometry homework?" she asks.

One of the things that Emiliano likes most about Perla Rubi is how seriously she takes her responsibilities as his tutor. He got to know her thanks to Brother Patricio, who arranged for her to tutor Emiliano when his grades fell below the average required to play soccer. They met for an hour once a week at first, and then Perla Rubi increased the meetings to twice a week. If it wasn't for her, he wouldn't be on the team. Still, he wishes he didn't have to worry about things like trigonometry. "Triangles" is the only thing he can think of saying.

"Among other things," Perla Rubi laughs. "You have a test next Wednesday, remember?"

"I . . . I can't today. I'll study this weekend. I promise."

She shakes her head, pretending to scold him. "I don't want all of Juárez to blame me if the Pumas' star midfielder flunks out."

"I'm going to study so hard, really, I will. I'll get a C-minus in every course, even if it kills me." He grins at her.

"That's what I like about you. You're so ambitious!" She tugs his right ear.

"Ouch! Hey," Emiliano says, looking at the clock in the back. "Are you going to be okay after volleyball practice? Is someone coming to pick you up?"

"My mother. Don't worry. I'll wait for her inside the school. Cristobal will keep me safe. I'll walk you to your bike. I need a break anyway."

He stands when she stands and they walk out of the library together. Chela, mopping the floor, smiles at him conspiratorially as they go by. Everyone knows there is something between him and Perla Rubi. Maybe it's time to tell her how he feels.

He stops at the top of the stairs and looks around. They're all alone.

"Are you okay?" Perla Rubi asks again, this time concerned.

Emiliano takes a deep breath. "Everyone thinks we're boyfriend and girlfriend."

"Yes, I think they do." She looks down, and Emiliano notices her breath quicken. His has as well. "Is that bad?"

"No. I mean . . . are we? We've never talked about it."

"That's true. We never have."

"I'd like to be."

Perla Rubi nods, her eyes still on the steps. She's wearing a one-piece outfit that he's seen on professional tennis players. A pair of blue athletic shorts peek from under her short white skirt. Her skin is smooth, a shade lighter than his. A few strands of black hair stick to her temple. She raises her head, looks deep into his eyes, and then leans forward and kisses him on the cheek.

"What was that for?" Emiliano says.

"For being patient."

"Is that what I am? Brother Patricio thinks I'm impatient."

"You're patient with me." Then she says, "Do you want to talk about *us*? You've never needed to before."

He looks away for a moment and then at her. "I think I know how you feel about me. And you know what I feel. Don't you?"

Only a few seconds pass before Perla Rubi responds,

but they seem like a lifetime to Emiliano. "Yes, you do, and yes, I do."

Emiliano turns her slightly so that they are facing each other, their bodies almost touching. "Can I say how I feel? Can you tell me? I would like to hear it." Warmth spreads through him.

Perla Rubi touches Emiliano's lips with her index finger. Finally, she says, "Emiliano . . . my parents are very strict. They know we're friends. I don't want to have to lie to them. So it's better for me if how I feel about you, how we feel toward each other, remains unsaid. Everyone knows that we're together. And *we* know what we feel, and that's all that matters."

Perla Rubi's words make Emiliano feel desperately happy and desperately confused. "But . . ."

"What? Tell me."

"Your parents wouldn't be okay with me being more than your friend." He means it as a question, but it doesn't come out that way.

She puts her arm gently around his and they walk down the stairs. When they reach the bottom, she says, "Emiliano . . ."

"That's okay," he says. "You don't have to say anything."

Just then Perla Rubi's phone rings. She steps away to answer it, and while she's talking, Emiliano berates himself for starting a serious conversation when he's so pressed for time. He's grateful for what she's given him. She feels about him the way he feels about her. Does he really need more? Why should he feel disappointed?

Perla Rubi hangs up. "That was Mamá. She asked me if

you were here. Before we go outside, do you want to talk some more about this?"

"No, I'm good."

She studies him. Then she drops her backpack at her feet and hugs him. "Emiliano, my father worked very hard to be where he is and to give my mother and me the kind of life we have. So they're concerned that whoever I fall in love with will—"

"Take care of you in the manner you're accustomed?" He doesn't mean the words to sound as bitter as they do.

Perla Rubi's embarrassed silence is all the answer he needs. After a few moments, she says, "Tonight you'll meet my mother. I've told her about your business and all you do for the Jiparis. She says she wants to talk to you. That's a good sign. My mother will like you, I know she will, and then . . . we'll work on my father."

"You have it all planned out."

"Yes, I do." She looks into his eyes until Emiliano blushes. Then she grabs his hand and pulls him outside. "Come early tonight so you and Mamá have a chance to talk."

"What should I say to her?"

"Tell her about your business. She loves folk art. You'll see when you walk through the house. Tell her about the motor-cycle you're going to buy soon and the shops you hope to open when you get out of school. Just be yourself. How many times have you told me you want to make enough money that your mother doesn't have to work? Tell her that. I'm not asking you to say anything you don't mean or be anyone you're not."

They walk to the awning where the bikes are kept. Perla Rubi is right. Since Emiliano's father abandoned them, he's been filled with a wanting that's a lot like anger. Every month when he and Sara sit at the kitchen table to pay the bills, he wants more and more to be rich. He wants a nice house for his mother, the kind of house his father was planning to buy before he left for the United States. He wants a motorcycle so he can get Sara to and from work safely. He wants to give his family and himself all that his father promised to give but didn't. This wanting became more intense after he met Perla Rubi.

Emiliano rolls out his old bike with the trailer attached. "Got to go. Duty calls," he says.

"Whenever I see you on your bike, you remind me of a knight and his horse."

"That's it," he says, mounting the bike. "I'm the knight off to kill the dragon and you're the princess. My princess. Princess Perla Rubi de la Esmeralda."

She grins. "Go slay the dragon, my knight, Don Emiliano de la Zapata. I'll be here waiting."

CHAPTER 3
SARA

Sara gets a call from Lupita, the secretary who Felipe and Juana share. "The big bad boss wants to see you. Like now."

When Sara gets to Felipe's office, he is, as usual, doing three things at once: talking to the staff photographer, Elias; holding a phone to his ear; and typing on his keyboard. "You're on with the Boy Scouts article. Wednesday's edition," he tells Sara. "Elias will take pictures."

"What?"

"He means the Jiparis," Elias says.

"Wednesday? This coming Wednesday?" Sara says.

"A week from this coming Wednesday. So we got time to do some deep, undercover, investigative research together." Elias waggles his eyebrows at her. "He wants us to go on an overnight trip with the group. We'll have to share a tent."

"In your dreams." Sara says. "Oh, I think I may need some pictures for the article I'm writing on the new city buses."

"Anything for you," Elias says.

Sara rolls her eyes. Why should Elias be any different today? Back at her desk, she looks at the business card that Juana gave her. Enrique Cortázar. She doesn't recognize the name. A rich developer willing to advertise in *El Sol*. How can interviewing someone about a mall be more important than investigating the disappearance of young girls?

Every job has its bad parts. She opens her top drawer and places the card in there. First she has to write the Jipari article. On the group's website, she finds a piece about how the Jiparis got started. The name *Jipari* comes from the Tarahumara, an indigenous people in the western part of Chihuahua. The Tarahumaras played a game called *rarájipari* with a wooden ball. Teams of four kicked the ball over many miles, and when one got tired, the person running behind him continued the game. The Jiparis try to support one another in that same fashion.

Sara knows she needs a specific example of how the Jiparis changed the lives of one of their members. Emiliano's story would be perfect. Two years ago, after their father left, he was caught shoplifting an expensive video camera from an electronics store. He would have gone to jail if Brother Patricio had not intervened. A week later, Brother Patricio took Emiliano on a hiking trip to the Sierra Tarahumara. Emiliano has never talked about that trip, but something important happened there, because when he returned, the shoplifting and petty theft were over and he and Brother Patricio founded the Jiparis. There's no better Jipari story than that.

But she would need to get Emiliano's consent to write about him, and there's no way he would agree. The delinquent period in his life is not something her brother likes to talk about. Maybe she can interview his friend Javier. Emiliano told her that Brother Patricio found Javier in a juvenile detention center where he was sent for stealing to support a heroin addiction. It was Emiliano who discovered Javier's talent for making paper piñatas and all kinds of papier-mâché animals. Now Emiliano sells his sculptures in folk art stores around Juárez, and Javier helps support his mother and three sisters while going to school. Javier lives in one of Juárez's worst slums, so a photograph of Javier in front of his house would be good. She stands to walk over to Elias's desk, but then sees Ernesto and Guillermo, one of the senior reporters at *El Sol*, talking to each other. Guillermo motions for her to come over.

"Sara, can you believe this guy is not coming to my daughter's quinceañera tonight? Tell him that's not acceptable," Guillermo says.

"I don't believe in quinceañeras," Ernesto says to Sara. "It's ridiculous to spend all that money on dresses and hairdos. Why? Just so his daughter can boast that her party was better than some other girl's. He should put the money into a savings account for college."

Sara happens to agree with Ernesto, but she knows how much Guillermo loves Aracelis, his only daughter. "I think the quinceañera obviously means a lot to Aracelis," she says, "and we should respect Guillermo's wishes to make her happy."

Ernesto gives her one of those *I expected more from you* looks. "That's why we never get anywhere in this country. Sentimental crap."

"You have a computer chip for a heart," Guillermo says.

"And you have a sponge for a brain."

"Why do we have to work with people like him?" Guillermo asks Sara.

"You know I'm right, even if you don't admit it," Ernesto tells him.

"You're coming, right, Sara?" Guillermo says to her.

"Yes, I wouldn't miss it. And thanks for letting me bring my mother as my date. Ernesto, you should come. Even if you dislike quinceañeras on principle, Guillermo is your best friend here at work. That counts for something, doesn't it?"

"I'll think about it," Ernesto says. "Hey, do you have a few minutes, Sara? I have something for you."

"Yes." Ernesto starts walking toward the stairs. Sara says to Guillermo, "Don't mind him. He only pretends to be a jerk."

Guillermo waves. "Don't worry, I know he's a teddy bear deep down. *Way* deep down."

"See you tonight," Sara says, laughing.

The IT department is one floor below the main newsroom in a windowless space that is always cold. When Sara started working at *El Sol* as an intern, the only empty desk she could find was in that room, and she learned to love the quiet and the air-conditioning. Now, whenever she has trouble writing something, she goes down there to work, away from the noisy telephone conversations and heat of the news floor. Unlike the IT room, which needs an air conditioner to keep the servers from overheating, the news floor is kept "cool" during the hot summer months by a dozen or so floor fans that whir and clang like the propellers on early planes.

Ernesto sits at his desk and clicks on the screen. Then he begins to type.

"Damn place," he says, noticing Sara. He seems to have forgotten that he asked her to come down. "Juana wants me to revise my budget proposal. Year after year I ask for new computers and year after year I get shot down." He hits the side of his computer screen. "This equipment is so old the company that makes the computers doesn't exist anymore. How are we supposed to do our work driving cars from *The Flintstones* when the rest of the world is zipping around in BMWs?" He stands and pushes his black thick-framed glasses up the bridge of his nose. "What's up?"

"You said you had something for me. Maybe the e-mail I gave you? Did the Jaqueros find anything on it?"

"Oh, yeah." He looks around like he's making sure no one else is near. "We weren't able to trace the e-mail fully, but the person who sent it"—he peers down at his screen— "jeremias28@gmx.at, is no dummy. The methodology used to hide its origin is super sophisticated, like I told you. Jeremias is probably not a guy but a moniker for an organization."

"If that's the case," Sara says, "whoever sent the message must know it wouldn't take us long to find that out."

Ernesto grins. "Glad to see someone around here has some actual brains! Yes, you can say that with this e-mail, the medium is the message."

"The sender wants us to be aware of his power."

"Or *her* power. Why do women always assume that evil is masculine?"

She gives him her best *get real* face.

"Yeah. Okay. *He* may have wanted you to know generally of his clout, but I don't think he meant for you to find out where he was clouting from."

Sara feels her heart rate pick up. "So you found out where it came from?"

"Not precisely. But Tovar, one of our best Jaqueros, recognized the encryption method from a corruption case he investigated a few years back. The same foreign bounce points used to hide the source of those e-mails were used with this one."

"What kind of case?"

Ernesto lowers his voice and glances at the door. "He was investigating some e-mails from cartel members, and he found communications between the cartel and the State Police."

"The State Police?" Sara sits down. She remembers the State Police officer telling Mrs. Fuentes that Linda was probably having a drink with a boy. The lack of sympathy, the repugnant smirk on his face. How many times has she gone to the State Police headquarters to ask if they have any news about Linda, only to wait for hours on those hard orange chairs while officers come and go? They laugh and talk about where to go for lunch, not giving a damn about the missing girls. Their unconcern is one thing, but this direct involvement is quite another. It is the worst fear of the mothers of missing girls coming true.

She thinks. "There's no way of finding out who in the State Police is involved exactly? Or where?"

"These people are good, technologically speaking. Tovar thinks someone detected his search this morning."

"Oh. Is that dangerous?"

"They're good, but we're better. The thing is, these people are very bad people. You should see some of the e-mails they've sent the Jaqueros."

"So you've taken this as far as it can go," Sara says.

"We'll keep going if you want us to," Ernesto answers. "But the more we dig, the more you and your family are in danger. This is not your run-of-the-mill threat. They already know we're up to something, and soon they'll figure out you're with us. We'll stop if you tell us."

"Thank you," Sara manages to say. She stands and walks back to the newsroom, dazed. If Ernesto can find the source of the e-mail, that might lead to an actual person involved in the abduction of the girls. Investigating that person might take them to Linda. She finally has a lead on the people responsible for the Desaparecidas and maybe even on Linda's whereabouts. It's a tenuous lead, but a lead nevertheless.

She sits at her desk and takes out the picture of Linda that she keeps in the middle drawer. Linda was beautiful. Five feet seven, slim, long black hair, big hazel eyes. But more than that, she had a pulsating sun of happiness inside her that shone day or night. Sara doesn't remember ever seeing her sad or moody. In the picture, she's laughing, reaching out for the dangling string of a purple helium balloon that has just escaped her grasp.

Sara goes over Ernesto's words. There's no doubt that they are dealing with people who would kill her in the blink of an eye. She's done too many stories about dead girls not to be afraid, not to know what these people are capable of doing. But this is Linda. Her best friend. And even if she wasn't Sara's best friend, she's a human being. Sara thinks of all the suffering people who pray that they are not forgotten, that there are others brave enough to keep believing every human life matters.

She opens a new e-mail and directs it to Ernesto. Then she types "Linda Fuentes" on the subject line. Below that she writes:

Proceed.

CHAPTER 4

Emiliano

Emiliano takes Calle Ignacio Mejía toward Zaragoza Boulevard. The sky is pale blue and cloudless. It's perfect weather to bike the twenty or so miles he'll need to cover today. He rings the bell on the old bike a couple of times and waves at Cristobal, who is coming back from the corner store with a soda.

"I'll take good care of Perlita," Cristobal yells after him.

Emiliano picks up speed going downhill and a cool breeze brushes his face. He's got to hurry if he wants to get to Taurus in time to see Armando. He could head there first, but Javier's neighborhood is closer. Javier will have at least three piñatas. Maybe his sister Rosario will have made something like the mask she made last week. But it is Doña Pepa's beaded purse that will bring in the big money today. The last time she made one, he got nine hundred pesos for her.

He turns right on Avenida Juárez, staying as close to the side of the road as he can. Even so, he can feel the cars whizzing by, inches away from him. Some sick people think it's fun to come as close as they can to his trailer and bike. He ignores them. Life's too short to waste valuable energy on imbeciles. Anger is energy, and energy needs to be carefully preserved, like water on a three-day desert hike. He slows down. Of all the things he's learned from the desert, knowing how to pace himself is probably the most important one. "Slow and steady, lads," as Brother Patricio likes to say. "Do not haste but do not waste."

Emiliano prefers to go to Javier's house in the early morning when most of the residents are sleeping. Last month, two guys about Sara's age stopped him on the dirt road and pointed pistols at him. He's alive only because he had cash to give them and they were in a rush to get their next fix. But what can he do? Javier is one of the best contributors to Emiliano's business. The smaller the papier-mâché object, the harder it is to make, and Javier's miniature piñatas are incredibly popular with American buyers. Lalo sells them to airport shops in Houston and Austin.

Emiliano dismounts his bike to climb the hill to Javier's house. He maneuvers around the potholes that fill the dirt street and holds his breath when the smell of a sewer becomes unbearable. Javier's house, like most of the dwellings in this barrio, is really more of a shack, made from discarded construction materials like chipped cinder blocks and cracked bricks, as well as rusty pieces of tin and used plywood. Despite this, it's still one of the most carefully constructed houses in the whole place. Where most of them look as if a desert wind will blow them down, Javier's home is sturdy, built with the same care as his piñatas.

Emiliano knocks gently on the plywood board that serves as a door. The littlest girl, Nieves, sticks her head out and smiles shyly.

"Is your brother home?"

She shakes her head. The door opens fully. "Emiliano!

Come in, come in!" says Mrs. Robles, her face lighting up. She would look not much older than Sara if it weren't for the tired, dark circles under her eyes and the white streaks in her hair. "Javier had to go to the store to buy supplies. He left three piñatas for you. Come in."

"Thank you, but I have to get going. I got a late start today."

"Still, sit down for a moment. Have a glass of water. You look hot. The girls want to show you something." Emiliano steps inside. It took him thirty-five minutes of pedaling and breathing diesel smoke to get here, not to mention the climb up the hill. He can sit for a moment. "Rosario, can you put the fan on for Emiliano?"

Rosario, Javier's older sister, rises slowly from a cot in the corner where she's been sitting. "Hello, Emiliano," she says warmly. "I made something for you." She bends down to get something from under the cot.

"The fan first, girl. You can show him later after he's cooled down."

"I'll get the fan." It's so dark in the shack that Emiliano did not see Javier's middle sister, Marta, sitting on another cot. She reaches for a small electric fan on top of the only dresser in the room and brings it to the table, her arm shaking. She climbs up on a chair and tries to plug the fan's cord into the outlet with the room's only lightbulb. Every person in the room, it seems, holds their breath until the fan starts to whir. Mrs. Robles leads Emiliano to a chair in front of the fan.

"Look." Rosario presents him with a rag doll dressed like a Mayan princess. The doll has a white dress with purple embroidered flowers on the hem and a white blouse with intricate pink designs on the sleeves. The head is covered with a scarf lined with tiny blue stars. The doll's face is primitive looking but friendly, warm.

"I didn't know you made dolls," Emiliano says, admiring it. "I really liked that jaguar mask you made. This is pretty amazing."

"You think someone will buy it?"

"Yeah, definitely," Emiliano says, squeezing the doll. He imagines a little girl hugging it for comfort.

Mrs. Robles takes a jar from a plastic cooler on the floor and fills a glass with water. "It's good water," she assures him. "We always boil it first."

"I'm making stuff too," Marta says. "Javier's teaching me to make papier-mâché animals. Want to see?"

"Let's not bother Emiliano with all our handiwork," Mrs. Robles says. Then to Emiliano, "The girls enjoy making things for you." Nieves, standing next to Mrs. Robles, pulls at her mother's dress. "What is it, little one?"

"I made something," Nieves whispers to her mother.

Before Emiliano can say anything, Marta drops some kind of multicolored creature on his lap. "A leopard," she tells him. "Only the spots are different colors."

"It's different," Emiliano says. Something's not right with the leopard, but he doesn't know what.

"It's the tail. The tail's too short. And he doesn't have any ears," Rosario says, reading his mind.

Marta sticks her tongue out at Rosario, even though the words were said with kindness. "If the tail was longer it could be a rat. And he does have ears. He's a baby leopard, so his ears haven't grown."

Now Nieves is tentatively presenting him with an ordinary piece of cardboard. She turns it over. Bottle caps have been glued on to form a picture. "Wow, you did this?" Emiliano asks her, taking the cardboard from her hands. She nods and hides behind her mother.

"Nieves and Marta collected the bottle caps and glued them," Mrs. Robles explains. "It gives them something to do while Javier is in school and Rosario and me are out working."

"I don't go to school," Marta says, a note of sadness in her voice. An assortment of her medicine bottles sits on the table. "It's the Popocatépetl, see?" She points at a volcano in the center of the cardboard. To the right of the volcano there's a sun. Marta sniffs and says, "It still smells like beer. The only yellow caps we could find for the sun were from beer bottles."

Emiliano can't imagine how five people can live in this minuscule space they call home. The inside of the shack is clean and there is no clutter. Everything seems to have an essential purpose. The floor consists of wooden pallets covered with remnants from various rugs. Two cots are joined together in the far end of the room where, Emiliano supposes, Mrs. Robles sleeps with the three girls. He can tell that Javier sleeps on the remaining cot because he can see three piñatas on top of it. The red plastic cooler with the white top sits behind the door. A wire stretches between two nails, holding dresses and flimsy jackets. Emiliano can see cracks of light between the walls of the shack. How do they keep warm in winter? How does Javier work on the piñatas at night with only that dim lightbulb? How do they not roast to death in the summer months, with only one window high up in the back wall? Against the other wall stands the dresser, with an iron crucifix on top, and a bench with a double-burner petroleum stove, where a pot is gurgling with something that smells like his mother's stew.

"We were waiting for Javier to eat. Will you join us?" Mrs. Robles says.

"Thank you, no. I have another stop after this. And then I have to go downtown to sell the merchandise. I'm late already."

"Oh, and here we are detaining you with our chatter. Rosario, can you help Emiliano with the piñatas?"

"I got them," Emiliano says, standing. He goes over to Javier's cot and reads the note on one of the piñatas.

Hey, Emiliano. Sorry I missed you. Can you bring whatever you get for the piñatas tomorrow? We need to get some medicine for Marta. Thank you. Javier.

Emiliano puts down the piñata and takes one thousand pesos from his wallet. He brought the money from his savings at home to buy Perla Rubi's mother a birthday present, but he can figure out something else for that. "This is for the piñatas," he says to Mrs. Robles. "I'll give Javier the rest tomorrow. I'm sure I'll get at least four hundred for these."

"Thank you," Mrs. Robles says, taking the money. "God bless you."

He takes two piñatas and Rosario takes the third. The whole family walks out with him.

"I'll come and get the doll next Saturday," Emiliano tells Rosario. "It's really beautiful."

"What about my leopard?" Marta asks, pouting.

He smiles at her. "Your leopard also. But see if you can get the ears and the tail to grow. And your volcano too," he says to Nieves.

"Thank you for all you do for us," Mrs. Robles says, taking his hand in hers. He squeezes it and lets it go.

Now it's time to fly. After Emiliano says his good-byes, it takes him thirty minutes to reach the commercial district where the Taurus nightclub is located. Thai and Indian restaurants line the streets, and boutiques with dresses so flimsy Emiliano can't imagine anyone wearing them. The six blocks surrounding Taurus are what everyone points to when they want to show that the old Juárez is gone and a new one has arrived. No one wants to think about Javier's neighborhood just forty blocks away.

Taurus has a hot pink facade with black music notes popping out of saxophones. There are no windows anywhere, and inside it's all black leather, chrome, and mirrors. It's the hot spot in Juárez, Emiliano knows, where all the kids with rich parents come to drink and dance. Some day, he imagines, he'll drive up to the club on his motorcycle with Perla Rubi behind him. But right now he is here for business and not to fantasize about the future.

The owner's son, Armando, is kind to him. He always asks about his mother. Likes to talk with him about soccer. Emiliano wants to ask him now about the empty beer cans he's seen in garbage bags at the back of the club. There must be at least one hundred cans in those bags, and that's just from one evening. Taurus is open six days a week. If Emiliano can take all those cans to the recycling center and keep a percentage of the fees, he could be making serious money. Armando is a friendly guy. He might go for a fifty-fifty split.

Emiliano needs to make at least two thousand pesos every month. Half of what he makes he gives to Sara so she can pay the monthly bills for cable and their cell phones. The other half goes inside the fake Bible on his desk, his savings for a down payment on Paco's brother's motorcycle. Once he gets the motorcycle, he can make twice, maybe three times what he's making now. He can also take Sara to work and pick her up again afterward. Riding those buses is too dangerous. He doesn't want what happened to Linda to happen to his sister.

Emiliano's heart jumps when he turns into the alleyway to the nightclub. There in the parking lot is Armando, walking toward a black Mercedes. Armando waited for him like he said he would. The day is looking good.

"Emiliano Zapata!" Armando practically shouts when he hears the rattle of the bike. "How are you?"

Emiliano dismounts and pushes the bike toward Armando. From the corner of his eye, he sees four garbage bags bulging with empty beer cans. "Good to see you." He stretches his hand out to Armando.

"Hold on," Armando says, shaking his hand. "I have to get something from the car." He clicks the car doors open and retrieves an envelope from the glove compartment. "Come on in. You want a beer?"

"No, thank you." Emiliano told Armando once that the Jipari code prohibited drinking, and now Armando jokingly offers him a beer every time he sees him. "I just need to get a purse from Doña Pepa."

"How about a cup of coffee? Doña Pepa made a fresh pot a little while ago."

"Maybe some water."

"You got it." Armando is wearing white chino pants and a soft black T-shirt that makes his biceps bulge. Emiliano knows he likes to work out. They go through the back door into Taurus's small office. "Pepa! Emiliano's here!" Armando shouts through the door that leads to the nightclub. He opens a small refrigerator next to the desk and takes out two bottles of water. He gives one to Emiliano. "Sit for a second," he says. "I got a proposition for you, like I told you."

Emiliano sits on a brown ottoman next to the sofa. "I wanted to ask you something too."

"Yeah? One second." Armando gets up and disappears into the darkness of the club. A few moments later, he returns and sits again. "I wanted to make sure Pepa was okay. The other day I found her on the floor. She blacked out. She really shouldn't be working, but she insists on coming in. She says she'd go crazy with nothing to do at home. She used to take care of my father when he was a kid, and he's sixty-eight, so you do the math." He raises his bottle and drinks. Emiliano does as well. "So, you go first. What did you want to ask me?"

"I was wondering about all those beer cans you throw away every day. I could take them to the recycling center and we can split the profits."

"The recycling center. That's, like, on the other side of town. You're going to bike all the way over there?"

"It's not a problem."

Armando studies Emiliano for a few moments and then laughs. "Okay. They're all yours."

"Sixty-forty?" Emiliano says. He knows you should always ask for a little more than you expect to get.

"Me sixty, you forty. Right?" Armando asks.

"The other way. I'm doing all the work. You're just throwing the cans away now," Emiliano responds in his best poker voice.

"All right," Armando says, laughing. "You're tough. But listen, I need a favor from you."

Doña Pepa hobbles in with something folded in newspaper. Emiliano stands and she hands him the package. "Here's the purse, Emiliano. I hope your buyers like it."

"If it's like the other three you made, I'm sure they will. As many as you can make, I'll find the best buyers for you."

"Those little beads are a big strain on my eyes," Doña Pepa says, blinking. "And my hands are stiff always. But I like keeping them busy. And the money is for Memo to buy one of those little computers. He loves those Piparis. He's been talking about that thing where he gets new shoes for weeks."

Emiliano nods, deciding not to tell her that it's *Jiparis*, not *Piparis*.

"You go home now. You're only supposed to work until twelve," Armando says to Doña Pepa, concern in his voice.

"Just have to do the women's toilets." Doña Pepa walks away slowly.

Emiliano finishes the water in his bottle. "You said you had a proposition for me."

"That's pretty impressive, that little business you got going." Armando nods in the direction of the newspaper package. "You like doing business, don't you?"

"I like making deals. It's about the only thing I'm good at."

"Oh, come on. Don't put yourself down. You're the best high school soccer player in Juárez, maybe in all of Chihuahua. I've seen you play. You're a natural-born leader. You single-handedly got this city its first state championship."

"Thank you."

"How are your grades?"

"Nobody's perfect." Emiliano shrugs.

Armando laughs. "Listen, here's my proposition. My father saddled me with taking his car, the Mercedes out there, to the repair shop. It's supposed to be just an oil change and tire rotation, but the dealership is going to find something wrong with it, because that's what they always do. So this morning—it came to me when I saw Pepa wrapping the purse—I said to myself, 'Emiliano is going to come to pick up that purse. Why not help him and myself by giving him a little money to take the car to the dealership? He needs the money and I need the time.' What do you think?"

"What exactly would I do?"

"You drive the car to the dealership on Mariscal. You wait there, watch some TV on the big screen in the air-conditioned room they got there, drink all the sodas you can drink, and then bring the car back here and go on your way a little better off financially than you started. Say, five hundred pesos better off."

Emiliano tries not to react, but it's too late. Armando sees the surprise in his eyes. "It's probably, what? Twice what you're going to make today after you sell all your things?" he says.

"A little more," Emiliano admits.

"So?"

"Why? Why so much for doing nothing?"

"Honestly?"

"Yes."

"You're going to be at the dealership for at least two hours, maybe three. Three hours of my day is worth five hundred pesos. And I get to help you out a little. I know you can use the money." Armando reaches into a pocket and takes out a shiny brown wallet. He opens it and offers Emiliano five crisp bills. "Take them. This is for three hours. And if it's more than three hours, I'll give you one hundred for each hour after that. If by some miracle it's less than three hours, you still keep the five hundred. And I don't care if you use the car afterward to do everything you were going to do on that antique you call a bicycle."

"I don't have a driver's license," Emiliano says.

Armando takes a card out of one of the wallet's compartments. "If a cop stops you, show him this and ask him to call me. I'll take care of it. You got nothing to worry about. And the insurance on that car is probably more than you'll make in your lifetime."

Emiliano thinks. Five hundred pesos, and he can do all his folk art business tomorrow after the exhibition game. That's maybe seven hundred pesos net in two days. That will go a long way to paying the monthly bills, and he'll be that much closer to owning the motorcycle. "Okay," he says.

"There you go." Armando hands Emiliano the car keys. "You don't need to call me when they tell you they found something that needs fixing. Whatever it is and whatever the cost, just let them do it."

They walk outside. Emiliano pops open the trunk and places Doña Pepa's purse in there. Then he walks over to his bicycle, takes Javier's piñatas from the trailer, and puts them in the trunk as well. Armando, standing by the trunk, picks up one of the piñatas and examines it.

"So who do you sell these to?" he asks.

"Stores near the bridge to El Paso. Mostly to Lalo Torres. He owns a folk art store downtown."

"And tourists buy them?"

"He ships to stores in the United States. One of his clients owns a chain of stores at airports."

"How does he get them across the border?"

"A shipping company. He knows all the customs regulations. He does it so much everyone knows him."

"Interesting."

Emiliano waits for Armando to finish inspecting the piñata. After a few moments, he takes it from him and places it in the trunk with the others. "I better get going. I'll bring the car back in the afternoon. Will you be here?"

"It would be better if you took the car to my house. I'll give you a ride back here to pick up your bike."

"Can I just bring it here and leave the keys with the bartender? This is closer to my house. I have to be at a birthday party in Campestre by six."

"Really? I used to live in Campestre before I got my own place. My father and little brother still live there, you know. Who's having a birthday?"

Emiliano closes the trunk. "The Esmeraldas. Mrs. Esmeralda. The mother of one of my classmates."

"No way! Jorge Esmeralda is my father's lawyer! You're invited to Judith Esmeralda's birthday party? Emiliano, you never cease to amaze me. I knew you were a mover and a shaker, but this takes you up a few notches in my already high estimation."

Emiliano waves to him as he gets in the car. Is it wrong to feel flattered and even honored by Armando's words?

No. Maybe. Whatever. It still feels good.

CHAPTER 5
SARA

FRIDAY, MARCH 24
2:45 P.M.

Sara tries to put the threatening e-mail out of her mind long enough to do her daily assignments. One of these jobs requires reading all the e-mails people send to the *El Sol* news "hotline" and deciding whether any are worthy of follow-up. The hotline is the special inbox where readers send anonymous tips about suspected crime and corruption (or simply complain). Most of the e-mails are about potholes that never get filled or garbage that is never picked up. It's work Sara usually does not mind doing and even enjoys—but today all she can think is she's wasting time that could be better spent on Linda.

She usually checks the hotline as soon as she gets to work, but she skipped yesterday, which means she'll get all the e-mails from Thursday as well as those that have come in so far today. She clicks on the link to the hotline inbox, but there is nothing there.

That's strange. Sara has been covering the hotline since she was a high school intern, and there has never been a day with no tips, no complaints, no nasty retort to one of Felipe's editorials. Maybe something is wrong with the site. She sends an e-mail to Ernesto asking him if he sees any technical problems. Five minutes later, Ernesto calls.

"This is very weird," he says.

"What is?"

"Someone deleted all of the hotline e-mails for Thursday."

"What do you mean, *deleted*? I thought you, me, and Juana were the only people who had access to the hotline."

"That's correct. Someone logged on to Juana's terminal this morning at five a.m. Whoever it was deleted all the e-mails from the previous day. There were fourteen of them. All gone."

"How do you know they were deleted?"

"Every keystroke you make on a computer creates a track that can be traced. The person who did this obviously wanted us to think we didn't get any e-mails."

"But how? You said they were deleted from Juana's terminal. Juana didn't delete those e-mails. She doesn't even know how to access them. Whoever did it would need to know her password."

"Everyone knows Juana keeps her latest password under the *P* in her Rolodex. I bet you always write your passwords on the last page of your address book."

"Oops," Sara says.

"Yeah, oops. But listen, I installed a program that saves all the e-mails we receive to the cloud. It's a precaution I took after our system started dying of old age. I'll send you a copy of the deleted e-mails in a few minutes. There must be something in there that someone doesn't want us to see." He laughs. "If this turkey had only deleted the one e-mail that worried him instead of all of them, we never would have known."

"Ernesto, I have a bad feeling about this."

"You must be thinking what I'm thinking . . ."

"This is related to the e-mail about Linda."

"That's what I think. Stay put."

"Thanks, Ernesto."

A few minutes later, Sara gets an e-mail from Ernesto.

Take a look at the third e-mail attached. The one from atlas444@gmail.com. It came in Thursday morning at 2. Pretty weird to get an e-mail with only a picture and no text. It's the only one that stood out to me. Who's the girl in the picture? One of your girls, maybe?

Sara clicks on the third e-mail and her heart stops. The subject line says *puchi*. That's Linda and Sara's secret word.

Heart racing now, Sara clicks on the attachment. It's a picture. It isn't Linda, but another beautiful young woman, about sixteen or seventeen, grimacing as if she smells something bad. She's sitting in what looks like a nightclub booth, next to an older man whose bald head has fallen to his chest as if he's passed out. On the table in front of them are an empty bottle of expensive Scotch whiskey and two thick crystal glasses. Next to the man is an ashtray with a cigarette still burning. Everything looks expensive in a cheap kind of way. The picture is off-center, rushed, like someone got up, leaving his cell phone behind, and someone else snapped a picture and sent it.

Someone else. Linda. Linda knew that one of Sara's jobs at *El Sol* is checking the hotline. And only Linda would use "puchi" for the old man.

Sara's head spins. She doesn't recognize the nightclub, but she doesn't go to places like that often. And this wouldn't be just any club, otherwise Linda would come home. This must be a place where girls are kept against their will. If Linda was at the table with the puchi guy, she must be kept by these men too.

Then she realizes: Someone deleted the hotline e-mails. That means the criminals know Linda sent the e-mail. The thought of what they might do to her takes Sara's breath away.

She calls Ernesto. "Hey," she says, struggling to keep her voice calm. "Any way you and the Jaqueros can find out who the guy in the picture is?"

"Hold on. Okay, I'm looking at it now. It's kind of hard to see his face. I'll send it to my guys. There's a ring on his finger that might help. That e-mail address is clearly an alias. We'll see if we can trace it. What are you thinking? Is the girl in the picture a Desaparecida?"

"I'm about to check the files now. She looks familiar for some reason. But the e-mail was definitely sent by my friend Linda." Sara swallows. "You know, the one I talk about all the time."

"You positive?"

"*Puchi* was a special code word we used. Ernesto, this is really serious and . . . urgent," she says. "The bad people know the e-mail was sent. They had someone in here delete it. So Linda and the other girl—"

"I know," he interrupts. "I know what that means. I'll get on it."

Ernesto hangs up, and Sara takes one deep breath and then another. Electricity zips through her veins. She needs to find a way to slow down. She needs to *do* something. There is an evil place where attractive girls are kept for the pleasure of men like the drunk in the picture, and Linda is there. She looks at the picture again. This club is a place of fake luxury with garish booths and expensive Scotch. The men who go there are likely men of wealth and power. The man's left hand lies limply on the table, and Sara can see a thick, platinum, expensive watch peeking from the edge of his sleeve. His giant gold ring with four small diamonds is ostentatiously rich. If the Jaqueros can discover the identity of the man, and she can discover who the girl is, she may find Linda. Because Linda is alive.

Alive.

In spite of the danger, Sara can't help but smile.

CHAPTER 6
EMILIANO

Emiliano sits on a white leather sofa in front of a giant-screen television, waiting for Mr. Cortázar's car. As Armando predicted, an inspection revealed that the brake pads were ninety percent worn out, and it will take a couple more hours to get the parts and install them. Emiliano is bored out of his mind. Earning good money by doing nothing is not what it's cracked up to be. The only things saving his sanity are the English soccer games on an obscure cable channel and texting with Perla Rubi.

He's also solved the problem of Mrs. Esmeralda's birthday present. A commercial for a chocolate candy reminded him that Mami makes the best coffee liqueur chocolate cake anyone has ever tasted. A call to her at the bakery, a little begging, a little sweet-talking, and Mami agreed to bake a cake for Mrs. Esmeralda. It's a perfect gift. Personal. And he doesn't have to spend any money on it.

A friendly man wearing a wide purple tie comes in to inform him that they need to replace one of the calipers as well.

"How long will *that* take?" Emiliano asks. He doesn't know what a caliper is but it sounds serious.

The man smiles as if he's used to that being the first question out of people's mouths. "I'll have the car ready for you in an hour. I promise."

He leaves. The man's smile and the sincere way he said *I promise* remind Emiliano of a conversation with his father the week before he left for the United States. His father had taken him to the construction site where he was working. Emiliano's job was to pick up debris in a wheelbarrow, take it to the front of the site, then load it into the dump truck when it came. They sat together under a skinny tree eating the lunch Mami had prepared for them. When they finished eating, Emiliano began to peel the blisters from his hands.

"Tough job, huh?" his father said.

"It's not so bad." But it was bad. His brain was fried from working in the ninety-degree heat. And there were still four more hours of the same.

"It's no way to make a living," his father said. Emiliano knew how much his father disliked construction work.

"But it's a living."

"That's what your mother says. She says I'm lucky to have a job."

"She's right." In the never-ending discussion of whether his father should go to the United States or stay and be happy with what they had, Emiliano was on his mother's side.

"I have a brain," his father said. "Not much of one, but one that can do more than spread stucco. If we have brains, we should try to use them, don't you think? To try to do better."

"You can try to do better here in Mexico."

"I've tried, son. I've tried. The only way I could find to do better here is the illegal drug business. I'm not going to do that. Do you understand?"

"Yes."

"I'm going to America and getting enough money that

when I come back, we can do something together. Open up a business. Our own place. We'll call it Zapata and Son."

"What kind of business?" Emiliano asked.

"I don't know. Over in El Paso they have these food trucks that go to construction sites. We could buy one of those. Take the truck to the factories and to the sites. Then after that, who knows? It's more about being our own boss. Finding different ways to make money and going for it. Making our own decisions. When I get back, you'll be done with high school, and we'll have the money to start our own business."

Emiliano chuckled. He liked talking to his father about the future. His father was strict in many ways, but when he talked about what they would do together in years to come, he was more of a friend. It was like when he and Paco sat around talking about the kind of car they would buy if they were rich. There were no limits to what they dreamed up. It was fun to be with someone that way. But the reality was that, if his father went to America, he would not be around for a long while.

His father must have noticed the sad look on his face, because he said, "I'll be back. I promise you. And when I come back we'll work together on something we both like." He shook Emiliano's arm affectionately. "You got to take care of your mother and sister while I'm gone."

"Why four years? That's a long time."

"I'm not going to find a good-paying job right away. It's going to take time to save up what we'll need. And I'll be sending your mother a lot of what I make. So if I'm going to go, I might as well go once and do it right. And when I come back, we'll . . ."

"Buy a food truck."

"Maybe something else. Anything. If I can learn to be an electrician or pick up a trade while I'm over there, I'll do it. I'm not going to waste my time. You can be sure of that."

Emiliano nodded, not very enthusiastically.

"Listen, I need you to believe in me. I need you to see that this kind of thing"—his father gestured at a pile of bricks—"would eventually kill me or drive me back to drinking. I think your mother and Sara are beginning to understand why I need to leave, but I need you to understand as well. I need your support. You of all people have to know that I am doing it for *you*. For all of you, but for you most of all. So you and me can be a team someday and do stuff we enjoy. Okay? I will return, Emiliano. I promise."

I promise, Emiliano repeats to himself and shakes his head. Words are cheap. But it doesn't matter. All that his father promised they would do together, he will do on his own. He will be a better provider than his father could ever be. And, unlike his father, he will keep the promises he makes.

It's three thirty when the car is finally done, and Emiliano is more exhausted and depleted than if he had biked a hundred miles. His cell phone rings just as he drives out of the dealership. He pulls the car over to the curb and stops. It's Armando. Emiliano tries to tell him about the brake job, but Armando doesn't let him finish.

"Yeah, yeah. Listen, man, I had this brilliant idea. It came to me after you left and I've been thinking about it ever since. It was like a lightbulb clicked above my head, you know? Are you there?"

"Yes, I'm here."

"You're not driving and talking on your cell, are you?"

"No, I stopped right outside the dealership. I need to make a couple more pickups and then get to the shops downtown. What is it?"

"I thought of a way that you can make a lot, I mean a *lot* more money with your folk art business."

Emiliano pauses for a moment. His folk art business is *his* business, and the fact that Armando has been thinking about it annoys him. But the purpose of the business is to make money, right? So he is also curious. "How?"

"Look, this is what I want you to do. I'm going to text you the address of one of my father's business partners. I want you to head over there now. His name is Alfredo Reyes. All you have to do is show him the folk art objects you have with you today and tell him how you run the business. You know, who makes the objects, who you sell them to, who they sell them to."

"I don't know. I don't know if I have time today."

"Emiliano, don't be stupid. This is a once-in-a-lifetime opportunity. All you have to do is see Mr. Reyes. Just listen to him, that's all. I called him a little while ago and he's expecting you. Look, I'll pay you for your time, okay? I'll give you two hundred pesos just for going over to his house and talking to him."

"What does Mr. Reyes do?"

"Just a guy trying to make some money. Like all of us. Hey, I got an idea. Why don't you keep the car tonight? Bring it to my house tomorrow morning. You can drive it to Mrs. Esmeralda's birthday party. How were you going to get there anyway? You were going to show up at Jorge Esmeralda's house on that bike of yours? Emiliano, Emiliano. Come on, optics are everything."

Emiliano imagines driving up to Perla Rubi's house in the elegant black Mercedes. He does need a way to get there tonight, and it would be kind of nice to show Perla Rubi's parents that he's—well—important.

"Listen, I have to go. I'll text you Mr. Reyes's address as soon as I hang up."

"Wait," Emiliano says. "Assuming I like what this Mr. Reyes has to say, what's in it for you?"

"That's my boy!" Armando crows. "You have a great head on your shoulders. We can talk about that later. But this isn't about me. It's about you right now. Say hi to Mr. Reyes for me. And listen, if you don't like whatever he proposes, don't be rude and say no to his face. Just say you need time to think about it. I'll call him later and give him a good excuse. If the deal he offers you doesn't sound right to you, you don't have to take it. This is business, pure and simple, Emiliano. Got it?"

"Got it."

He waits a few seconds for Armando to text him the address and then he loads the coordinates into the car's GPS. He pulls out onto the street. This car is luxury on wheels. It responds to the slightest touch on the steering wheel or the gas pedal. What a difference from Brother Patricio's old Honda, in which Emiliano learned to drive. He speeds up. According to the GPS, the place he needs to go is thirty-seven minutes away with no traffic. Perla Rubi wanted him to be at her house at six, and it's almost four, so he's cutting it close.

He should probably swing by Paco's house on his way home and borrow Paco's loafers. Paco is the snappiest dresser of all the Pumas and possibly all of Colegio México. Should he wear socks with Paco's loafers or go sockless like Paco sometimes does? Maybe no socks is a little too informal. Perla Rubi told him to dress casual, but he's going to be talking to Perla Rubi's mother about his business, and business talk requires socks. That much he knows. He'll wear his best pair of denim pants and a black crewneck T-shirt that's a good imitation of the super-soft, expensive shirt Armando was wearing this morning. His only problem is the shoes. He'll call Paco on his way home after he sees this Mr. Reyes.

As he leaves the city behind, Emiliano thinks that maybe, just maybe, this is his lucky day. He's going to come out of today and tomorrow with nine hundred pesos. That's next month's rent payment right there. He's on his way to talk to someone who will help him expand his folk art business. He's going to see Perla Rubi later, and he'll drive up to her house in a Mercedes. Perla Rubi's plan feels clear to him now. She invites him to her mother's birthday party. He meets her mother and impresses her with his ambition, so even though he's poor today, he will be successful in the future. The mother likes his drive and determination, his level-headedness, and, of course, the respect he shows for her daughter. Perla Rubi's mother then convinces her husband that Emiliano is solid, a good prospect, and he and Perla Rubi can date openly. That's Perla Rubi's plan. No doubt about it.

The lady inside the GPS tells him that in five hundred feet, his destination will be on the right. He has traveled for thirty-seven minutes in the blink of an eye. Emiliano slows down and stops. He can see a two-story white house behind a tall gray wall that takes up the rest of the block. He gets out of the car and walks to a black iron gate. He's about to push the white button on the intercom when the gate opens magically. Only then does Emiliano notice the camera on the side of the wall.

He drives into the compound. There's a separate garage-like building next to the three-story house. A man wearing a blue blazer has come out from a side door and waves him over. Emiliano parks the car and rolls down the window. Before he can say anything, the man says, "Mr. Reyes is waiting for you."

They walk across a courtyard toward the front door of the house. Inside, the house is cool—not air-conditioned cool, but cave cool. Leather chairs and dark antique bureaus line the hallway, and on the wall hangs a painting of a dark volcano spewing ash and lava that reminds Emiliano of the picture Nieves and Marta made with bottle caps. In the air is a smell he can't identify, something flowery, as if there were a garden of roses inside the house.

The man in the blue blazer leads him to what looks like a dining room. Mr. Reyes is sitting at the head of a long table, and Emiliano stops at the other end. The man's thin white hair is carefully combed, and his gray suit jacket and purple tie make him look distinguished and wealthy. He is thin but not frail. A bowl of soup in front of him gives off steam. Beside the bowl sits a plate with one piece of bread, a roll. A woman dressed in black enters from a door behind him with a saucer and a cup. Mr. Reyes waits for the woman to place what looks like hot chocolate on the table and gestures with a nod for her to leave. Only then does he look at Emiliano.

"Emiliano Zapata, correct?" Mr. Reyes says, pointing at a chair in front of him.

Emiliano pulls out the chair and sits. He watches the man

dip a large silver spoon into the soup and then raise it slowly to his mouth. Mr. Reyes grimaces slightly when he swallows. The man in the blue blazer stands in the corner of the room.

"Armando tells me you have a business. Tell me about it."

Emiliano should be nervous but he isn't. He feels the same confidence that comes to him on the soccer field when he knows he can outrun the player in front of him. "I belong to this explorers' club called the Jiparis," he begins. "One time, when we couldn't hike because of the weather, we made papier-mâché animals. Some of the kids were good at it, and I thought I might be able to sell the things they made. So that's what I do. I sell them to shops by the bridge to El Paso, shops that sell mostly to Americans. The kids—the Jiparis and their families—make different folk art objects. My job is to get the best price for them. I take a ten percent commission. I have some objects in the back of the car."

Mr. Reyes nods. The man in the blue blazer moves next to Emiliano and stretches out his hand. Emiliano hands him the car keys and the man walks out. Mr. Reyes drinks from the cup and wipes the foam on his upper lip with a crimson linen napkin. He raises his eyes and fixes them on Emiliano.

"How often do you sell these folk art objects?"

"Every week. There are always new things to sell. The families of the kids who make them need the money."

"But there must be lots of competition for these objects, no? So many places make them."

"The ones that my kids make are the best. I don't take any pieces that aren't well made. You can tell they're different, they're quality. The shop owners like them. They can't get enough of them. One of them, Lalo Torres, he sells them to stores at airports in the United States."

Mr. Reyes smiles for the first time, and so does Emiliano, although he's not sure why. The man with the blue blazer enters the room with a cardboard box in his arms. He places it on the table and then goes back to the same corner where he stood before. Mr. Reyes pushes himself slowly away from the table and stands. Emiliano does as well.

Mr. Reyes lifts the package with Doña Pepa's purse out of the box and unwraps it. He examines the colorful design. Doña Pepa used thousands of tiny beads to make a red-and-silver rooster crowing at a golden sun. Emiliano watches the man for signs of approval, but there is no change in his expression. Then Mr. Reyes picks up one of Javier's piñatas. Now a tiny grin appears on his wrinkled face, as if he's remembering something from his childhood.

"How are these made?" Mr. Reyes asks, dangling a small purple burro by the string on his back.

"Usually, you blow up a balloon and glue pieces of paper around it until you get your base shape. When it dries, you pop the balloon and construct the rest."

"But the balloon could be filled with something solid."

Emiliano is not sure what Mr. Reyes is getting at or whether he is even asking a question. "It doesn't matter so much with these small piñatas, because they're just used for decoration. But in a bigger piñata, you want the inside hollow so you can fill it with candy."

Mr. Reyes makes a sign with his hands that Emiliano does not understand, but apparently the man in the corner does. The man takes a penknife from his pocket, opens it, and hands it to Mr. Reyes. Mr. Reyes stabs the center of a star-shaped piñata with the knife. Emiliano tries not to gasp. What is he doing?

Mr. Reyes proceeds to cut a square-shaped hole in the piñata. When he finishes, he sticks his finger inside the star and pulls out a deflated blue balloon. Then he covers the hole with the piece he just cut out and again examines the piñata. He gives the piñata to the man in the corner, who removes the cut piece and also sticks his finger inside.

Emiliano watches the man shake his head. Somehow, the inside of the piñata is not good enough. Good enough for what? He does not want to believe what is slowly becoming obvious to him.

Mr. Reyes sits back down in his chair and waits for Emiliano to do the same before he speaks.

"We are not a big operation here. On the other hand, we are allowed to operate because we're not a threat to the major players, and we pay our dues . . . and our respect. Your business would be so small it's not worth our while. But Armando trusts you. Otherwise he wouldn't have sent you here. And Armando is the son of my good friend Enrique, and, frankly, I like you— the star midfielder who won the state championship and brought honor to our city. You have a good head for business, I can tell. I want to work with young people like you. So, Emiliano, if you want to do business together, we will do business together."

There's something about the quiet way that Mr. Reyes talks to him that makes Emiliano feel like he's respected, an equal. There's also a queasy feeling inside him that reminds him of the moment just before he was caught stealing, but the feeling is not strong enough to overcome his curiosity about what Mr. Reyes is offering.

"How would it work?" Emiliano asks.

"We give you a loan to buy the first batch of product. With the profits you make, you pay back the loan and buy more product. I suggest you do a dozen or so piñatas and other papier-mâché animals a week. No more. Instead of this Lalo Torres shipping to his usual shops, he'll ship to our stores. He will have to agree to do that, but it shouldn't be a problem. Our stores will give him a better price. But you should keep working with Lalo, since he is known and has been checked out by customs already." Mr. Reyes smiles a kind, reassuring smile. "A dozen piñatas like those"—he points to the star on the table—"will net you maybe thirty thousand pesos."

"Thirty thousand pesos," Emiliano repeats, stunned. "A week?"

Mr. Reyes smiles again. "It's a very small operation. I recommend you keep it small. Under everyone's radar. You keep going to school. Keep winning state championships for us." He nods. "Why don't you take a few days to think about it? One thing: The piñatas need to be loaded by the people who make them. It won't work if you have to cut a hole to insert the product after the piñatas are made. The opening could be detected."

Emiliano lowers his head. He would have to get Javier to stuff the piñatas with . . . "Loaded with what? What is the product?" he blurts.

Mr. Reyes lifts an eyebrow. "We can talk about that later. Once we're partners. There are options. Now, I'm afraid I have to make a business call. Oscar will help you with your box."

Emiliano and Mr. Reyes stand at the same time, and they shake hands. "It's good to meet you, Emiliano. I hope to hear from you soon."

"Thank you," Emiliano says. "It was good to meet you too."

When the box is in the trunk, Oscar motions for Emiliano to wait. Emiliano watches him walk into the building with the garage doors. A few moments later, he comes out carrying a white box with holes on the side for handles, the kind used to file documents. The box is sealed with black electrical tape. Oscar puts the box in the open trunk.

"Give this to Armando when you return the car," Oscar says, closing the trunk. "And one more thing. Please don't mention this location to anyone." He waits long enough for fear to make its way to Emiliano's face, and then he turns around and walks away.

Emiliano drives slowly. The last thing he wants is to be stopped for speeding. He keeps one eye on the rearview mirror to make sure no one is following him. There's an unexpected rush, scary yet exciting, from the knowledge that Armando is involved in the drug world. Armando's father too, probably. Mr. Reyes says Mr. Cortázar was an old friend. And if Mr. Cortázar is also a narco, then what about his lawyer, Perla Rubi's father? Emiliano's mind spins with connections, possibilities . . .

Back when Emiliano shoplifted, his first theft was a cheap watch he didn't even want. It happened a few days after his mother received the divorce papers from his father, who had gone to the United States two years earlier. His father had spent so much time preaching to Emiliano about what was right and wrong that the shoplifting felt like revenge. He wore the watch for a week, like a trophy. Then the stealing became more systematic. He's always been a good planner. He checked out the store, noticing where the surveillance cameras were located. He had a knife and pliers in his pocket to disconnect items from the sensors that would trigger alarms. He found a man who would buy what he stole. The money he got went to pay the family's bills, because the money his father continued to send was not enough. He always felt the same mixture of excitement and fear when he entered a store, like he stood on the edge of a deep canyon.

Then he was caught. A stupid mistake, not to have suspected a hidden surveillance camera in an electronics store. This proposal of Mr. Reyes's is different—not stupid. It represents big money and the risk is small. The need to pay the bills, to make his life and his family's life safer and more comfortable, is still there. Why not, if he's careful? He can proceed slowly. Not twelve piñatas, even. Six. Even one half of the thirty thousand pesos Mr. Reyes mentioned would bring happiness to his family, and make it easier for him to be with Perla Rubi.

He sighs and pushes the thought away. He forces himself to remember the three days he spent with Brother Patricio in the Sierra Tarahumara after he was caught stealing. They didn't have any food or water other than what they found, and Emiliano was full of anger, swearing and fighting. The desert taught him that unchanneled anger would destroy him, that anger needed to be converted into courage and determination to overcome the obstacles in his life. Success takes hard, slow, persistent work, Brother Patricio said. There are no shortcuts to getting what he wants. He must remember that. No shortcuts. He'll make money, but he'll work for it.

And Armando and Mr. Reyes? The main thing is that he can say no. No one is forcing him to do anything. He listened to Mr. Reyes, but tomorrow he'll tell Armando thanks but no thanks. Maybe he'll wait until Monday. It doesn't hurt to think about it over the weekend.

One thing's for sure: He's not going to lug that box full of whatever to Perla Rubi's house. If Emiliano gets stopped or someone steals the car with the box, that would be the end of him. What he needs to do is drive straight to Taurus right now and dump the car and the box. He looks at the clock on the dashboard. It'll be five thirty by the time he gets to Taurus. By the time he bicycles back home, showers, and then gets to Perla Rubi's house, it will be close to midnight. Perla Rubi wanted him to come at six. All right: He'll hide the box in a safe place and then drive to Perla Rubi's in the Mercedes. In the morning, he'll take the car and box to Armando. But what about tonight, after the party? He slows down and pulls into the gravel area on the side of the road, then takes out his phone.

Please, Paco. Please pick up.

"Hello?"

"Oh, man. I'm so glad you're home," Emiliano says. "Listen, I need to park a car in the back of your house for one night."

"What car?"

"It's a long story. The grandmother of one of the Jipari kids works at this club, and the owner paid me to take the car to the repair shop. It got too late and I have to keep it overnight. It's a Mercedes. I don't want to leave it in front of my house."

"A *Mercedes*? What are you up to?"

"Just let me park it in back of your house."

"Does this have something to do with that birthday party? Are you doing things to try to impress Perla Rubi's family?"

Emiliano closes his eyes. "I'll give you a hundred if you let me park in back of your house."

"How much did you get?"

"For what?"

"For taking the car to the repair shop."

Emiliano knows exactly where Paco is headed. Best friends think alike, unfortunately. "Five hundred."

"I'll let you do it for two hundred."

"Okay, okay. Two hundred. But you have to lend me your black loafers. I need them for this party."

"How are you going to get there? I thought you were parking the car in my backyard."

"I'm parking it in your backyard *after* I come home from the party."

"So you *are* doing this to impress Perla Rubi's parents. You think driving a fancy car is going to do it? Why don't you find a nice girl who likes your poor ass for what it is?"

"Are you going to lend me the shoes or not?"

"Fine. If you're determined to make a fool of yourself, you might as well do it with nice shoes. Don't step in any crap at your fancy birthday party."

"I'll be there in about half an hour."

"Oh, man, we're on our way out to dinner. I'll leave the key to the gate under the Virgen in my mother's garden. Careful with the flowers. If we're asleep when you get back, make sure you lock the gate after you park the car."

"And the shoes?"

"I'll leave them on a chair on the back porch."

"Thanks, man."

"Hey, Emiliano. You're not doing anything illegal, are you?"

"Bye, Paco."

Oh, thank God. Someone is watching out for him. He's not religious, but at moments like this, it's hard not to believe in the guardian angel his mother claims is always by his side. He was wondering how he was going to explain the Mercedes to Sara and his mother.

It's ten after five when he pulls up in front of his house. He looks around to make sure no one is on the street or looking out their windows. He pops open the trunk, lifts out the box with the black tape, and takes it to the toolshed in the back. He moves the shovels and picks and rakes and places the box in the farthest corner of the shed. Then he covers it with a canvas splotched with paint. The boxes with the folk art he takes inside the house. He showers, dresses, and is out the door carrying the beautiful chocolate cake Mami left for him on the kitchen table, next to a note from Sara:

We're on our way to Guillermo's daughter's quinceañera.
Mami wants to go to the Mass first. Behave at the party.
How did you ever get Mami to bake you a cake? You owe her
big! Be good.

He texts Perla Rubi.

I'm on my way. Running a little late.

He drives the two blocks to Paco's house and finds the loafers. Paco even shined them for him. Paco may say that Emiliano and Perla Rubi are not long term, but deep down, Emiliano knows, Paco is rooting for him to succeed. If he makes it permanently into Perla Rubi's world, there's hope for everyone. Paco is also a thief, given that Emiliano has to pay him two hundred pesos for one night's parking and the use of the loafers. Still, the peace of mind he gets from not leaving the expensive car out on the street is worth it. He locks the gate and places the key under the statue of the Virgen de Guadalupe. He pats the Virgen's head for good luck.

CHAPTER 7
SARA

FRIDAY, MARCH 24
5:15 P.M.

In the last remaining box of the newspaper's archives of material on the missing girls, Sara finds a picture of the girl in the e-mail. She's younger and happier looking and doesn't appear worn out yet. The words *Erica Rentería* are written in pencil on the back. Sara looks for the letter from the mother or father that always accompanies pictures of the missing girls, but there's no message or envelope or anything else she can use to contact the family.

She studies the picture. Erica is standing in front of some kind of monument made of white marble. She has a white blouse buttoned all the way to her neck and a pleated black skirt. Her shoes are old but clean. And white socks? What teenager wears white socks these days? It looks almost like she's wearing a school uniform, or dressed for a very conservative church. Her smile is the opposite of her clothing, though—open, generous, excited. Her expression reminds Sara of Linda, so much so that she has to close her eyes. If she finds Erica, she'll find Linda. The next step: talking to Erica's family.

As Sara walks up the flight of stairs from the file room to her cubicle, she suddenly feels very tired. She can look in the phone book for the Renterías, but most poor people don't own

74

landlines. Even if they do, there must be hundreds of Renterías in Juárez. She'll have to call them one by one. And when she finds the family, they won't know where Erica is. In the meantime, God only knows what is happening to the girls.

It's after five. All of this will have to wait until tomorrow. Tonight is the quinceañera.

Back at her cubicle, Sara is getting ready to leave when the phone rings. It's Ernesto.

"We're still trying to find out who atlas444@gmail.com belongs to, but I think we got our man anyway. That ring on his finger and the bald head? His name is Leopoldo Hinojosa. He's the head of the Public Security and Crime Prevention Unit of the State Police."

"Oh, God." A sense of powerlessness comes over Sara. How many times has she gone to the State Police to ask about Linda?

"Have you told anyone? About the deleted e-mails? About the picture?" Ernesto demands.

"No."

"Well, don't tell anyone. I mean *anyone*, Sara. Not Juana. Not Felipe. Don't even tell your family. We're safe now because people think the e-mail with the picture was deleted before anyone saw it. But this is big, Sara. Big. This guy will kill to protect his identity. It's not just him, it's the organization he's associated with."

Ernesto is saying out loud what she knew immediately. She forces herself to speak. "Okay."

"Go home. We'll talk tomorrow."

"Guillermo's quinceañera . . ."

Sara has never heard Ernesto swear until that moment. "I'll see you there. Might as well act normal in case someone is watching us."

"Like who?"

"Like whoever deleted the e-mails from Juana's computer."

Sara goes out the back door to the building and walks four blocks so she can catch her bus at a different stop. She finds a seat in the way back, squashed between two men, and ignores their thighs pressing against her. There are only so many battles she can fight.

She takes out her notepad and tries to write down everything that happened that day. Usually, writing helps her think, calms and consoles her. Today, it doesn't work. She pushes away the head of one of the men pretending to "accidentally" fall asleep on her shoulder and closes her eyes. Felipe ordering her to stop writing about the Desaparecidas seems a million years ago.

That e-mail threat about Linda. So much about it was strange. Most of the threats reporters and editors receive at *El Sol* come by regular mail. Why send an e-mail, which can possibly be traced? Sara remembers what Ernesto said: The threat came via e-mail because whoever sent it wanted them to know about his power. That much is clear.

But why mention Linda specifically? Hinojosa and his people had to know that the e-mail with the picture had been deleted from the *El Sol* hotline, so there was no need to threaten Sara. She's received death threats before, and they typically start after she talks to family members or the missing person's friends, or she's known to be digging around in the public records. People who are afraid of publicity find out quickly when *El Sol* is on the scent. But no one at the paper has done anything on Linda since Sara wrote about her. The last time she went to see Mrs. Fuentes was over two weeks ago, and it was just a friendly visit; they didn't go see the State Police. Why the need for a further threat?

Unless . . . Sara opens her eyes. Unless there was something *else* that they thought Sara had, or was about to get. Something incriminating that they were afraid she'd see—*so* incriminating that they had to threaten her family. But what? She needs to dig into that possibility tomorrow.

Should she tell Linda's mother and father that Linda might be alive? It's such a hard thing to decide, whether to give someone a hope that may turn out to be false. Is the hurt worse for having hoped? But this hope is real. *Puchi:* Linda wrote that a little more than a day ago. *One more day,* Sara decides. She'll wait one more day, doing all the research she can, before she speaks to Mrs. Fuentes. Maybe by the end of the day tomorrow she can give Linda's family something a little more solid. There has to be something out there, anything that will connect Hinojosa to the place where Linda is being kept.

I'm going to find you, Linda. I promise.

CHAPTER 8
EMILIANO

Emiliano drives the car down the Esmeraldas' long driveway. The boy who will take the car and park it in an empty lot down the street is only a year or two older than he is. "I'll take good care of it for you," he says, but Emiliano still hesitates a moment before handing him the keys. He will have to give the boy a tip on the way out, and all he has are the five hundred-peso bills that Armando gave him. One hundred pesos is too big a tip. Maybe he can get change from Perla Rubi. No, that's ridiculous. He can't ask Perla Rubi if she has change for a hundred pesos. He'll work it out inside.

He walks to the front door of the Esmeralda residence, holding the platter with his mother's cake in both hands. A man in a shiny brown suit and skinny black tie opens the door for him. "I can take that for you, sir," he says, gesturing to the cake.

Sir? "Thanks," Emiliano says. "I can do it."

"Certainly, sir. Your name, please?"

"Emiliano Zapata."

The man shines a thin flashlight on a sheet of paper. When he lifts the paper closer to his eyes, Emiliano sees the holster on the man's hip. After he finally finds Emiliano's name, at the very end of the list, the security guard opens the door.

The foyer inside sparkles in the light of a chandelier with hundreds of prisms in the shape of frozen tears. The trumpets from a mariachi band blare from somewhere in the back of the house. To the right of the foyer is a dining room with a table covered with wrapped presents and vases full of roses. Two women stand in front of the table holding champagne glasses. Their necks, wrists, and fingers glitter with jewels. To the left, a step below the foyer, Emiliano sees a room with a blue-felt pool table, brown leather chairs, and lamps that glow with soft yellow light. Encyclopedia-looking books line one of the walls, while the other is covered with colorful paintings of Mexican villages and bustling marketplaces. In this room, men in dark blue and gray suits stand with thick tumblers in their hands. Despite Paco's loafers, Emiliano feels shabbily dressed. He's glad he opted for socks.

He stands paralyzed, dazed by the opulence. Everything looks luxurious but also comfortable. He could easily imagine himself in one of those brown chairs or playing pool. Which way does he go? Should he put the cake on the table next to the silver-wrapped boxes with silky red ribbons? Sooner or later he has to do something, take a step in one direction or another. No one has noticed him standing there like a scared rabbit, but that could change any second.

The end of the foyer seems to lead to another hallway. That hallway seems to point north. *When in doubt, follow Polaris, the North Star.* That's a Jipari rule. The mariachi band is playing one of his mother's favorite songs, and he draws comfort from that.

He's about to leave the foyer when a young woman in a black dress and frilly white apron turns a corner and almost bumps into him. She smiles a beautiful smile that instantly reminds Emiliano of his sister. "Emiliano?" she asks.

He nods, grateful to find a friendly face.

"Perlita told me to look out for you. I recognized you from your picture in the newspaper."

"Newspaper?"

"When you won the big soccer game in Chihuahua." Her eyes fall on the cake. "What a gorgeous cake!"

"For Mrs. Esmeralda. My mother made it."

"Those little whirls of frosting are very difficult to make." The young woman starts to take it from his hands, but stops when Emiliano hesitates to let it go. "I'll put it in a safe place and let Mrs. Esmeralda know it's from you and made by your mother."

He allows her to take the cake. "It's a liqueur cake, my mother's specialty," Emiliano tells her.

"I can't wait to taste it when no one's looking," the young woman whispers to him. "Come, I'll take you to Perlita. She's by the pool."

They walk to the end of the hallway and stop in front of some glass doors, through which he can see a stone terrace full of people, and beyond that, the turquoise light of a pool. Emiliano hesitates.

"Go on," the young woman says. "The rich people's bark is worse than their bite."

He laughs. How does she know he's not one of the rich people? Is it that obvious? She smiles at him one more time before she walks away.

That was pleasant, Emiliano says to himself as he opens the glass door and steps bravely onto the terrace. Pushed against the walls of the house are tables with dozens of hot and cold dishes. There's more food and more different kinds of it in one place than Emiliano has ever seen. It's like a banquet scene from a movie about the Roman Empire. When he looks at the abundance of desserts on one of the tables, he feels a pang of sadness. His mother's masterpiece will be lost in all that richness.

But the sadness dissipates when he sees Perla Rubi sitting at a table by the pool. She's with a group of people her age—their age. When she sees him coming down the steps from the terrace, she jumps up and walks toward him, arms outstretched, to hug him as if he was lost and is now found.

"I was worried about you!"

"Why?"

"You're so late. I thought you were going to get here around six."

"It was a rough day."

"You'll have to tell me about it. Come on, I want you to meet my cousins."

Emiliano is used to shaking hands when being introduced, but neither of the two young men nor the young woman sitting at the table gets up when Perla Rubi introduces him, so he simply nods and gives a babyish five-finger wave to each one. He tries to remember their names, but the only one that sticks with him is the name of the last person: Federico. Perla Rubi drags a chair from the next table and Emiliano sits.

"He's a hunk!" the young woman whispers in Perla Rubi's ear, loud enough for Emiliano to hear. Blood rushes to his face. "Look, I made him blush. How cute!"

"Veronica, behave!" Perla Rubi says. Emiliano repeats the name to himself so he won't forget.

One of the male cousins is looking at his phone and laughing to himself. The other, the one named Federico, is staring at him with cold intensity. There is something about his ears that seems out of proportion with the rest of his head.

"Are you hungry? Want something to drink?" Perla Rubi waves her hand until she catches the attention of a boy with a tray at the other end of the pool.

Emiliano notices that the tables are decorated with miniature piñatas, and the image of Javier's shack, with its plywood walls and tin roof, flashes in his mind.

"So all of you are related?" he asks, for something to say. He instantly feels stupid. Perla Rubi already told him they were cousins.

"Carlos is my mother's brother's son. Veronica is the daughter of my aunt, my father's sister. And Federico is the son of Veronica's father's uncle, so we're distant cousins, I guess."

"Extremely distant," Federico adds, looking at Perla Rubi in a way that makes Emiliano immediately dislike him.

Carlos reaches for his can and chugs whatever beer is left in there. When the boy with the tray reaches them, Perla Rubi says, "Mario, bring us plates of different things. A little of everything. As many of those small plates as you can fit on your tray."

"Bring me another one of these." Carlos shakes his empty beer can.

"Three more?" the boy asks.

Emiliano shakes his head. "A Coke for me, please."

"You don't like beer?" Federico asks.

"I like it. I just don't drink it."

"Rum? Tequila? Wine? Scotch? Do you like anything a man would drink?" His tone is not friendly. The guy is a jerk.

"I don't drink alcohol," Emiliano says, forcing a smile.

"Oh, how sad!" Federico exclaims.

"Why?" Veronica asks Emiliano, serious.

He shrugs.

"Emiliano belongs to an explorer group," Perla Rubi jumps in, pride in her voice. "Part of their code is not to drink or do drugs. Isn't that right, Emiliano?"

"An explorer group? Like the Boy Scouts?" Federico asks.

"I love their cookies!" Carlos says, clapping his hands. "We buy them when we go shopping in El Paso."

"That's the Girl Scouts, idiot!" Veronica says.

Emiliano reminds himself that these are Perla Rubi's relatives and he should be nice to them for her sake. "There are some similarities with the Boy Scouts, but we're more focused on desert survival."

Perla Rubi moves her chair closer to him. "Emiliano's the captain of our school's soccer team. We won the state championship last year, as you know." She directs these words at Federico.

"Anyone can play soccer," Federico responds. "Try hitting a tiny ball with a wooden mallet while your horse is at a gallop."

"Federico is on our country club's polo team," Veronica tells Emiliano. "They think they're oh so hot, even though it's the horse that does all the work."

"Very funny," Federico says. He turns around. "Where the hell is that kid?"

"He's trying to figure out what to bring us," Veronica says, glancing up at the terrace.

"You could walk up and get your own beer, you know," Perla Rubi says. "Moving your own legs now and then would do you good."

"Ooo! Touché!" Carlos laughs and picks up his phone again.

Federico says to Emiliano, "Ever been on a horse?"

Emiliano thinks of his bike. When Sara gave it to him, she said it reminded her of Don Quixote's horse, Rocinante. "I've been on a burro. He had these really big, ugly ears." Emiliano stares for a few moments at Federico's ears. "Does that count?"

Federico's smirk changes to a frown. Perla Rubi giggles, then pulls Emiliano out of his chair. "We'll be back," she tells the group. She's walking with him, laughing, waving at someone on the terrace.

"What?" he says to her when they're away from the group.

"I had to get you out of there before you lost it and beat the crap out of Federico."

"I wasn't going to lose it."

"They're just silly—don't mind them. Let's see if we can find my mother so you can wish her a happy birthday like we planned." She squeezes his arm. "Are you all right? You seem upset about something."

"I'm sorry. It's been a very strange day."

She stops in the middle of the steps and turns to him. "Anything bad? Are you sure you're okay?"

"Everything's okay." He notices for the first time the soft, white dress that Perla Rubi is wearing. Not white, exactly, but the creamy color of a pearl. She seems so rich, like everything else in her house. Not just money-rich, but rich with life and color and happiness.

"Did you have trouble getting here? How *did* you get here anyway?"

"I drove here in a Mercedes." Did he really have to mention that it was a Mercedes?

"What?"

"It's a long story. I did a friend a favor and took his father's car to the repair shop, and then it got too late to take the car back to him and still make it here in time, so he let me keep it overnight."

"Mmm." The look on Perla Rubi's face says she doesn't quite believe him. "I didn't know you had those kinds of friends."

He smiles and squeezes her hand. "Stick with me, young lady. I am full of surprises."

Perla Rubi smiles back and blushes.

Mrs. Esmeralda is waiting for them at the edge of the terrace. He's met her before, when she's come to pick up Perla Rubi from school. Emiliano extends his hand, but Mrs. Esmeralda hugs him instead. It's a delicate hug that makes him think of a monarch butterfly, the kind he saw on the Sierra Tarahumara.

"Thank you for the beautiful cake," she says, smiling at him. "Diana told me your mother made it."

"It's her specialty. It has coffee liqueur."

"I hope you don't mind," Mrs. Esmeralda says, "but I told Diana not to put it out with the other desserts. I'm going to keep it all for myself. Maybe I'll let you have a piece, Perla Rubi, if you are good."

"I will be. I'll be very good."

Mrs. Esmeralda hooks her arm through Emiliano's and tells Perla Rubi, still smiling, "I'm going to take him to meet your father."

"Papá?" Perla Rubi asks, surprised. "Why?"

Mrs. Esmeralda shrugs mysteriously. "I don't know. Your father told me he wanted to talk to him."

"Don't worry," Perla Rubi says to Emiliano. "His bark is worse than his bite."

Emiliano grins as he tries to remember where he heard that phrase recently. It's supposed to make people less afraid, but it usually has the opposite effect. There's no need to be nervous. He should be excited. This is his opportunity to show Perla Rubi's father that he is worthy of his daughter. Isn't that the plan? "I'll see you," he says to Perla Rubi.

"Bye!" Perla Rubi says, excited. She's happy that he's getting all this attention from her parents, he can tell.

Mrs. Esmeralda is wearing a silky, soft, pale green dress with her hair flowing over her shoulders. A silver-and-emerald necklace jiggles gently when she walks. Emiliano is glad he chose the cake as a present. Whatever he was going to buy her with his thousand pesos would have looked pathetic on Mrs. Esmeralda.

"I hope you didn't have too much trouble getting here. I know you live far away," Mrs. Esmeralda says. They are walking through a kitchen that seems larger than Emiliano's entire house. The girl who took the cake smiles at him, or at Mrs. Esmeralda, he's not sure. "Don't forget to take your mother's platter when you leave. Diana will have it ready for you."

"Thank you."

"I could get Jaime to take you back home if you wish."

"Thank you. I have a way to get home."

They walk up a staircase made of white granite. Mrs. Esmeralda stops and says to him, "I wanted to tell you how glad I am that you and Perla Rubi are good friends."

"Thank you," Emiliano says. Does he imagine a slight weight on the word *friends*?

"It's really been good for Perla Rubi to help you with your studies. I've noticed, I don't know, a greater maturity and sense of responsibility ever since she started tutoring you. And, of course, Jorge and I are very grateful that she has you to watch over her at school."

"Thank you" is the only thing he can think of saying. Sometime in the near future, he hopes he will come up with something to say other than *thank you*.

Mrs. Esmeralda continues, "Jorge and I don't care about material things, believe it or not. We care about hard work. Perla Rubi has told me how hard you work with the school's soccer team and helping poor kids with Brother Patricio and the . . ."

"Jiparis," Emiliano says.

"Jiparis. What a nice person Brother Patricio is, isn't he?"

"Yes. He's a good man."

"We're always happy to contribute to his causes. Oh, look." They stop by a small table placed against a wall. On top of it is a vase with black and white designs. "Perla Rubi told me about your Mexican folk art business. How enterprising on your part. I collect folk art too! This is a vase made by the indigenous people of Michoacán. Isn't it beautiful? Do you work with pottery in your business?" She looks at him expectantly.

"No, pottery like that requires special clay and paints and

furnaces. The folk art objects that my kids make are from everyday, easy-to-find, inexpensive materials."

"Your kids?"

"The younger Jipari kids make things for me to sell."

She smiles. "That's sweet."

Mrs. Esmeralda starts walking and Emiliano follows her. Javier and Memo and the other Jiparis *are* his kids, kind of. He got them interested in creating things once he saw they had the patience and attention to detail needed to be good craftsmen. He gives them money for materials when they don't have any. He sells their work at the best price he can get. He gets a fair fee for what he does. He never thought of the arrangement as "sweet."

Emiliano thinks of the miniature piñatas that Javier makes. If he accepts Mr. Reyes's offer, he'll need to convince Javier to load the piñatas. Javier's family is barely surviving. The money that they make from the loaded piñatas would make their lives so much more comfortable.

They turn left at the top of the stairs and stop in front of the first closed door. Mrs. Esmeralda raps on it gently.

"Come in," a man's voice says. It is difficult to determine whether it is welcoming or not.

"Don't let him intimidate you," Mrs. Esmeralda whispers to Emiliano. "Sometimes he interrogates people like the lawyer he is. If he asks you a question you don't feel like answering, just say, 'That's a very good question. I'll have to think about that.' It's what Perla Rubi and I do." She winks and then opens the door for him to go in alone.

The room is dark except for the pale glow of the open laptop on the glass desk. Emiliano waits for his eyes to adjust and then sees the back of a reddish-brown leather chair with the top of a man's head over it. The man swings the chair around and covers a cell phone with his left hand. He's younger than Emiliano imagined him, with a closely shaved face, a light blue shirt with a white round collar, and a thin lavender tie—all elegant, handsome, refined. "I'll be right with you," Mr. Esmeralda says. "Emergency. Have a seat."

Emiliano sits in one of two beige chairs. The leather on the chair is buttery soft, and Emiliano has to keep himself from sliding to the front of the seat. The built-in bookcases are full of crystal bowls with glittery engraving that Emiliano cannot read. Prestigious awards, probably. There's an order and simplicity about the room that reminds Emiliano of a very exclusive jewelry store where people walk softly and speak in whispers. He has never met Mr. Esmeralda, though Perla Rubi told Emiliano that her father saw the Pumas play in the state championship. She said he thought Emiliano was the reason the Pumas won that day. Sitting there in the semidark room, listening to Mr. Esmeralda talk, Emiliano remembers the winning goal: a perfect cross from his foot to Paco's forehead and into the net.

So much is happening so fast. He is either getting "checked out," or Perla Rubi's parents want to make sure that he knows his place and stays there. They would be doing these things only if they know Perla Rubi likes him. The conversation with Mrs. Esmeralda was more positive than not, all things considered. What matters is that she recognized he's a hard worker, and the Esmeraldas believe in hard work. What was it she called him? Enterprising. That's a good thing, isn't it? That's what he likes to do—"enterprise," whatever that means. He leans back a little into the chair. He's not nervous now. On the contrary, he feels like he sometimes does out on the soccer field, like he belongs here and can move freely.

Mr. Esmeralda puts the cell phone faceup on the glass desk, rises from his chair, and walks around the desk, hand outstretched.

"Jorge Esmeralda."

"Emiliano Zapata." He tries to stand, but Mr. Esmeralda pushes him gently back in the chair. The man sits down in the adjacent chair, putting his right foot over his left leg.

"You must get a lot of comments about your name," Mr. Esmeralda says.

"Yes. 'Like the revolutionary hero?' is what people usually say."

Mr. Esmeralda laughs. "I shouldn't laugh. I named my daughter Perla Rubi."

"It's a nice name. I like it."

Mr. Esmeralda studies Emiliano for a few seconds, then uncrosses his legs. "As my wife no doubt told you, we are very grateful that you are Perla Rubi's friend." This time Emiliano doesn't mind being referred to as a friend. Mr. Esmeralda says it without any emphasis, in the same tone as the rest of his words. "To tell you the truth, I wasn't sure Colegio México was the right choice for Perla Rubi. It's not in the best part of town and the security is not—well, it doesn't really inspire confidence." Emiliano laughs and immediately feels guilty for doing so. He likes Cristobal. "But Perla Rubi wanted to go there. She wanted to play for one of the best volleyball teams in the city and she wanted to be challenged academically. Colegio México has a very rigorous academic curriculum."

"Yes," Emiliano says, "extremely rigorous."

The way he says it makes Mr. Esmeralda laugh again. "So I was happy to hear that someone like you was watching over her. With all the kidnappings that still take place, it made me feel better that you were with her after school. Thank you for that."

"You're welcome." It never crossed his mind that he was protecting Perla Rubi. He always stayed with her after school because he did not want to miss a single second of her company. But maybe that's how rich parents think: that bad people want to kidnap their kids for ransom.

There's a long moment of silence, and Emiliano wonders if the conversation is over. He shifts in his seat as if to stand.

"Stay a little longer," Mr. Esmeralda says. "Although you're probably eager to go downstairs and spend some quality time with Perla Rubi's cousins."

"Yes. We have a lot of polo to discuss."

Mr. Esmeralda laughs a third time. Who knew Emiliano could be so funny? "I understand. I don't really care that much for those spoiled brats myself, but they're family."

"They're okay," he says cautiously.

"They are rich, arrogant, lazy dandies who think they're better than people like you, and you know it."

Emiliano smiles.

"Perla Rubi is not like that. Don't you think?"

"Yes. I mean no, she's not arrogant . . . or lazy."

Mr. Esmeralda stretches out his left hand and rests it on the glass desk. He taps his fingers on an imaginary piano as he looks around his office. Emiliano follows his eyes and notices the same colorful Mexican paintings he saw throughout the house.

"When I was your age"—Mr. Esmeralda sits back and returns his gaze to Emiliano—"I also made papier-mâché animals and sold them to tourists from El Paso. My father had a small store that sold Mexican souvenirs. The whole store was about the size of this office. I stood on the main street with my parrots and bulls and tried to lure tourists down an alleyway to the store. My parents insisted I finish high school, but after that, I went to work in a factory, making those famous Mexican tiles everyone loves so much. I helped my parents and made sure my younger sisters finished school. I saved, invested, and went to law school eventually, and after a few years, I started my own firm. All I have today is the product of hard work."

Mr. Esmeralda pauses. "The parents of Perla Rubi's cousins were just as poor as I was. But somehow they forgot to pass on to their children all the values that got them where they are now."

The cell phone vibrates on the glass desk and Mr. Esmeralda reaches for it and reads a message. He puts the phone on the desk facedown.

"When I opened my own firm, I tried to take the kind of cases that helped people. Poor store owners like my father who were losing their businesses or their homes. I helped the small guys. I was a good, conscientious, clean lawyer." Mr. Esmeralda clears his throat. "But things happened. I wanted to grow, personally and professionally. I wanted to take care of my family but . . . it was not possible to do that without being a part of this city, such as it is."

There is a note of regret in Mr. Esmeralda's voice. His openness and vulnerability surprises Emiliano. Then he slides to the front of his chair, an intense look in his eyes.

"There's no way to be successful in Mexico without getting dirty. The best one can do is control the degree of dirt. Do you understand what I'm saying?"

Emiliano nods involuntarily.

"Do you understand what I'm telling you?"

The way he asks, as if he really wants the truth, makes Emiliano respond with what is foremost in his mind. "What do you mean, 'getting dirty'?"

Mr. Esmeralda pauses. "Good, good," he says, sitting back, crossing his arms. "Now I see why people are impressed with you. You remind me of myself when I was your age."

"Thank you."

Mr. Esmeralda stares at him, a serious look on his face. Emiliano stares back, trying not to feel uncomfortable or speak just to fill the silence. Finally, Mr. Esmeralda says, "I got a call an hour or so ago from Enrique Cortázar. One of my clients. You know his son, Armando, I believe."

A current of fear travels through Emiliano. Is he going to get accused of stealing the car?

"Enrique tells me that you made a good impression on a business associate and close friend of his, Alfredo Reyes."

"You know Alfredo Reyes?" Emiliano doesn't mean to sound as shocked as he is.

"Of course I know him. This city is a like a spiderweb. Every thread is connected directly or indirectly to every other thread. Enrique Cortázar, Alfredo Reyes, myself, we are businessmen. The success of any organization depends on the quality of the people who work there. These people, they see potential in you. That is very special. The kind of trust that was shown to you today is not given easily. Not many people are invited to Alfredo Reyes's house or are offered an opportunity to work with him."

Emiliano rubs the back of his scalp. "They want me to . . ."

"Stop," Mr. Esmeralda commands. "I don't need to know the details. All I want to do is tell you that . . . growing up means, unfortunately, expanding our views of what we consider good and bad. Within that larger view, we do what we can for our families, we create jobs, we help the less fortunate." He pauses and takes a deep breath. "You asked me what I meant by 'getting dirty.' Getting dirty means doing what we have to do for our families and for those around us, given the realities of where we live, in this mess of a life that is good and bad."

"Good and bad," Emiliano says to himself.

"Do you know how Colegio México is able to give soccer scholarships to young men like you? Because of businessmen like Mr. Cortázar and myself. When Brother Patricio asked for help, I called Mr. Cortázar and others, and we gave. You are already part of the web, if you think about it."

Emiliano remembers the calls for donations Brother Patricio makes every year.

Mr. Esmeralda continues, his voice soft and warm, the way Emiliano's father sometimes spoke to him. "I know a little bit about you from what my daughter and my wife have told me, and I know that your first instinct is to reject Mr. Reyes and his offer. Part of you is probably disgusted by what he proposed."

Emiliano is silent.

"I know because that was my first reaction to a similar offer when I was only a little older than you, and like I said, you remind me of me. But look." Mr. Esmeralda opens his arms.

"I'm also a good person. I want the best for my wife and daughter. I'm not greedy. I make enough to live comfortably. I could be making more, but I don't. Do you understand?"

"Yes."

"So. Think about what I said to you today. Think about the offer that Mr. Reyes made to you. Consider all the implications, said and unsaid, and get back to Mr. Reyes one way or another. Don't make him wait too long. Get back to him no later than Monday. All right?"

Emiliano nods. "All right."

Mr. Esmeralda stands and Emiliano does as well. "Come on. I'll take you back to Perla Rubi and her scintillating cousins."

They walk through the house in silence, Mr. Esmeralda half a step ahead of Emiliano. As they go down the stairs, he notices a series of photographs of Perla Rubi. They are posed portraits, the kind done in a studio or by a professional photographer who comes to your home. Mr. Esmeralda sees Emiliano looking at a photograph of Perla Rubi when she was four or five. She's wearing a charro outfit and holding a lasso in her hand.

"You know," Mr. Esmeralda says, putting his arm around Emiliano's shoulders, "children don't grow up as well as Perla Rubi has without rules. One of the rules we have been very strict about is that dating and boys are not going to be a part of her life until she graduates from high school. Her focus during these years needs to be on school, and whatever extra energy she has, she can use in volleyball."

Now it makes sense to Emiliano why Perla Rubi did not want to say openly that they were girlfriend and boyfriend. He shouldn't have resented her for that. He should have understood.

"On the other hand," Mr. Esmeralda continues, "I'm no fool and neither is Judith. If the rope is too tight, the horse will break it. That's why we didn't mind when Perla Rubi told us you had become a good friend to her. Someday she'll find the right person and fall in love and get married. But I will tell you this: When that day comes, I am going to make sure that the man she marries is a hardworking man who has the courage to do whatever it takes to care for her. To make whatever sacrifice is needed on her behalf. Do you understand what I'm saying to you, Emiliano?"

Emiliano gazes into Mr. Esmeralda's eyes for as long as he can. Finally, he has to look away. He stares at the picture of the child Perla Rubi in front of him. She's confident and secure, even a little cocky. She's felt no hardship in her life and sees no hardship in her future. Emiliano wants to take care of her, to do whatever it takes to give her everything she wants and needs. He knows Mr. Esmeralda wants that too.

"I understand what you're saying," Emiliano says.

"Good."

They walk through the rest of the house, Mr. Esmeralda speaking quickly as he waves and nods to guests. "I saw you play in Chihuahua, you know."

"Perla Rubi told me you were there."

"Your technical skills are superior and your stamina is impressive. I don't think you were even breathing hard at any point in the game. But you know what I liked the most about how you play?"

Emiliano shakes his head. They pass through the kitchen. He sees his mother's cake platter on a counter next to a huge stainless steel refrigerator.

"I liked how you played with a kind of controlled anger. You know what I mean?"

Emiliano has never thought of his concentration on the field as anger, controlled or otherwise. What he had when he played was not anger but an ability to see the whole field, almost as if he were calmly hovering above it. They stand in front of the closed glass doors that lead to the terrace and the party. Mr. Esmeralda puts his hand on the handle of the door.

"That kind of intensity is a precious gift, Emiliano. Don't waste it."

He looks at Emiliano one last time, making sure all the implications of his message are received. Then he opens the door and waves at Perla Rubi and his wife at the other end of the terrace.

"What were you guys talking about for so long?" Perla Rubi asks when they approach.

"A little business, a little getting to know each other," Mr. Esmeralda says. "Right, Emiliano?"

"Right," Emiliano answers. The expectant looks on Perla Rubi's and Mrs. Esmeralda's faces indicate that more explanation is needed. "I . . . we . . ." he stammers.

"One of my best clients called me this afternoon to tell me that a very influential business associate had been very impressed with Emiliano. He wants Emiliano to do business with him."

"Really?" Perla Rubi asks, excited.

"My folk art business," Emiliano says. Hopefully, they can leave it at that.

"And?" Perla Rubi asks, raising her eyebrows expectantly. "Are you going to do it?"

Emiliano knows that a yes will light her face with joy. Mrs. Esmeralda watches her like a parent watching a child unwrap a Christmas present. If he says yes, Mr. Esmeralda will know he'll be the type of man who can take care of Perla Rubi. But the image of little Marta setting up the fan with her trembling hand flashes through his mind.

He forces himself to speak. "I'm going to seriously consider it. I'll think about it this weekend and let him know on Monday," he says, glancing quickly at Mr. Esmeralda.

"That's right," Mr. Esmeralda says. "All important decisions should be considered carefully." Looking at his wife, he adds, "Right, sweetie?"

"Yes. They *should*." The way she says it makes Emiliano think Mr. Esmeralda has on occasion acted on important decisions without consulting his wife. She smiles. "Now, enough business talk for one day. Go dance, you two."

Perla Rubi takes Emiliano's hand and leads him to the section of the terrace where a DJ has set up. She puts her arms around his shoulders, and they begin to dance to a slow ballad. There is space between them, and yet Emiliano can feel her warm breath on his neck. "They really like you," she says, pulling back to look at him.

"Who? Your cousins?"

"Very funny. You know who. My parents. Papá wouldn't have talked to you for so long if he didn't. You have to tell me every single thing he said. And Mamá, she wouldn't say 'Go dance, you two' if she didn't really like you."

"They like me," Emiliano teases, "because I'm the big tough guy who protects you while you're waiting for your mom or Jaime to pick you up after school."

"Stop it." She laughs. "First of all, you're not big and tough, and second of all, I can take care of myself." She moves a little closer. Emiliano can smell wildflowers in her hair. "I'm glad they like you," she says softly. "I hope you say yes to my father's client. Papá knows everyone. He'll help you." The music stops, but Perla Rubi keeps her head close to his. "I like thinking you'll be connected to my father's work. It's like you'll be part of the family."

Emiliano feels a knot in his throat, hot liquid in his eyes. He brings Perla Rubi closer to him. He hugs her silently until he can feel the wave of emotion recede. Then, when the music starts again, she starts to sway softly and he follows her movement. They dance like that, hardly moving, and when the song is over, Perla Rubi holds his hand and meets his eyes. "Thank you."

"For what?"

Perla Rubi touches his heart. "For this."

He smiles.

"Do you want to sit down?" she asks. "You haven't had anything to eat."

"Listen," Emiliano says, biting his lip. "Would you mind very much if I went home early?"

"Why?"

He tries to smile. "Honestly, this dance and this

conversation are so nice that I don't want the moment to be ruined by what's coming next."

Perla Rubi follows Emiliano's eyes and sees Federico raising a bottle of champagne. He motions for them to come to his table, but she ignores him. "I'm sorry. He's a harmless snob. Don't worry."

"I'm not worried," Emiliano says. "But I am kind of worried about the Mercedes I drove here. I want to make sure I park it in a safe place tonight. Paco said I could leave it in his backyard, but I don't want to get there after everyone's asleep."

"It's only nine o'clock, Emiliano. No one goes to sleep this early."

"I know. It's just been a long, long day and I . . ."

"Okay. Go. I'll see you tomorrow, don't forget. We're playing Sacred Heart at home. Come by and say hello."

"I'll be there."

She takes his hand and leads him down the back stairs of the terrace. She glances around to make sure no one can see them, and then she leans over very slowly and kisses him on the lips. The kiss is soft, lingering, full of more to come.

"Good-bye, Emiliano Zapata."

"Good-bye, Perla Rubi Esmeralda."

The way she looks at him, the smile she gives him, tells Emiliano that the kiss meant all that it promised.

CHAPTER 9

SARA

***

The banquet room of El Camino Real Hotel can barely fit all of the guests attending Guillermo's daughter's quinceañera. The twenty round tables are supposed to sit ten people each, but that's not enough space for everyone who showed up uninvited, so two additional people have been squeezed around each table. Sara sits between Mami and Juana, so she doesn't have to engage in small talk with strangers, but she finds herself wishing she wasn't sitting next to Juana. Juana is her mentor, the person who gave her an unpaid internship when she was in high school, permanent employment as soon as she graduated, and progressively harder assignments so that she could grow as a reporter and as a writer. She fought Felipe to have Sara's article about Linda printed, even though it was not written in the objective journalistic style that Felipe insisted on. Most of all, Juana is a relentless advocate against all the different forms of violence, physical and otherwise, perpetrated against women. But Sara promised Ernesto she would not tell anyone about Hinojosa, not even Juana, and with her mind full of Linda and Erica, she's afraid she will break that promise.

When Ernesto shows up late, he squeezes in at their table, and Sara can tell by his fake smile that he's as unhappy to be there as she is. As the evening wears on, she can almost see his mind tallying up the cost of each champagne bottle popped, each cocktail served at the open bar. Every time a tuxedoed waiter brings yet another dish or a new bottle of wine to the table, Ernesto sighs, shakes his head, and rolls his eyes at Sara. Watching Ernesto's various grimaces is the only enjoyable part of the evening for her. That, and seeing her mother laugh.

During one of the old Mexican rancheras, Mami leans over to Sara and says, "Whenever I hear that music, I think of your father."

"Does that make you sad?" Sara puts her hand on top of her mother's.

"Yes, but not in a bad way."

Sara lets her mother listen to the song, watches the beautiful, peaceful smile on her face. That smile makes Sara remember a conversation with Linda after her mother signed the divorce papers. They were in Sara's backyard, sitting sideways on a hammock tied between two elm trees.

"It's sad, but your mother's right, you know," Linda said. "Love's not enough."

Sara leaned away to look at her. "What else is there?"

"I don't know what you call it. People have to hope and want similar things."

"And Papá and Mami didn't?"

Linda shook her head quietly. "Think about everything you've told me. All the ways they're so different."

"My dad is outgoing. My mom is shy and quiet. Is that what you mean?"

"No, it's not about personality. It's about what each of them wants out of life. Your mom is happy with what she has.

If she has a roof over her head, some beans and tortillas, and her family—what else is there?"

Sara nodded, understanding her point. "And Papá wants more."

"Yes. He had a steady job building houses here, right? But he wanted more than he could ever have in Mexico, and that's why he went to the United States. There's nothing wrong with his ambition. Your mom doesn't fault him for that. She realizes that what makes him happy is not what makes her happy. She's accepted that it's okay for the two of them to go their separate ways. They'd be miserable together, just like he was already miserable before he left. Everyone could see that. You did too, admit it."

Sara lowered her head. Yes, she knew he was unhappy.

Linda continued, "He'd blame her for holding him back, and she would fault him for not paying attention to what she thinks is really important."

"But he left us," Sara argued. "He went away and never came back. Doesn't he have obligations to us?"

"He's doing what he can, isn't he?" Linda said. "He sends money. He's not rejecting you and Emiliano. That's not what the divorce is about. If anything, he's showing you how important it is to do what you really like."

Sara thought about it. Linda's words made sense to her, but she knew her brother was struggling with Papá's decision. "Emiliano sees it as a rejection."

"You have to help him think differently."

"How?"

"By doing what your mami's doing. Understanding that the

divorce is for the better. That there is love, but love is not enough. Then eventually Emiliano will understand."

Sara put her arm around Linda's shoulders. The two girls were quiet for a long time. Two cardinals perched on the branch above them. "You better not poop on us," Linda warned them.

"How'd you get to be so wise anyway?" Sara asked her.

"Telenovelas," Linda answered.

Sara smiles, remembering Linda's words and seeing her mother rock gently to the rhythm of the music. Then a man's hand stretches out in front of her. "May I have this dance?"

It is Elias, staggering a little as he speaks. Sara can tell that he's made several trips to the open bar, in addition to the champagne and wine served at the tables.

"Elias, I'm a terrible dancer. I would kill your feet. But you're very kind to ask." She's as nice and polite as she can be, especially with the whole table looking at them. The male ego, Elias's especially, is fragile.

"Come on. Just one dance, please." Elias goes down on one knee. "Please."

"Okay, okay." Sara stands up, pulls Elias from the floor and then steadies him with her hand on his waist. She lets go of him when he seems stable enough to walk by himself, and they proceed to the dance floor.

"You are radiant tonight. Like the sun," he says as they start dancing.

"That's the margaritas speaking," Sara says, stepping back to create a respectable distance between their bodies. She tries to block out the words of the beautiful love song. There's something incongruous about the pure kind of love that the lyrics are proclaiming and dancing with Elias.

"You know what I like the most about you?" His voice has a slight slur to it.

"Hey," Sara says, trying to change the subject. "You know that camping trip with the Jiparis next Saturday? I was thinking of getting some pictures of the kids setting up camp and maybe a few of them hiking at night with the stars shining above them. What do you think?"

"Stop talking shop for a minute. I want to tell you something."

Sara is surprised at the brusqueness in Elias's tone. *It's the alcohol*, she reminds herself. *Humor. Get through the dance with humor.* "Okay, but keep it clean."

Elias giggles like he thinks she's joking. Flirting, maybe. "You're not going to believe this, but what I like the most about you, what I really, really like about you, is your dedication."

Oh, God, Sara thinks. *He's going to get sentimental on me.*

"I mean it," he continues. "You're different than all the other women . . . I know. You . . . you're committed to a cause. To those girls who are, who have gone missing. Who turn up dead after a while. There's not that many women like you."

She turns her head slightly so she doesn't have to smell his breath. "There's lots of women like me. You just need to look at women a little differently than you usually do."

"No, no. I've looked. Trust me. In this very room"—he lets go of her hand and makes a circle in the air with his index finger—"I probably looked extremely close at half a dozen women. Including women you'd never guess."

"Wonderful." She exhales and tries to listen to the words of the song.

"I'm not trying to boast or anything." Elias takes her hand again and squeezes it. "I'm saying that to show you how I see you is different. You know how I found out that I care for you?"

Sara stops dancing. "I think I want to sit down."

"No, wait. Let me finish what I want to say!"

The volume of his voice makes people glance in their direction. Sara starts dancing with him again to dispel the attention. "Elias, you've had too much to drink," she says. "You're my colleague. Don't say anything that will make it hard for us to work together."

"You know what they say, drunks tell the truth. Just let me finish. I knew I had feelings for you when I noticed I was worried about you."

"Worried?"

"Those articles you write. The threats you get. I've never been worried about anyone before. You understand? It hit me that I was falling in love with you when I worried that something might happen to you."

The song ends, but Sara stands still, looking at Elias. It isn't his declaration of love that startles her; it's the way he says that something might happen to her. Up until then his speech has been sweet, dramatic, with the kind of exaggeration peculiar to inebriation. But those last words were cold and totally sober, and they sounded very much like a threat.

Someone at *El Sol* is working with Hinojosa. Someone went into Juana's office and deleted the hotline e-mails. Someone knows that her life has been threatened.

The band starts playing Ricky Martin's "La Vida Loca" and people begin shaking and jumping all around them. Sara lets Elias take her in his arms again, and they continue dancing softly. Her mind is spinning, but her reporter instincts tell her one thing: Being close to Elias, as painful as it is, may be an opportunity to gather information, or to convey information to the people who are threatening her. She should go along with him, pretend she knows nothing.

"What should I do?" she asks. "About the articles I write?"

"You need to stop. Write about those Boy Scout kids, about all the happy things going on, like Felipe says. There's nothing you can do about the missing girls. Leave them alone."

"I've stopped," she says as convincingly as possible. "I'm not doing anything about missing girls. No articles. No investigations. Nothing. I'm done. From now on, happy stuff."

"Good." He pulls her tighter against him. "Please don't do anything that puts you or your family in danger."

She shivers. How does he know about the threat to her family?

Elias whispers in her ear. "Sara, do you think that you and I—? Do you think there's any chance . . ."

Sara moves away from him and pretends to cough. She's not good at this kind of game, and she can't stand being close to him a moment longer. "No," she says firmly but kindly. "There's no chance of any relationship between us other than as colleagues who respect each other. I'm flattered you think of me that way, but no. Thank you."

She walks back to her table, aware that she has left Elias standing alone on the dance floor. She sits down and tries to smile at the people looking at her. Juana has a strange, disapproving look on her face. Sara wants to tell her what she just realized about Elias, but she can't without revealing all her other secrets. Mami pushes her glass of water in Sara's direction, and she empties it in one long swallow.

Mami leans over and whispers in her ear, "Luisa says we can go whenever you want."

"In a little while," Sara says. She needs a few minutes to recover, and she does not want people to see their departure as related in any way to Elias.

She sits there quietly, listening to the music and watching people dance. Elias is at the bar getting another drink. Juana has spent most of the evening flirting with the man next to her, an anchor for one of Juárez's television stations. He's a handsome man in his forties with a deep, almost musical voice, and he's there alone, although Sara knows he is married. When the man gets up to talk to one of the young men sitting at Elias's table, Sara asks her, "Is everything all right?"

"That's what I should be asking you," Juana says.

"What do you mean?"

Juana reaches over, grabs a half-full bottle of red wine, and fills her glass. "That little scene with Elias. What was that all about?"

"Too much tequila," Sara says.

"What do you mean? Be specific."

Sara stares at her for a moment, wondering if the wine is responsible for Juana's tone of voice. She hates what alcohol does to people. Emiliano feels the same way. Once when she was ten and Emiliano was eight, Papá came home drunk, and in a voice loud enough to wake them up, proceeded to tell Mami their marriage was a big mistake. Mami waited until the tirade was over and then calmly told him that if he drank again, she would leave him. The next day he went to a meeting of

Alcoholics Anonymous, and he never touched another drop of alcohol. He still goes to meetings in the United States and he's still sober—that's what he says in his letters. But not everyone has that discipline.

"He claims he has feelings for me," Sara says to Juana.

Juana snorts and drinks the wine in her glass. "And you said?"

"I was nice. I thanked him. I told him I was flattered—I *am* flattered. But no. He's not for me. I'm sure he won't remember a thing tomorrow."

Juana pours the remainder of the wine in the bottle into her glass. She turns her chair in Sara's direction and takes a deep breath, as if to clear the cobwebs created by the wine. When she speaks again, she sounds totally sober and in control.

"Do you know why you will never be as good a reporter as me?"

Sara shakes her head, surprised.

"You feel too much," Juana says, without any humor in her voice.

Sara laughs, relieved. She thought Juana was going to say that Sara wasn't as courageous as she is, which is true.

"No, really. I'm serious," Juana continues. "I can do my job well because I don't let things get to me. I focus on what needs to be done and I do it. You feel too much. You put too much of yourself into your work. Sometimes the job requires callousness."

"You're not callous."

"Let me tell you something," Juana slurs. "The only thing that matters to me is my work. And my work is, for better or for worse, tied to *El Sol*. At my age there's no way I'd get a job anywhere else. And anyway, that paper is my baby. Felipe and I founded it. We kept it going through the worst of times. Two of our reporters got killed. When Felipe was ready to fold, I found the money to keep us open. You don't think I'm callous? Who do you think fired, I mean laid off, two-thirds of the staff? Who decided to go from a daily to a weekly? Felipe didn't have the heart or the guts or whatever it is you need to make those kinds of decisions. Who do you think is keeping *El Sol* going now? Felipe talks a tough line but he's a softy . . . like you." Juana drains the last drop of wine from her glass. Then, looking into the distance, she says, "That job and two stupid cats is all I got." She raises the empty glass at a passing waiter.

"Are you all right? We can drive you home," Sara says.

"I'll call a taxi," Juana says. Then, "Your father lives in the United States?"

"Yes, Chicago."

"So he's an American citizen?"

Sara can't help smiling. Where is that question coming from? "No," she says patiently, "he's got a green card. I think he's waiting for his citizenship papers."

"He married again?"

"Yes. They're happy, from what he tells me."

"What does he do?"

"He worked in construction for a while, like he did when he lived here, until he saved enough money to start his own business. He sells and fixes air conditioners."

"So he's a good man? You like him."

"He has a good heart. He does what he can to help out."

"Why are you smiling?"

"Oh, nothing. Just before Elias asked me to dance I was

thinking about my father and my mother, and how Mami accepted him leaving and is okay with it. She can even remember the good times she had with him without any bitterness." Sara looks at her mother, who's laughing over something Luisa has said.

Juana grabs Sara's arm and leans close to her face. "Why not get your father to help you get your residency or a work visa? Once you're legit, find a job in El Paso. The *El Paso Times* loved that article you did on the joint task force—the one between the FBI and the Mexican Attorney General's Office. Your English is excellent already. You'll start at the bottom just like you did at *El Sol*, probably making photocopies or something, but knowing you, that wouldn't be for long."

"Are you firing me?" Sara asks, laughing.

"I'm thinking of what's best for you. What did you say in that article about the task force? Remember, 'the U.S. legal system is not perfect in practice, but it may be as good as it gets'?"

"Mmm," Sara says. "I'm very flattered that you think I would be a good reporter in America. But this is my home, and here is my family. Mexico is where I belong, even with all its problems. As much as I admire the laws and the freedom of the United States, I love my Mexico more. I love this stupid city. I don't know why, but I do." She stops, a little embarrassed. It sounded like she was making a speech.

Juana sits there, looking at her. After a while, she speaks in a different, sober tone. "You also have to consider the fact that your life may be very short if you stay here. Especially if you keep investigating that e-mail."

The e-mail. So somehow Juana knows that she's continued looking into it.

"I want you to leave it alone, Sara. I mean it."

"I can't. Not yet." Sara catches her breath, tries to explain. "Linda was . . . *is* my best friend. I'll work on it on my own time if you tell me absolutely as my boss that you want me to stop." Sara waits for her to respond, but all Juana does is glare. She goes on, "You know you're my role model, don't you? You know I'm only doing what you taught me to do."

"Go ahead, then, get yourself killed. See if I give a damn."

Sara knows that Juana doesn't mean that. It's the alcohol speaking. Right?

CHAPTER 10

EMILIANO

Emiliano, lying on his bed, picks up the letter and reads:

I wanted to talk to you tonight but you didn't want to come to the phone. I don't write very good. But I am still your father, even if you don't think so. Your mother told me about the shoplifting and how you were caught. Why, Emiliano? Because you are angry at me? Why do you want to hurt your mother and sister and your future just because of me? You and me spent a lot of time talking about what is right and wrong. It is the most important thing a father can teach a son. When you came home from school with those binoculars you took from a friend, didn't we take a bus all the way to his house so you could return them and apologize? Stealing or doing other wrong acts is not about me, Emiliano, or what you think of me. It's about the kind of person you are. Even if I was the worst person in the world and as bad as you think I am, that would not make it right to be a criminal or even dishonest. I'm not perfect but at least I can say that I'm not a criminal. I want to do well doing honest work. It would have been easy enough for me to make lots of money doing something illegal, trust me on that. I hope you find it in your heart to love me again. You don't know how much it hurts

*me that you may think I don't love you. What I want most
of all, with all my heart, is for you to know that I do. I do
love you, Emiliano. I hope someday you understand that
divorcing your mother was something I believe is best for all
of us, including you. Most of all, I have not stopped being
your father and I am going to continue to remind you to
be a good, honest, kind person, just like I did when I was
with you.*

He hears a knock on the door and for a moment he thinks
it's his father. Emiliano puts the letter down.

"You decent?" It's Sara. He looks quickly at the digital
clock on a stool next to his bed. Three a.m.

"No."

Sara opens the door anyway. He's fully dressed. He didn't
even bother to take off Paco's loafers. He got home before Sara
and Mami were back from the quinceañera and threw himself
on the bed. Then, when he thought that Sara and Mami were
asleep, he got up and took a shoe box full of unopened letters
from his father out of his closet. He searched for the only one
he ever opened and read, and when he found it, he read it again.
Now the shoe box is on the floor and the letters are scattered
over the bed. He's been lying there staring at the ceiling.

"What are you doing?" Sara asks. Emiliano sees her look at
the shoe box on the floor. When he doesn't answer, she says, "I
can't sleep either."

He closes his eyes. Why he thought of reading that particular letter now is something he doesn't fully understand. It has
something to do with the decision he needs to make, he realizes
that. But how is that letter going to help one way or another?

And, besides, hasn't he already decided? Didn't the conversation with Mr. Esmeralda and that kiss with Perla Rubi pretty much seal the deal?

"How was Mrs. Esmeralda's birthday party?"

"Okay."

"Did something happen? With Perla Rubi?"

Emiliano shakes his head. Then, with his eyes still closed: "Why can't *you* sleep? Did something happen at the quinceañera?"

That's enough of an invitation for Sara to pull out the desk chair and sit. Emiliano opens one disapproving eye but doesn't say anything. The truth is that his sister's presence makes him feel better. "It's not just the quinceañera. Stuff at work." She grabs her head with both hands.

Emiliano pushes some of the letters out of the way and sits up. "Like what?"

Sara raises her head. He sees her hesitate. "Oh, things, you know. My work with the Desaparecidas. It gets to me sometimes. My bosses don't want me to write about them anymore. I'm supposed to write about happy things. Show how much better Juárez is now than five years ago. So tourists and businesses can come back." Her words have a bitter tone.

"Things *are* better. Aren't they?" *Or maybe the bad people look more like the good people*, he thinks. Armando, Mr. Reyes, Mr. Esmeralda. They don't look like your typical narcos.

And what about you, Emiliano? You getting ready to be a narco too?

The words in his head sound distinctly like his father's. In place of reprimands, he liked to ask questions. *How do you think Paco is going to feel when he finds his favorite marble is missing? He knows he didn't lose it. He loves that marble. He'll know it was stolen. What if someone stole that collection of soccer cards you treasure so much?* Those kinds of questions.

"Are you sure you're okay? You're white as a sheet. Tell me," Sara insists.

"I hate parties."

"I know. They can be hard if your mind is full of other things. They're probably more fun if you drink. Although, I don't know, Mami had fun tonight and she didn't drink."

Emiliano is quiet. It's not really true that he hates parties. What exactly did he hate about Mrs. Esmeralda's birthday party? He loved Perla Rubi's house. The terrace, the turquoise pool, the kitchen the size of his own house, the Mexican paintings adding touches of color to the solemn rooms and halls. It's the kind of house he would like to have someday. The kind of house he dreams of building for his mother and sister. Perla Rubi was beautiful. That Federico guy was a jerk, but he doesn't hate him. And Mr. Esmeralda? He made clear the conditions under which he would be allowed to be Perla Rubi's boyfriend.

It's those conditions that you hate. The conditions for having a house like Mr. Esmeralda's, for being allowed to be his daughter's boyfriend. That's why you didn't like the party.

Emiliano shakes his head. He folds the letter next to him and sticks it in the envelope. Then he places it and the other unopened letters back in the shoebox. What would Sara say if he told her everything that happened that day? It's clear she's preoccupied with something heavy—probably another threat. The last thing he wants to do is add to her worries.

"Speaking of happy things," Sara says as Emiliano puts the letter in the envelope, "I'm supposed to do an article on the Jiparis." She waits for him to say something. When he doesn't, she continues, "I told my boss that I would try to go on an overnight hike with you guys. I know you have one next week. Do you think it would be okay if I come with you? Interview people, take some pictures?"

"Yeah, sure."

"The article will be great publicity for the Jiparis. Brother Patricio will get some good donations, I'm sure."

Emiliano had forgotten about next week's hike. He wishes he were out there now, under the stars where things are clear. He could use a few nights by himself to think things over.

Do you really need time to think? Haven't you already made up your mind? You've already decided deep down. You know you'll say yes to Mr. Reyes.

"All right," Emiliano says, louder than he intended. "I'll check with Brother Patricio. I'm sure it's okay. We have a soccer game in a few hours."

Sara and Emiliano are quiet for a few moments. Sara is looking at Emiliano's desk. The three piñatas from Javier that he has yet to sell lie there with Doña Pepa's purse. Emiliano tried to glue the square that Alfredo Reyes had cut out of the piñata back in place when he got home from the party, but the best he could do was tape it. He doubts that he'll be able to sell it.

Sara picks up the purse. She touches the beads and then puts it back on the desk. Emiliano watches her face. How long has it been since he has seen Sara so sad?

"You going to tell me about the stuff at work or not?" he asks.

Sara doesn't respond to him, or maybe she doesn't hear. She reaches for Emiliano's fake Bible and opens it. Finally, she smiles. "I still can't believe Linda gave you this."

"Best birthday present I've ever gotten. Well, second best. The knife she gave me was the best."

"I was with her when she bought it," Sara says, closing the Bible. "She knew it would be the perfect gift for you." She places the book on her lap. "You had a crush on her, didn't you?"

"Who didn't? Me, Paco, Pepe. Every kid in the neighborhood except maybe Joel. For some reason he preferred you. That guy never was the sharpest pencil in the bunch."

"Hey!" Another smile from Sara. That's two. "So, you're going to tell me what happened at the party?" she says.

"So, you're going to tell me what happened at work?"

Sara lowers her head, thinks, and says softly, regretfully, "I can't."

"I can't either," Emiliano says.

"So something did happen?"

He shrugs.

Sara's eyes focus on the shoe box. "Why did you decide to take out his letters tonight? I always thought you were throwing them away." She looks at the sheet of paper with her father's handwriting next to Emiliano. "I guess I was wrong."

"I don't know why I saved them. I thought maybe someday I'd open them . . . in case they had money."

His sister grins the way she does when she doesn't believe something he says. He doesn't know why he saved the letters or filed them in the shoe box in the order they were received.

"What does he say?"

"He writes to you too, doesn't he? What does he tell you?"

"He talks about his new business. His new family. Life in America. He really likes to work, like you. He asks about you, you know. He misses you. Wants to know when you'll forgive him."

"Is there something to forgive? You and Mami don't seem to think so."

Sara exhales. "I think Mami and me accepted that some relationships are not meant to be. That it doesn't do any good to force parts that don't fit together, or people who don't fit together. But yes, we forgave him. It's not good for anyone to live with anger."

"Anger is good sometimes. It's energy." That's what Mr. Esmeralda said.

Sara shakes her head. "There are better sources of energy. Like love, or wanting to do something with your life. Anger makes you sick. It makes you go after hurtful things, as if hurting yourself is a way to get revenge on the person who hurt you."

Emiliano slides down on the bed and folds his hands on his chest. He stares at the peeling paint on the ceiling. He feels his anger most on the first days of the month, when the three of them sit at the kitchen table to pay the coming month's bills. Every month is a mental struggle harder than a trigonometry problem, trying to figure out who gets paid and who can wait another month. Every month he has to dip into his motorcycle savings. In the meantime, his father is in Chicago, living in an air-conditioned home, supporting his American wife and blue-eyed baby. So what is there to forgive?

Sara is still sitting there. It's nice to be with someone in silence. Linda liked to play a game with him that he always lost. They would stand in front of each other, stare into each other's faces, and see who could last longer without making a sound. They could not move anything except their eyes. But Linda had the ability to cross hers, which always made him laugh.

Sara was right. He had a crush on Linda. But that crush was different from what he feels for Perla Rubi. There's a hunger inside of him for Perla Rubi's touch, for her whispered words, for the mischievous way she sometimes looks at him. With Linda there was humor and ease. With Perla Rubi there is an electric restlessness. Every time he thinks of her, he wants to hurry up and have more of the kinds of riches she has, so that he can be with her, in her world.

"Some good things came out of Papá leaving." He opens his eyes when he hears Sara speak, but he doesn't look at her. "You joined the Jiparis. You discovered the desert. You started your folk art business. You give us some of the support that used to come from him. You became a man in his absence." She stands. "I better go and try to get an hour of sleep. Of all the nights not to be able to sleep! I need to have my mind working well tomorrow . . . later this morning. I have to."

The way she says that scares Emiliano. Sara may not be powered by anger, but she always seems to have access to another constant, even deeper source of energy. Convictions, purpose, whatever it is, he wishes he had it. Except that, for the first time, Sara's source seems to be depleted. What is happening to her?

"What time you going to work?" Emiliano asks.

"Early."

"I'll go with you." Then he remembers that he can't go with her. He has to take the car back to Armando's.

"You don't have to. It's out of your way. I'll be all right."

"You got another threat, didn't you?"

Sara shrugs. "It comes with the territory."

"I'll leave some money on the kitchen table so you can take a taxi. Don't do anything stupid."

"Me? Never. Good night, little brother. Be good."

He watches her close the door.

Be good. What is good? Isn't helping his family a good thing? If he accepts Mr. Reyes's offer, he'll make Sara's and his mother's lives easier. He'll buy Joel Cardenas's motorcycle and get a sidecar so Sara won't have to walk through dark streets or wait for buses in dangerous places. He'll buy his mother a commercial stove so she can bake at home. He and Perla Rubi can be long-term. There are little goods and bigger goods. A person needs to choose. He will choose what is good for his family, for everyone. He will do what his father promised to do. Whatever it takes.

He places the letters back in the shoe box, no longer worried about the order.

CHAPTER 11
SARA

"God, help me today to do all that you would have me do."

Sara hears someone breathe next to her and nearly jumps out of her chair. Elias is leaning on the partition of her cubicle, looking down on her.

"Geez, you scared the heck out of me." She tries to laugh. "How long have you been standing there?"

"Long enough."

Sara knows he heard her say her morning prayer. She pushes her chair back to see his face. He has dark circles under his eyes and he smells like stale perspiration. He looks as if he slept in his black silk jacket. "You look worse than usual."

He doesn't smile at her attempt at humor. "It's not human to make people come in on Saturdays," he says.

"That's what happens when you have to put out two newspapers every week." Sara pauses, lowers her voice. "Hey, I'm sorry about . . . last night." She knows there's nothing for her to feel sorry about, but she does have to work with the guy.

He shrugs and makes a face as if to say that rejections from insignificant people like her could never hurt him. "Listen," he says, businesslike, "what's the status of that camping trip for your article on the explorer kids?"

"It's next Saturday evening. I told you at the quinceañera, remember?"

"I don't remember anything that happened at the quinceañera," he says curtly.

"Oh." *God*, she thinks, *he's really, really upset* . . .

"Luis, you know, the kid from the mailroom? I've been training him in photography for the past couple of months. I told Felipe this place needs more than one photographer. I think it would be good experience for him to go with you. Pictures of kids in the desert, how difficult can that be?"

"But—"

"I'll clear it with Felipe and tell Luis to come see you."

Before she can say anything, he walks away in the direction of the mailroom.

Sara spends a good fifteen minutes trying to calm down. Was Elias really in love with her? Had she misled him in some unconscious way? Didn't she respond to his comments and flirtations with the same deadpan, professional silence that she used with everyone? She treated his advances as if he were joking, ribbed him back whenever possible. Elias's comments were at least on the witty side of the harassment spectrum, and she laughed sometimes. Was that what gave him the impression he could take his joking one step further? Sara thought he was a friend and treated him like a friend. *Big mistake, I guess.*

She reminds herself one more time that she is not responsible for Elias's anger or hurt or humiliation or whatever it is that he is feeling. Then she gets her mind back to her work. She reads the threatening e-mail again.

If you publish anything of Linda Fuentes we will kill your
reporter and her family.

Why did the sender of the e-mail feel *El Sol* needed to be told not to publish anything about Linda Fuentes? If the puchi e-mail was sent to the hotline at two a.m. on Thursday, and the hotline e-mails were deleted at five a.m. on Friday, why send a threatening e-mail one hour later that would only attract attention? And why *of* Linda Fuentes instead of *about* Linda Fuentes? *Of* could mean "about," but it could also mean "from." Reading the e-mail as "If you publish anything *from* Linda Fuentes" means that Hinojosa thought something even more incriminating than the puchi message had been sent to *El Sol*.

Sara jumps out of her chair and almost runs to the mailroom, a small closet-like space at the other end of the floor. Luis—her new photographer for the Jiparis' overnight trip, apparently—is sorting mail into different piles, though it is impossible to tell where one pile ends and another begins.

"Hey, Luis," Sara says as politely and as calmly as possible. Luis does not deal very well with urgency.

"Hey," he says. He looks upset.

"Is something the matter?"

"Someone came in here and messed up all my mail. I still can't find some things. They tried to put things back where they were so I wouldn't know, but they put things in the wrong place. I've told Juana the mailroom needs a door with a lock." He turns to face her. "Sorry. Hey, Elias just told me about the camping trip next Saturday. That's so cool. But we should plan to get some shots before it gets dark. I'm not really good with night photography yet."

"Yes, we can do that." She tries to smile. "But I'm here about something else. I was wondering if by any chance I had received a package or letter?"

"No. No packages. Just the envelope I put on your chair yesterday."

"Envelope? Yesterday? When?"

"Around six thirty in the morning. I found it in the mailbox downstairs—you know, the slot on the side of the building. I always look in there on the way out. It was around ten p.m. on Thursday and I was too tired to come back up. So I put the envelope in my backpack, and then yesterday when I came in, I put it on your chair. I figured you lost your cell phone and someone was returning it to you."

"My cell phone?"

"It was a small, white, square envelope with something heavy in it. I'm pretty sure it was a cell phone. It felt like one. It had your name written on it in not very good handwriting. Like a kid wrote it, or maybe someone in a hurry."

"You put it on my chair?"

"Yes. I put it on your chair when I came in. You didn't see it?"

"No." Sara grabs on to the counter. For a moment there, it seemed as if the floor had tilted. But it isn't the floor that's moving. It's her mind trying to comprehend the implications of what Luis is saying to her.

"You okay?"

"Yes. Why did you put it on my chair?"

"I thought it was safer than in your inbox. People sometimes don't bother to look in their inboxes. I placed it on the middle of your chair and then tucked your chair under your desk so no one would see it. Things sometimes disappear around here. I don't know if you've noticed."

"Thank you, Luis." Sara turns around and hurries back to her desk. She rolls her chair out of the cubicle and inspects the floor, then gets on her knees and searches under her desk. She peers behind her computer screen and empties her inbox, just in case. Nothing.

She sits down and puts her head in her hands. How could an envelope disappear? Yesterday, she came in around seven because she needed to finish an article about some energy-saving buses the city was buying. That was only half an hour after Luis put the envelope on her chair. Who else was there at seven? Only four people were in the office that early: Sara, Juana, Guillermo, and Elias.

Elias never gets to work that early. He must have taken the envelope—an envelope that contained a cell phone related to Linda and Erica. That's why the threatening e-mail was sent even after the hotline e-mails were deleted. Linda's e-mail was no longer a threat, but the cell phone was. She checks the time-stamp of the e-mail threat again, then opens up her notepad and jots down a time line of events.

Thursday 2:00 a.m. Linda sends e-mail with picture.
Thursday 10:00 p.m. Luis finds envelope in downstairs mailbox.
Friday 5:00 a.m. hotline e-mails deleted.
Friday 6:00 a.m. threatening e-mail sent to Felipe.
Friday between 6:30 a.m. and 7:00 a.m. envelope with cell phone taken from my chair.

Sara stands up and heads to Juana's office. She's working on her computer, her glass door closed. Sara barges in.

"What is it?" Juana sounds as if talking to anyone is the last thing she wants to do.

"Did you take an envelope from my chair?" Sara blurts. Maybe Juana wanted to protect her, didn't want her to get killed like those two reporters.

Juana grimaces. "Lower your voice, please. What envelope?"

"Luis put an envelope on my chair yesterday morning. It had something to do with Linda. I just know it did."

"Slow down, slow down." She turns to face Sara. "So you got an envelope in the mail. You don't know it was related to Linda Fuentes."

"It was a white, square envelope with something heavy inside—like a cell phone, according to Luis. Someone dropped it through the slot downstairs Thursday evening and Luis picked it up on his way home. It had my name on it. Luis put it on my chair when he came in yesterday. And then it disappeared."

"You searched . . ."

"Everywhere. Someone took it—there's no other explanation. That's why we got the threatening e-mail. Whoever sent the e-mail was worried about us getting the cell phone. It must have information about Linda."

"Let's think through this. One step at a time. Sit." Juana gets up, walks very slowly to the door, and closes it. Sara sits on the edge of the chair, hands clasped. Juana goes back to her chair. "What else have you found out about the threatening e-mail?"

Sara remembers Ernesto's warning, and for the first time since she started working at *El Sol*, she lies to Juana. "Only that Ernesto thinks it was sent by someone with a lot of sophisticated technical knowledge."

"That's all you know? I want you to tell me everything."

"Ernesto thinks the e-mail could have been sent by someone in law enforcement."

Juana stares at her with the same cold stare that makes people spill their secrets to her in interviews. But Sara holds off. She's afraid to get Juana involved and bring the same danger upon her that Sara's bringing upon herself.

"I see," Juana finally says.

"That cell phone had to be related to Linda. It's the only explanation."

"Who could have taken it? Yesterday morning, you say?"

"Luis dropped it on my chair at six thirty and the envelope was gone when I got here at seven."

"I was here at seven yesterday working on the budget. I didn't see anybody except you, Luis, and Guillermo." Juana pauses, glances at Sara. "Maybe it was Guillermo. He sits across from you and can see when a package is delivered to you."

"No, I know Guillermo. He's trustworthy. Besides, if he was working with bad people, he wouldn't have had to borrow money from Ernesto for the quinceañera." Sara thinks for a moment, then decides to take the risk. "Elias was here early as well."

"Elias?"

"Have you ever known him to get here before ten? And it's not just that. He said some things at the quinceañera . . ."

"What kind of things?"

"That I shouldn't write about the Desaparecidas, that it was too dangerous for me and my family. The e-mail also mentioned my family, and he never read that e-mail. How did he know to use that word? It's too much of a coincidence. And the way he said what he said at the party—it was creepy."

Juana huffs out a breath. "Hell, *I* also told you that what you were doing was dangerous for you *and* your family. Not that you listen." She pauses. Then, "There's one quick way of finding out if he's a rat."

"How?"

"I'll call him in here and talk to him for ten minutes while you search his desk. If he took the envelope, he might still have it. He didn't go out yesterday. He was with me until late, working on an article, and I know he went straight to the quinceañera with only a quick stop at his gym to change." She rushes through her words, as if she's embarrassed to know so much about Elias. "You want to check his desk or not?"

"I don't know. Are you sure?"

"We might as well find out if he's bad."

"Okay. I'll wait until he's in your office. We should do it before everyone starts coming in."

"We'll do it now. And Sara—" Juana waits until Sara's eyes are on hers, then says sternly, "You are not to keep anything from me, do you understand? If you find something, you come straight to me. I'm not talking only about the cell phone. I'm talking about anything whatsoever related to the e-mail. You come tell me immediately. And no one must find out about this. Is that understood? Who else knows about the missing cell phone? Ernesto?"

It is the second time in two days that Juana has surprised

Sara. Last night, maybe it was the alcohol speaking, but here it is again—something different about Juana, harder somehow. Sara waits a few moments to respond. "No. No one else knows about the cell phone. I told Luis I didn't get the envelope. But I could tell him I found it under my desk."

"Yes. Do that."

Sara goes back to her desk and waits for Elias to walk past on the way to Juana's office, his black silk jacket still on. Then, after he shuts the door, she walks to his cubicle and pretends to write him a note. Fortunately, Elias's cubicle is in the farthest corner of the room and none of the reporters who work nearby have come in yet. She bends down and rifles through his gym bag. Nothing.

The desks at *El Sol* have a middle drawer and four side drawers, the bottom one large enough to hang files. When she pulls open the first drawer, she almost laughs out loud. Elias's drawers are full of personal grooming items: a nail clipper, tweezers, scissors, combs, brushes, a nose-hair puller, razors, talcum powder, ChapSticks of assorted flavors, hand lotion, teeth whitening strips, mouthwash, a pumice stone, and, surprisingly, one of those little gadgets that curls a person's eyelashes. She also finds camera parts and batteries and invoices and more information about Elias's private life than she ever wants to know, but no envelope. Before leaving, she looks in the plastic garbage can beneath his desk, but it too does not contain any traces of a white envelope. Due to budget cuts, the offices are cleaned and garbage receptacles emptied only on Wednesdays and Sundays, so the envelope would be in the garbage can if Elias put it there yesterday.

She goes to the coffee pot for another cup. This is not a morning to be a stickler on caffeine limits. On the way back to her desk, she passes by Juana's office and shakes her head. Elias is a rat in many ways, but he does not appear to be the rodent who stole her envelope.

There is nothing else she can do about the cell phone at the moment, so she decides to resume her search for anything that could lead her to Erica Rentería's family. Any hint of Erica's whereabouts could be helpful in finding Linda.

She studies the picture of Erica that she found in the file room the day before. Erica stands in front of some kind of monument made of white marble, wearing a white blouse, pleated black skirt, white socks, and old-looking but clean shoes. Sara remembers thinking that she was dressed as if she were going to a conservative church. What if she *was* going to church? What church has that kind of wall? White marble. Sara does an Internet search for Juárez churches and looks at the pictures. There must be a hundred churches, but not many are made of white marble.

And then she sees a picture of a beautiful, gleaming white building: the Templo Mormón on Calle Paraguay. Sara's heart races. This is the building where the picture was taken. Erica Rentería, with her white blouse and pleated black skirt and demure white socks, was going in or coming out of the temple when she posed for the photograph. Sara feels sure of it.

On the website for the Church of Jesus Christ of Latter-Day Saints in Ciudad Juárez, she finds the name and number for a mission president and his wife.

"Hello," a woman's voice answers.

"Yes. Hello. Is this Mrs. Mirabiles?"

"Yes," the woman replies tentatively.

"My name is Sara Zapata. I'm a reporter for *El Sol*. I'm trying to reach the family of Erica Rentería. I believe her family attends your temple."

Silence.

"Hello. Hello?"

"Are you calling about Joselito?"

"Who?"

"Joselito Rentería. Manuel and Rosa's son."

"Erica's brother?" Sara says, guessing.

"Are you a friend of Erica's?" The woman's voice brightens.

"Yes." She is a friend of Erica's, in a way. "Who am I speaking with?"

"This is Hortencia Mirabiles, President Mirabiles's wife. My husband is at the hospital with Manuel and Rosa. People have been calling us to see how Joselito is doing since Rosa and Manuel don't have a telephone."

"Did something happen to Joselito?"

Mrs. Mirabiles pauses. "You better talk to my husband. Do you have a pen? I will give you his cell phone number. He's at General Hospital with Mr. and Mrs. Rentería."

Sara writes down the number. "Can you tell me what happened?"

No answer. The woman is gone.

Sara has the horrible feeling that whatever happened to Joselito is connected to Linda. She starts to call Mr. Mirabiles, then stops. She grabs her cell phone, sticks it in the small backpack she uses as a purse, and heads to the coffee shop down the street. After her sleepless night, she needs something more powerful than *El Sol*'s cheap coffee.

Thinking about last night reminds her of Emiliano. He was already gone when she got up this morning. Something heavy must have been on his mind to make him read Papá's letters. Sara decides that tonight, she will tell Emiliano everything that's happening with her. Maybe he will tell her what's happening with him in return.

She orders a café con leche and sits down with it at an empty table close to the bathroom. She dials the number that Mrs. Mirabiles gave her on the phone.

"Hello, this is Alberto Mirabiles. Who is this?" The man's voice is barely audible, as if he is whispering.

"It's Sara Zapata from *El Sol*. Your wife gave me your number. I called her about Erica Rentería, but then she said that something happened to Erica's brother."

"Yes." He says it as if he already knows the reason for her call.

"Is Joselito all right? Your wife told me you were at the hospital because of him."

"No. He's not all right. Did you get the cell phone?"

"What cell phone?" But she doesn't really have to ask. Her beating heart tells her exactly what cell phone he is referring to.

Silence.

"Mr. Mirabiles, are you still there?"

"Is this your own private phone?"

"Yes."

"I can't talk to you here. I will call you back at this number in ten minutes."

Sara sits there for a few moments trying to make sense of it all. There is no question now that the threatening e-mail, the missing envelope, and the picture of Erica and the bald man are all related. For the first time, she feels scared, truly scared. More than anything, it's the fear she heard in Mr. Mirabiles's voice that frightens her. He wasn't whispering because he was in the hospital. He was speaking softly because he did not want to be heard. He hung up so he could find a place to talk without being watched, and he thinks watchers are everywhere.

When the phone rings and she picks it up, she notices sweat on the palm of her hand.

Mr. Mirabiles speaks in a low, clear tone. "Listen carefully. This will be the only time that I will talk to you. Don't call me at home or on my cell anymore and don't try to see or get in touch with any member of the Rentería family. I am telling you this not only because I'm afraid for my family but also for Manuel and Rosa and their other son and . . . for you and your family. Do you understand?"

"Yes." Sara clears her throat. "I'm listening."

"I'm going to tell you all I know and then I'm going to hang up. No questions or interruptions, please. I am calling you from a phone in someone's office here at the hospital. I only have two or three minutes. If the owner of the office comes in, I'll hang up."

"Okay."

"After I hang up, please erase the call you made to my cell a few minutes ago."

"Okay."

Mr. Mirabiles inhales deeply and exhales. Then he begins slowly, as if he expects her to write down his words. Sara searches in her backpack and finds a small notebook and a pen.

"Last Thursday, early in the morning, Joselito happened to be coming home from work when he saw a young man put a package in front of the Renterías' front door. Then the young man walked to the corner, where he got on a scooter and rode away. Joselito recognized the young man because he used to go to our temple. The package was a box of the kind laundries use for clean shirts. Hidden among many pages of newspaper there was a cell phone and a napkin. The napkin had a message that says, more or less—I'm trying to remember the exact words— 'I'm alive. Don't know where. Like a ranch. Airplanes fly real close. My friend says to give the phone to Sara Zapata at *El Sol*. Don't tell anyone else. Not even the police. I love you.' I might have mixed up the order or left out a few words, but that was generally what was written on the napkin. Manuel recognized Erica's handwriting. You can see the place in the napkin where his tears fell. Erica had been gone for two months.

"That day, around noon, Manuel and Rosa came to my house. We talked about it and decided not to involve the police, as Erica had requested. There must be a reason she said that, right? All we could do is what she asked and send the package to you. Around eight p.m., Joselito took an envelope with the cell phone and napkin to *El Sol*. We waited until after the newspaper was closed because we were afraid. The owner of the cell phone might be watching Erica's family or watching *El Sol*. We thought dropping it in the mail slot was best. You'd get it first thing on Friday."

"Just the cell phone and the napkin? That's all that was in the envelope?" Sara asks.

"Why are you asking? Didn't you get it?"

"I never got the envelope. It was taken from my desk Friday

morning before I could open it. Someone at *El Sol* wanted to make sure I didn't get it. Please tell me everything you know. It's our only chance of finding Erica."

There is a long pause. Mr. Mirabiles begins to speak again, slowly and with difficulty, like someone whose mouth has gone dry. "The only thing in the envelope besides the cell phone and Erica's note was a letter to you from Mr. and Mrs. Rentería, explaining how they got the package and pleading with you to find Erica."

"What about the young man who delivered the package? Maybe . . ."

"I'm not going to tell you his name. That young man risked his life. He's in enough danger already."

"Please. We may still be able to help Erica and other girls."

Another long pause, then Mr. Mirabiles says again, "I'm not going to tell you his name. All I can tell you is that he works for a commercial laundry place. You know, the kind that picks up and delivers linens to hotels. The business is called La Vaquita."

Sara writes the name down. "Thank you, Mr. Mirabiles." She is afraid to ask the next question, but then, she already knows the answer. "And Joselito?"

"Thursday, only a few minutes after Joselito got back from dropping off the envelope, three men showed up at the Renterías' house in a brown car. Manuel, Rosa, and their two sons were home. They asked Manuel about the cell phone. At first he denied receiving anything, and then one of the men began to hit Manuel with his fists. When he still refused to talk, they tied Joselito's hands behind his back and beat him on the legs and arms with a rubber tube, the kind that policemen carry. When they started to strike Joselito on the head, Manuel had no choice but to tell them that they had dropped the cell phone in *El Sol*'s mail slot earlier that evening . . . with your name on it."

"Oh, God."

"They asked Manuel if he knew the identity of the man who owned the cell phone. Manuel told them that he didn't know. That was the truth. No one in the family has any idea who the phone belongs to." Mr. Mirabiles can barely speak. "They told him that if he said anything else, they would come back and kill his wife, his other son, and him, in that order."

Sara presses her thumb and index finger hard against her eyes.

Mr. Mirabiles continues, "Joselito is in a coma. We don't think he'll make it. The doctors say there's bleeding in the brain. You say the envelope was taken deliberately from you?"

"Yes, it was taken deliberately."

"If you didn't get anything, how did you know to call me? Sara explains how she found his name. "Mr. Mirabiles . . ."

"Listen, if you didn't get the envelope, everyone thinks you don't know anything. It would be better if you let this be. Stay out of this, for your own sake."

"And Erica? And the other girls? There are good people who can help us. There are honest people in the police department and in the military."

"Do you know the kind of people we're dealing with?" His voice is sharp. "They beat a young man nearly to death and hit an old man. Doesn't that tell you what kind of people they are?

You and your family are in danger. So am I and my family, just by talking to you. I urge you to stop whatever you're doing. Please."

She can't answer.

"Good-bye. God bless you." Mr. Mirabiles hangs up.

Sara puts the phone down and holds her coffee mug in both hands, thinking, thinking. What is her best chance for saving Linda and keeping everyone safe? Everyone, including her mother and Emiliano. The owner of the cell phone and his people know that the envelope was addressed to her, but they also know it never reached her. They think the e-mail with Erica's picture was deleted. If she doesn't do anything more, there's a possibility that the bad people will leave her and those she loves most in the world alone.

There is a line in front of her. One more step on behalf of Linda and her life will change forever. How does she decide between safety and the risk that comes from doing what her heart knows to be right?

A memory comes to Sara: Linda sticking her tongue out as the bus pulled away the day she disappeared. Other memories follow: Linda getting chased by Mr. Lozano's tom turkey when they climbed into his yard to steal peaches. Linda playing "who makes the first sound" with Emiliano. Linda giving her instructions on how to kiss before her first date with Joel Cardenas.

"Just turn your head away for a second when you think Joel's about to kiss you and moisten your lips with your tongue," Linda said. "The kiss has to be a little wet, and make sure you open your mouth a bit like this."

"You look like a fish. And where did you learn all this?" Sara asked.

"I don't tell you everything."

"Yes you do."

"Okay, a girl at work loaned me her *Cosmopolitan*. Want to know the twenty things a woman most likes to have done to her?"

"No!"

Sara smiles at the memory and then feels very alone. She knows what lies ahead of her and it makes her want to find a source of strength somewhere. She needs to talk to Emiliano. If there is anyone in the world who would understand what she has to do, regardless of the risks involved, it is her little brother. She calls him but there's no answer. She texts him to call her as soon as he can. Then she calls Ernesto, her friend and ally.

"Hey, what was all that with Elias last night?"

She ignores his question. "Ernesto, before I tell you what I've found out, you have to know that this is getting more and more dangerous for all of us, including you. You may want to bow out. It's okay if you do."

"Yeah, yeah. What do you have?" He sounds almost bored.

"Are you sure?"

"Sara, I don't have much time here. I have two computers that crashed and Juana and Felipe are insisting I submit a budget for IT that's fifty percent lower than last year's. I'm thinking of sending them a piece of paper with the words *Five typewriters*."

She tells Ernesto everything that Mr. Mirabiles told her.

"Bastards! I think the Jaqueros can figure out where these girls are being held," he says.

"Really? How?"

"We'll hack into La Vaquita's computers and then look for any deliveries to places near the airport. La Vaquita is a big laundry outfit. Their trucks run all over the place. They probably have better IT than *El Sol*. I'll call you back. What *you* have to do is figure out who in law enforcement can go out there and rescue the girls. It's pathetic. I don't know a single person in law enforcement I can trust. Do you?"

Sara remembers an American FBI agent from El Paso she met while reporting on the joint task force. He told her to call him with any leads. "Maybe. I think so."

Ernesto's tone changes, gets serious for once. "Listen. If things get real hot, I have places where I can disappear. But you need to start thinking about what you're going to do when the caca hits the fan. This Hinojosa guy has a lot to lose if it gets out he's involved with sex trafficking or slavery or whatever this is. He and whoever . . . are involved with that place will figure out who screwed them, and they will come after you and me. All right. You should go home. Call you soon. Let's do this."

"Yes," she says, mustering all her courage, "let's do this."

CHAPTER 12

EMILIANO

Emiliano is standing in the middle of the soccer field as the two teams go through their pregame drills. He's looking in the direction of the opposing team, the North El Paso High School Conquistadors, but his mind is preoccupied with the conversation he needs to have with Javier as soon as they get back to Juárez.

"Man, can you believe American schools? I could get used to playing here." Emiliano snaps out of his reverie and follows Paco's eyes to the lush green grass under their feet. "No wonder the Rio Grande is a trickle of warm piss. All the water's used for this field."

Emiliano taps the ground with the point of his shoe. It is a big difference from the patch of dirt where the Pumas practice.

"And look at the shoes on those guys." Paco points at a player retrieving a ball. "That's one year of my father's salary right there." He looks at Emiliano suddenly. "Hey, are you going to tell me what you're up to? What's with the Mercedes?"

"I told you. I had to take the car to the dealer's for a friend, and it got late. I have your money in my pants. I'll give it to you after the game."

"Come on, man, it's me, remember? My parents are all like, *What is going on with Emiliano?* You park a fancy car in our backyard at night and then you drive it out at five this morning. You have to admit it's a little suspicious. And, by the way, you got my loafers all muddy."

"That's from your mom's flower beds when I was putting the key under the Virgen."

Paco shakes his head. "She waters those flowers every day as soon as the sun starts to go down. So how was the birthday party? Did you make the big-shot impression you wanted to make with the car? This is all about Perla Rubi, isn't it? God, you're so unbelievably stupid."

"Leave it alone, man."

Paco takes a step closer to Emiliano, faces him. "Leave it alone? Since when? You don't think I can tell when you're doing something bad? Whenever you're bad or thinking about doing something bad, your eyes go left and right, up and down like they did just now. First time I saw your eyes do that was when you threw a marble at my head and gave me this scar." Paco lifts the hair on his forehead. Emiliano looks at the scar and then looks away. "You drive a Mercedes to impress a rich girl who, when the chips are down, is going to dump you. Come on, talk to me."

Emiliano should feel anger, but he doesn't. What comes up is sadness at this breach between him and his best friend. He could close the separation, he knows. All he has to do is tell him the truth. But Paco would not like the truth.

They both turn when they hear Brother Patricio's whistle. Paco walks toward Brother Patricio. Emiliano waits a moment and then follows. The Pumas gather around and bow their heads.

"Okay, before we pray, a reminder," Brother Patricio says. "This is a friendly game where we hone our skills. It took me a long time to get a school in El Paso to agree to play with us. So keep it clean and let's play them with the respect they deserve. Let's pray. Lord, keep us and our opponents safe. Help us to be humble in victory and grateful in defeat. May this contest be an opportunity to increase our courage and our desire to do all we do for your greater glory. May all our actions on and off the field show that we love God with all our soul, heart, and strength, and our neighbor, including our opponents, as ourselves. We ask this in the name of your son, Jesus Christ."

"Amen," respond the Pumas as they cross themselves—all of them except Emiliano.

It is the exact same prayer that Brother Patricio repeats before every game. Emiliano doesn't mind people praying. Mami and Sara pray. Colegio México is, after all, a Catholic school, run by Salesian Brothers like Brother Patricio. But today the words *grateful in defeat* annoy him. Why should anyone be grateful for losing? Losing feels bad and winning feels good. It's a natural thing to want to feel good, and God, if there is a God, shouldn't have any problem with that.

Emiliano waits for Brother Patricio's last-minute coaching instructions, which also never vary. Defense, defense, defense. Don't let anyone get through and then wait for the right moment to counterattack. Only this time, his instructions are different. "Let's concentrate on execution of plays and not on scoring," Brother Patricio says. "They are the best team in the city of El Paso, so maybe we can learn a few things from them."

"We're the best team in the state of Chihuahua," Pepe says, "so maybe they can learn a few things from *us*."

Laughter and cheers. Pepe is the goalie and, besides Paco, Emiliano's favorite teammate.

"Yes," Brother Patricio says, "they will undoubtedly learn some things from us as well. This is a great opportunity to . . . rectify some misconceptions that Americans have about people from Juárez. So just have fun." Then he looks directly at Emiliano. "I'm counting on you as the captain and midfielder to control the energy level. Keep it nice and smooth. Even tempered. No need for the usual high intensity today."

"Yes, Brother. Nice and easy today. Let them win," Emiliano echoes sarcastically.

Brother Patricio pauses. "I didn't say that, necessarily. 'Don't concentrate on scoring' is not the same as letting them win."

"Yes. I understand," Emiliano says. He tries not to sound angry, but there is anger in his voice.

Brother Patricio notices his tone, because he takes Emiliano aside and says, "Emiliano, don't turn this game into a personal vendetta."

Emiliano looks at Brother Patricio for a few moments. What vendetta is Brother Patricio talking about? Then it comes to him: the conversations they've had where he expressed anger at his father for staying in the United States. Does Brother Patricio think he blames the United States for his parents' divorce, for his father never returning? He's wrong. The United States didn't force his father to stay there, to abandon his family. That was all his father's decision.

"No vendetta here," Emiliano answers, then walks away before Brother Patricio can say anything else.

Where is all this anger coming from? He wishes he hadn't read that letter last night, inviting his father's voice to enter his head after all his work getting it out. But he also knows that the whole team will ignore Brother Patricio's instructions. The soccer field is the one place where they can shine and be admired, the one place where they are rich—not with money, like all the other teams they play, but with skills and courage. It's the one place where anger, properly managed, is permitted.

Nevertheless, throughout the first half, Emiliano does his best to ignore the gnawing in his stomach urging him to go all out. He plays relaxed and without urgency, and the rest of the Pumas follow his example. His passes to Paco from midfield are off-mark and easily intercepted. Paco's few shots on the opposing goal dribble meekly into the goalie's hands. The Conquistadors score an easy goal. The locker room is quiet at halftime.

Then in the second period, a shot from the top of the box rolls lazily into the corner of the Pumas' goal. Emiliano notices that the Conquistadors are all laughing, and the crowd in the stands begins to chant: "USA! USA! USA!"

That's not so bad. People have the right to cheer for their team.

But then the chant changes and the crowd shouts: "NAR-COS! NAR-COS! NAR-COS!"

That, on the other hand, is the wrong cheer. It is the wrong cheer any day, but today it loosens a fury in Emiliano. The gnawing in the pit of his stomach turns to a simmering fire and then it starts to boil.

Emiliano dribbles the ball through two defenders. Paco is ahead of him on the right wing. Emiliano lifts his chin, signaling that no mercy will be given, and their eyes meet in complete understanding.

His pass drops twenty feet behind the last defenseman for the Conquistadors, and Paco outruns a kid who looks like he's more interested in not messing up his golden locks than in playing soccer. Now Paco's alone with only a scared-looking goalie in front of him. Paco waits for the goalie to charge him and then lobs the ball over the boy's head into the net.

Their single-minded intensity wakes up the Pumas, and there is no stopping them after that. The friendly game turns into a war. Yellow cards fly left and right for both teams. By the time the Pumas are up four to two with ten minutes left in the game, Emiliano has started to feel sorry for the Conquistadors, who have abandoned any kind of discipline and are running around the field like angry hornets. Why not take the foot off the pedal, maybe even let them score another goal? Then the chant comes again.

"NAR-COS! NAR-COS! NAR-COS!"

Emiliano stops for a moment to look at the parents and students shouting in the stands. Two-thirds of them are brown-skinned Mexicans or of Mexican descent. He nods first to Paco and then to López. Two minutes later, Paco scores with a header from one of Emiliano's corner kicks. Thirty seconds before the end of the game, López scores with a vicious shot from almost midfield. They win the game six to two.

When the referee blows the final whistle, both teams line up to limply shake the hands of their opponents.

"Was that really necessary?" Brother Patricio asks Emiliano during the long, silent ride back home.

"Yes, Brother. Today that was necessary."

Brother Patricio doesn't say anything more. But Emiliano knows he has hurt him with his deeds on the field and now with his words and tone. First Paco and then Brother Patricio. Who else is he going to push away?

146

When they get out of the van at Colegio México and all the players are walking away, Emiliano goes to Brother Patricio and takes the bag of practice balls from him. "I'm sorry."

"Do you want to talk? I have time."

"No, not right now."

"Next week, maybe, on the hike."

"Maybe. Oh, I forgot. Sara is doing an article on the Jiparis, and she asked if she can come on the hike. She plans to do a big story. She says it's sure to bring in a lot of donations."

Brother Patricio opens a storage closet on the side of the building and Emiliano places the bag of balls inside. "Well," Brother Patricio says, "we could use the extra money."

"I'll tell her. She'll be happy. Thank you."

"Emiliano, I have a theory about why you were so angry out there. Do you want to hear it?"

"Sure." He doesn't really, but he's been mean enough to Brother Patricio for one day.

"Maybe playing in El Paso, at that rich school, reminded you of your father and his decision to leave you and your mother and sister and remain in the United States."

The vendetta thing again. Emiliano nods thoughtfully. He knows that besides hiking out in the desert, psychoanalyzing people is Brother Patricio's greatest pleasure.

"Maybe that 'USA' chant brought to the surface the anger you still have for your father."

"Maybe," Emiliano says. But no, it was not the "USA" chant that he minded. It was the "narcos" chant that hit home, in a deep, personal way that Brother Patricio cannot even begin to imagine. "I got to run. I have to go see Javier."

"Be safe. And Emiliano?"

"Yeah?"

"It's time to forgive."

As Emiliano walks slowly away, he does not let Brother Patricio see the grin on his face. Brother Patricio never gives up, does he? He takes out his phone and reads a text from Sara.

Call me as soon as you can. I need to talk to you right away. Be careful.

He calls her but her phone is busy. Something is going on with Sara. If only they could have talked openly about their problems last night. She needed to talk with him and he with her and neither one could do it. He texts her to make sure she takes a taxi home, hoping she saw the money he left for her on the kitchen table.

Then he goes to the text that he received from Perla Rubi the night before around midnight, when he was lying in his bed thinking, thinking.

What did you say to my father anyway? All he did last night is talk about you. He wants to know if you want to hit golf balls with him next Saturday. He wants to teach you how to play golf. Amazing! Stop by after your soccer game. I'd love to see you before our game against Sacred Heart. I miss you, Emiliano Zapata.

Golf? Emiliano Zapata playing golf? Maybe the game is not all that different from the walks he takes in the desert. You just hit a white ball with a stick now and then as you walk. He puts the phone in his pocket and takes a deep breath.

He stops when he turns the corner of the building. The girls' volleyball team is warming up by doing jumping jacks. The players from Sacred Heart High School stretch on the other side of the net. Perla Rubi is at the end of one row of Colegio México players. As if sensing his presence, she turns to where he's standing and waves at him as she jumps. Then she gestures to wait five minutes. After the warm-up exercises, they can talk.

The way she just happened to turn her head to the right when everyone was looking straight ahead. The way her face lit up when she saw him. Something happened last night. He's crossed some kind of threshold into Perla Rubi's life in a way he had not been allowed before. Even now, watching her, he feels different. No more of the usual doubts about them being boyfriend and girlfriend or whatever. He feels sure of himself. It's the way he feels sometimes during a soccer game: a confidence that comes out of nowhere and fills him.

He reminds himself that he has not yet decided if he will do business with Mr. Reyes. As he reasons out the pros and cons of Mr. Reyes's proposition, the one obstacle his logic cannot overcome is Javier. Brother Patricio rescued Javier from a life of truancy and addiction. Now Javier is going to school and helping to support his family with his piñatas. Javier is also the best Jipari that Emiliano has ever trained. The other kids call him the Turtle because he walks slow but somehow gets there faster than anyone else. And now? Now, Emiliano is going to ask him to stuff the piñatas with drugs.

Yes, but with the extra money, maybe Javier can get his mother and sisters out of the stink hole where they live. Life is messy.

And what about your Jipari pledge, Emiliano? "I will abstain from all intoxicants. I will be honest with myself and others. I will use the knowledge and strength the desert gives me for the benefit of others."

Emiliano shakes his head. This kind of internal talking is sheer craziness. It's part of him talking to another part of him, even if the voice is his father's. It was a big mistake to read that letter. Did he actually think he was going to find an answer to his moral dilemma there? Yes, it was his father who patiently taught him right from wrong. But look what he did when it came time for him to practice what he preaches, how he left his family and broke promises. All the letter did was remind Emiliano what a hypocrite his father is.

The volleyball team has ended their warm-up drills and Perla Rubi is walking toward him. She wears red shorts and a green T-shirt with the word *Pumas* in white letters. Her hair is pulled back into a ponytail. A radiant look of happiness lights her face, a happiness for him and because of him. How can it be that Perla Rubi likes him, maybe even loves him? He feels humble and proud all at the same time. So, so fortunate. So grateful. How can he possibly say no to this gift life is offering?

"I was worried about you," she says when they reach each other.

"Why?"

"You never answered the text I sent you last night."

"I was so tired. I put my head on the pillow and fell asleep." The volleyball coach blows her whistle. Perla Rubi and Emiliano walk toward the court side by side.

"Really? I couldn't sleep." She smiles.

The way she looks at him. She's telling him that she couldn't sleep because she was thinking of him. "Actually, I couldn't sleep either."

Perla Rubi stops and comes closer. "Is everything all right?"

"Yeah, yeah."

"Really? Truly? You seem different."

"Good different or bad different?"

She peers into his eyes. "I'm not sure."

"I've been thinking."

"Well, that explains it." They laugh. "Were you thinking about what you and my father talked about?" she says.

The whistle blows again, but Perla Rubi ignores it. Emiliano smiles at her and she smiles back. He's not imagining it: There is something new between them. Like a current of electricity flowing unimpeded in a complete circuit where before it traveled in spurts. She has given him something precious and in so doing made herself vulnerable. If he decides not to enter through the door she opened, she will be hurt.

"Yes," he says, "it's the job I talked about with your father."

"My father knows a lot about business. You can't go wrong with his advice." She says this as if she knows exactly what her father wants him to do.

"Would you like me to?"

"Would I like you to follow my father's advice?"

"Yes."

"You should do what is best for *everyone*."

"Everyone?" He's pretty sure that Perla Rubi and even the players down on the volleyball court can hear his heart pounding.

"Everyone that matters."

"*You* matter." He says it mostly to himself, but she hears him.

She lowers her eyes briefly as if considering whether to say what she wants to say. When she raises her eyes again, she says, "You matter too."

They are facing each other now. Emiliano's eyes fall to Perla Rubi's lips. She is a magnet and he is all iron. They are leaning, falling almost imperceptibly toward each other, when the whistle blows and Perla Rubi's teammates begin to chant: "Kiss! Kiss! Kiss!"

Emiliano and Perla Rubi pull back, blushing.

"See you in a while," she says, walking backward toward the court. "You better call me, Emiliano Zapata."

"I will, Perla Rubi Esmeralda." He watches her run to her laughing, cheering teammates.

He waits until she turns to wave and then he walks away, his heart bursting.

He matters.

CHAPTER 13

SARA

SATURDAY, MARCH 25
12:22 P.M.

Sitting there in the near-empty coffee shop, Sara reads Emiliano's text message again.

I won't be able to meet you after work today. Make sure you take a taxi home.

She remembers the two hundred pesos he left on the kitchen table this morning. She didn't take them, because she knows how much work that money entailed. What's going to happen to Emiliano's business when she tells him that their lives are in danger? That he can't go out bicycling all over the city anymore? Whatever she does to help Linda will affect Emiliano, Mami, Ernesto, Juana. She imagines someone hitting Emiliano on the back of the head with a rubber tube and it brings tears to her eyes.

"Are you all right?" It's the young woman who runs the espresso machine at the café. How long has Sara been sitting there? The young woman puts a cup down on the table. "I thought you could use this. It's not coffee. It's chamomile tea. My mother makes me drink it when I'm nervous."

"Thanks." She tries to smile. "I do seem nervous, don't I? I'll leave in a few minutes, I promise."

"No, no. Stay as long as you want. I don't know what it is about this table. Yesterday I saw a couple break up. The day before someone got some bad news when she was sitting here."

The girl is all of sixteen, maybe, and Sara can tell by the holes in her sneakers that she is poor, like Linda, like Erica. How can anyone hurt girls like her? What goes through the minds of men when they hurt them? Isn't there a spark of conscience somewhere in them telling them to stop? How is it possible that they forget their sisters or mothers when they abuse another woman?

"Thank you," Sara says. And then, as the young woman is walking away, "God bless you."

"You too," she says, turning around.

Sara sits there staring at the screen of her phone for who knows how long. Then she taps the icon for her contacts and scrolls down until she finds Alejandro Durand's number.

Sara met Agent Durand when she wrote an article on a joint task force between the FBI and the Mexican Attorney General's Office—a special investigation dedicated to the murders of six girls in one month on both sides of the border. She tried to get Agent Durand to admit that the Mexican State Police's investigation of the murders was at best negligent and at worst corrupt. He would say only that the State Police were doing the best they could with the tools they had. It was clear to Sara, as it was to the families of the missing girls, that there were many officers in the State Police who were not helpful. Many were sympathetic but seemed to lack the resources needed to do their jobs, while others acted as if they were afraid. There were even a few whose behavior could not be explained by anything other than bribery.

Although Agent Durand never said that corruption was the only possible explanation for the critical delays and loss of evidence in the investigation, Sara was able to get him to describe how the FBI would have handled the exact same situation. The comparison proved indirectly what everyone suspected—that people in the State Police were protecting the killers. Sara's article was reprinted by *La Prensa*, one of Mexico's most prestigious newspapers, and after that, it was translated into English by the *El Paso Times*. She received a letter from Agent Durand after the article was published: "Keep up the good work. You are on your way to becoming a good investigative reporter and a good writer, but most of all you have courage. If you ever get any good leads or if I can ever be of help to you, call me. You have my number."

It's that number she calls now.

"Agent Durand, this is Sara Zapata," she says when she hears his voice.

A few moments go by before he responds. "Sara! What a nice surprise."

"I need a favor," she says.

"Shoot."

Sara tells him her story from the beginning. She speaks as if she is writing a story for *El Sol*, making sure she mentions every detail, every person involved. She talks for ten minutes straight and he does not interrupt her once. Sara knows he is still on the line because she can hear him breathe, and when she tells him about Joselito Rentería, he sighs.

"My friend Ernesto thinks he can find the location where Erica and Linda and maybe more girls are being kept."

"Mmm."

"What do I do if Ernesto gets that information?" Sara asks. "Who can I call? Who can rescue the girls? I know this is not your jurisdiction. But you've worked with Mexican law enforcement agencies. Do you know anyone I can trust?"

"There are many good people within the State Police who can help. That's not going to be a problem."

"Really?"

Sara realizes she sounds incredulous when she hears a quiet laugh. "Believe it or not, there are lots of people in Mexico who are trying very hard to fight crime. It's an uphill battle against people with incredible resources of power and money, but they hang in there, doing what they can, like you."

"So you know someone?"

"Yes. But, Sara, let's think this through for a few minutes. The man in the picture, Leopoldo Hinojosa, he's powerful. Really powerful. He commands the Public Security and Crime Prevention Unit, one of the most important divisions of the State Police in Chihuahua. But it's his association with whoever is keeping the girls that makes him so . . . dangerous. It's not just him, it's the web of criminality he's a part of."

"You knew there were places where they took girls?"

"We suspected some of the kidnapped girls were being kept alive as sex slaves or sold to sex traffickers. You know that the bodies of most kidnapped girls show up sooner or later in fairly public places—almost as if the criminals want them to be found. So it didn't make sense that certain girls were never found. And when you look at the girls who are still missing, it's hard not to notice that they all fit a certain profile."

"They're all beautiful," Sara says, remembering Linda.

"Yes. Slim, tall, long black hair, dark skin. So, I'm not going to lie to you, this lead you have is very substantial."

"The way I picture it, there's this place where girls like Erica and Linda are kept like prisoners," Sara says. She swallows, thinking about it. "So Erica and Linda are with Hinojosa and another man. Hinojosa falls asleep, probably drunk, and the other guy goes to the bathroom. Linda grabs Hinojosa's cell phone, takes a picture, and quickly forwards it to the first e-mail address she remembers that won't track back to her family. She's afraid the other guy will come out of the bathroom at any moment, so she only has time to put *puchi* on the subject line, so I'll know it's from her. Then Linda or Erica hide the cell phone somewhere, and later that day, they find a way to sneak it out with the help of the boy who works for the laundry service."

"I agree that's probably what happened. Well, if that's Hinojosa's phone, you can be sure that it contains a lot of names, telephone numbers, pictures, and all kinds of information that would hurt a lot of people if law enforcement had it. That's why they did what they did to the Renterías."

Sara doesn't say anything.

Agent Durand continues, "I want to make sure, before you call me again with more information, you know what this will do to your life." She knows what he's going to say and part of her does not want him to say it. "I think that right now you are relatively safe. But once this horrible place is raided and any girls there are rescued, they'll know that it was you or the Renterías who were responsible. I think they'll rule out the Renterías because they'll know it takes some technical savvy to find the place. So they'll narrow it down to you, and maybe they'll figure out that you had help from your friend in IT and the Jaqueros."

"You know about the Jaqueros?"

"They're one of our biggest and best sources of information. So, what I'm saying is that Hinojosa will do everything he can to protect himself. And if he's threatened, he will stop at nothing."

Sara is silent.

"Sara, are you still there?"

"Yes."

"I'm sure my good friends in Mexico would love to go after a guy as important as Hinojosa. I just want to make sure you know what's at stake here."

She's trying to process what exactly this all means. For her. For Mami and Emiliano. For their lives as they're living them. "No one at *El Sol* knows where I live except Juana. I give everyone a post office box number. There's no trace of our address in any public records. I changed it to a P.O. box ever since I got that threatening letter—you know, after the article I wrote on the joint task force."

"I wish I could tell you that was enough to keep you safe. But I know the people we're dealing with. They're not human beings like the rest of us. I'm sorry."

Sara looks up at the café's ceiling fan going slowly around and around. She has no words, no response. Does she really have to give up her job? Will they need to leave their home? Where will they go? She feels like a small child who does not understand the overwhelming emotions she's experiencing and all she can do is cry. So that's what she does. "I'm sorry," she says after a minute or so. She blows her nose on a napkin.

"No. Don't apologize." Agent Durand's voice is kind. "Why don't you think some more about all this? Wait for your IT friend to call you with the location, if he finds it. Go home, talk to your brother and your mother. Their lives will change too, after all. I'll wait to hear from you."

"But don't we have to move fast . . . for Erica and Linda?"

"The only way Hinojosa's people could have known all they know is if they got the information out of the girls. It's likely that the worst already happened."

She gasps when she realizes what he's saying. "They were tortured? They're not alive anymore?"

"I think you should assume the worst."

Sara can't speak. Erica and Linda would be alive if it wasn't for her. The e-mail was sent to her. The envelope was addressed to her. If she had done something to discover the missing e-mail sooner. If she had gotten to work half an hour earlier yesterday and found the envelope. It suddenly seems as if there were hundreds of things she could have done but didn't.

"Sara," she hears Agent Durand say, "it's not your fault. Do you hear me? I know that's what you're thinking. It's not your fault. And it will be okay if you decide that you need to protect yourself and your family. I'll work with the Mexican Attorney General's Office. We'll put Hinojosa under constant surveillance. Sooner or later he'll take us to that place. We'll take our time and work discreetly, so if we arrest him you won't be implicated. Okay?"

"Okay," Sara says. She's too tired and confused to say anything else.

"If I don't hear from you later today, that's fine. We'll go with that. Take care, Sara."

"Thank you." She taps the red circle on her phone to end the call.

Sara doesn't know what to do next or where to go. The young woman who gave her the chamomile tea is wiping the table next to her. There is something very beautiful and soothing about the careful way she wipes the table. No one is in the café except the two of them, and Sara's sure she isn't being thorough just to impress her. It never ceases to amaze her how grateful poor people are for their jobs. Linda made six dollars a day in the shoe store where she worked. The young woman in front of her makes less than that. What if this young woman is kidnapped on the way home tonight and taken to that horrible place?

As long as that place exists, young women like her will be taken there, Sara knows. Closing one place or putting away one man will not make a dent in all the evil in Juárez, much less in Mexico or the world. She remembers something she read in school once: *The decision to act against evil is not measured by the impact it has on the evil but by the impact it has on the person who acts.* She can't remember who wrote it, but the words ring true. The only thing that matters is that she act in accordance with her conscience.

She digs in her backpack for the twenty pesos she hid there for emergencies and leaves them under her cup. On her way back to the *El Sol* building, she makes a mental list of what she must do next. She wants to see Ernesto, find out if he's gotten any more information on the location of the evil place. Then she'll go get Mami at work and take her home. Hopefully, Emiliano will be there. She'll tell them everything. They should be given the opportunity to decide their future, even if she already knows what they will say. Then, after that, she'll go to Linda's house and talk to Mr. and Mrs. Fuentes. They need to know all that she has found out.

Ernesto isn't in his office, so Sara leaves him a note on a sticky pad: *I'm going home. Call me as soon as you can.*

The news floor is quiet. Sara feels entirely alone. She knows what has to be done but she also wants someone to tell her what she should do. She goes over to Juana's office. She'll tell Juana all that is happening. Juana has always been the newspaper's biggest advocate for the Desaparecidas. That's the real Juana, not the one she's seen the past two days. It's the real Juana who Sara needs right now.

But Juana's office is empty. Sara stands in front of it for a few moments, not knowing where to go next.

"She's in the conference room with Felipe working on the budget," Lupita says behind her.

Sara starts to walk away and then remembers she gave away her emergency taxi money. Today is one day when she doesn't want to take public transportation home.

"Lupita, you think I could have a taxi voucher? I'm going home early today. I don't feel well."

"I don't get to give them out anymore. Queen Juana thought I wasn't mean enough when it came to giving out vouchers. Her Majesty is the only one who can give them out."

"I think you're a lot meaner than Juana," Sara says, only half joking.

"I know, right? Juana's a pussycat and I'm a tiger." Lupita roars.

Sara pretends to laugh. For a moment, she considers borrowing taxi money from Lupita but then thinks better of it.

Maybe she can wait for Ernesto in the IT room and borrow it from him when he returns.

"She keeps them in the bottom right-hand drawer," Lupita says, her fingers already flying over her keyboard.

"What?"

"The vouchers. Go ahead and get one. The drawer's locked but you can find the key under the lamp. Don't tell anyone I told you."

"Thank you," Sara says. "I really needed someone to be nice to me today."

"Yeah, well, don't get used to it. Hurry, before someone sees you."

Sara walks into Juana's office and sits in her chair. There under the lamp is the key to the drawer, just as Lupita said. Sara smiles when she sees Juana's old Rolodex full of contact cards. She can't help checking, and Ernesto is right: Filed under *P* is a series of passwords. The last one is Micifus#25. Micifus is the name of one of Juana's cats. Clearly, Juana does what Sara does and just keeps increasing the number every time Ernesto's harsh security system forces them to change passwords. Elias would have had no trouble coming into her office, logging on to her computer, and deleting the hotline e-mails.

Sara is still shaking her head as she unlocks the bottom drawer and opens it. The taxi vouchers are right next to a bottle of rum, which Sara knows Juana pours into a Coke at the end of a hard day. She removes a taxi voucher from the pad and is about to close the drawer when something makes her stop and look at a cigar box partially hidden under a notebook. It feels almost like a voice asking her to look inside. She takes out the cigar box and opens it.

There is only one item inside: a small manila envelope with an *H* on it. Sara picks it up, her hand trembling. The manila envelope is not sealed. She opens it and takes out the white envelope with her name on it. She can feel the cell phone inside.

At that moment, her mind goes blank. It clicks off. She can't think or feel anything, but she reacts instinctively: She takes the envelope with the cell phone and drops it in her backpack. Then she puts the manila envelope back in the cigar box, closes the drawer, locks it, and puts the key under the lamp.

Sara stands. She's not sure her legs will hold her up, but they do, barely. Lupita winks at her as she leaves Juana's office and her heart jumps, but then she remembers the wink is for the taxi voucher in her hand. Sara even manages to wink back.

She walks ever so slowly to the elevator and waits for it to inch its way up from the first floor. Why? What could Juana possibly gain by helping Hinojosa? She tries as best she can to remember the conversation she had with Juana at the quinceañera. Something about finding the money to save *El Sol*. Perhaps Juana is working under his protection and funding. Does that make her less evil? She doesn't have time to answer that question for herself because just then the elevator door opens and Elias steps out, black silk jacket and all.

"Going out?"

"Yeah," she mutters. "Home. Not feeling well today."

"You don't look good. I can drive you. My car is down the street."

Is he being kind or is he working with Juana and Hinojosa? Who is good and who is bad? She can no longer tell.

"Taxi," Sara says, waving the voucher as she steps onto the elevator. The doors close between them.

God, my God, she prays. *Please help me. Help all of us.*

CHAPTER 14
EMILIANO

SATURDAY, MARCH 25
12:35 P.M.

"Emiliano!" Javier says when he sees Emiliano at the door.

"Come in, come in!" Javier's mother says.

Everyone turns when Emiliano enters. The room is full of an energy that feels like happiness. Marta stands so Emiliano can take her chair. Nieves grabs his hand. Mrs. Robles goes to the red cooler to fill a glass with water. Rosario rises from the couch and turns the fan on. Emiliano notices that she has a beauty that reveals itself only slowly.

"I don't have any more piñatas," Javier says. "We had to take Marta to the emergency room yesterday."

Marta looks as if she will crumple to the floor any second. "Thank you," Emiliano says to her. "You sit. I can't stay. I need to talk to Javier for a few minutes." Then to Javier, "You want to take a walk?"

"All right," Javier says, with slight apprehension.

Javier is the most mature of all the Jiparis. Even at fourteen, he has lived more, seen more, and felt more than most adults. Emiliano has always felt close to him because they share a special bond: They both want nothing to do with their fathers. Javier's father is in Mexico City, maybe alive and maybe dead, no one knows. One day, while he was out on a binge, Mrs. Robles put everyone on a bus and came to Juárez, where she heard the assembly plants were hiring. The family lives in fear that one day he will find them.

Emiliano blinks a few times when they step outside.

"I know, it's like a cave in there," Javier says, laughing.

"How do you do your homework? How do you work on those piñatas with so little light?"

"You grow raccoon eyes after a while." Javier makes circles around his eyes with his thumbs and index fingers. Then, turning serious, he says, "That was a lot of money you left us yesterday. More than three piñatas' worth. Thanks."

Emiliano nods. They walk side by side toward the bus stop half a mile down the hill, then pause to sit on the rusty hood of an abandoned car. A squealing pig with two barefoot kids behind it runs on the dirt road in front of them. Javier watches with delight while Emiliano wonders how to say what he wants to say. He had a speech along the lines of Mr. Esmeralda's, but right there and then, with the smell of raw sewage making it hard to breathe, telling Javier that there's no way to be successful without getting a little dirty seems inappropriate for some reason.

"So what is it?" Javier asks. In the distance, it sounds as if the pig has been caught.

Emiliano takes a deep breath, which he immediately regrets. He searches for a source of the smell more specific than the whole neighborhood and notices a stream of water flowing down the hill behind them.

"Wouldn't it be good if you could get out of this place?" Emiliano asks.

Javier shrugs. "There's worse places."

Is he serious? Javier is smiling, but Emiliano can tell that he also meant what he said.

He decides to launch into it. "After I picked up your piñatas yesterday, I ran into some people who want to do business with me. With us, if you're interested."

"Yeah?"

"We wouldn't be working for them, like their employees or anything. We would have our own operation, but they would supply us with the product."

"Product? You mean they also make handicrafts?"

"No. We would continue to make the handicrafts. I mean, *you* would continue to make the piñatas and other papier-mâché animals."

"Along with the other Jiparis."

"Actually, this particular operation, this part of the business, would be just you and me."

Javier looks confused. "I don't understand. Why do we need these other guys?"

"They would supply the product to put inside the piñatas. Then the piñatas would be taken across the border to the United States, pretty much the way they're being shipped now, except they would go to shops controlled by our business associates."

Javier stares at Emiliano with open-eyed amazement for a long time and then laughs. " 'Product.' You mean cocaine, heroin, things like that."

"Yes. I think we could decide what kind, if we preferred one kind of product over another."

Javier shakes his head. He and Emiliano watch the barefoot

boys, who have now caught the pig. One boy holds its front legs and the other the back legs. The pig is breathing heavily and making tiny baby sounds. They carry the pig back toward the houses.

Emiliano continues, after the boys and the pig have gone by, "We would be in control of the operation. We would always keep it small. The same number of piñatas you're making now. No more. You stay in school. I stay in school. Nothing really changes. Let's say we do six piñatas a week. As I understand it, that amount will get us, after we pay everyone, around fifteen thousand pesos. Eight thousand for you and seven thousand for me. Or more for you, if you want, since you're doing most of the work."

Javier whistles. "That's a lot."

"Yeah, it is. That's just for six piñatas. The guy I talked to suggested twelve a week, but I think fewer is better."

"Eight thousand a week."

"Your mother and Rosario together don't make that much in a year."

"Gosh." Javier scratches his head. Then, "And if we're caught? I've been in a Juárez jail. You think this place stinks . . ."

"I thought about that a lot," Emiliano says. "If we do this, I want to make sure that no one knows who you are. You'll never have any contact with anyone but me. Not with the suppliers, not with the shop owners. No one. If something happens, they will only be able to trace the piñatas to me. I'll even start making some in my house so they believe me when I tell them it's just me."

"You're not afraid?"

"The main thing is to keep it small, not get greedy. If we can do that, we'll be okay. I'll continue selling other kids' handicrafts. Our operation will blend in unnoticed. Once I make enough to take care of my mother and sister, and you make enough to take care of *your* mother and sisters, we stop. I'm thinking maybe one year, two years at the most."

"Is that why you want to do this? So we can help our families?"

Emiliano swallows. Is that the only reason? Is it necessary to tell Javier all of the reasons? He exhales. He will answer truthfully. That's what he decided to do last night. "I guess there's another reason." He stares for a few moments at a puddle in the middle of the road. Where did that puddle come from? It hasn't rained in two months. "I . . . I like this girl at school. Her name is Perla Rubi. She's . . . Her family is very wealthy. Her father knows the people that we would be doing business with. Anyway, Perla Rubi's father talked to me and explained to me how things are, business-wise, here in Juárez, and maybe all of Mexico, how you can't really get ahead unless you're willing to do things you don't like."

"And Perla Rubi? She wants you to do it too?"

He remembers the promise of Perla Rubi's kiss. "I'm not sure she knows the details of what I'd be doing, but she's happy that her father likes me. It would be impossible for her to have me as a boyfriend if her family did not accept me. And from what her father said to me, they would not accept me unless I could take care of her. They want someone who will do all it takes—make all the sacrifices that are needed—for their daughter." He shakes his head. "Right now, how am I ever going to do that? I mean, look at me. I'm going to graduate from high school next year, and what will I do? I'm not smart enough to go to college. I'm good at soccer, but not good enough to make a living out of it. I want to own my own store, but how will I get the money for that? So what will I do? Work in an assembly plant?" Emiliano slides down from the hood.

Javier slides down too and stands next to him. They both lean on the car, looking at a little girl returning home from the water spigot with a plastic bucket. After she goes past them, Javier says, "It's okay with me. If you want to do it, I'll do it too."

Emiliano pushes himself away from the car. Javier looks as if he's holding something back. "Tell me," Emiliano says. "If we're going to be partners, we need to be honest with each other."

"'I will be honest with myself and others,'" Javier says, remembering the Jipari pledge.

"I know. I feel bad about our Jipari pledge too." Emiliano and Javier both stare at the ground for a few moments. "Maybe it's not realistic—that part of the pledge. We'll be faithful to the rest of the pledge. We'll abstain from all intoxicants and we will be doing something for the benefit of others."

"Others? You mean like the people who end up using the product?" Javier looks at Emiliano for a moment.

There's nothing Emiliano can say in response. Javier's right. He thought about that too last night. The only thing he can think of is that helping some people inevitably hurts others.

Javier speaks. "You're new at this. But I've been on the streets since I was eight, doing business with the kind of people we're going to be doing business with. Some of them were nice. Every one of them for sure was a lot nicer than my father. They treated me like a son, you know, and I liked that. But I found out after a while that they weren't all that nice deep down."

"You don't want to do this, then?"

"I'll do it if you want me to. God knows we can use the money. We can get Marta her medicine, find a good doctor, maybe even live in a place that doesn't make her sick. But I'm not fooling myself and you shouldn't either. These people we're going to do business with, the father of the girl you're in love with and all the others—they're not good people."

Emiliano nods. He respects what Javier is telling him, but he doesn't agree. Maybe Armando and Alfredo Reyes are shady, but Mr. Esmeralda is just doing what he has to do to be successful, to take care of his family. That doesn't make him a bad person, does it?

Javier continues, "And the other thing I know as an addict is that once you get that hunger inside of you, you can't control it. It's impossible."

"We're not going to *use* the product." Then it hits him. Unbelievably, it's the one thing he hadn't considered in all the meticulous thinking he did in the endless night. Javier is an addict. *Once an addict, always an addict, even if you stop using.* Isn't that what Brother Patricio says? How did Emiliano manage to overlook that small detail—how dangerous it would be for a recovering addict to handle drugs? "You probably shouldn't do this, then," he says.

Javier shrugs. "I'm not worried about me. I'm worried about you. You say we won't get greedy, that we'll stay small. But money is like heroin. Once you get it, you want more. It's just something you need to know."

Emiliano thinks. "Okay. I hear you. But since we know

that, can't we guard against it? We can keep an eye on each other. You stop me if you see me start to want more. And . . . we need to figure out a way for me to work with you on the piñatas. I don't think it's a good idea for you to be around the stuff alone. Tell me if this will be a problem for you. Do you want to do this or not? Do you think it's possible to keep it under control? The truth."

"Yes," Javier says. "I trust you, Emiliano. I'll do it if you want to do it."

"But do *you* want to?"

"If I said 'I'll do it,' it's because I want to. We'll help each other, like you say." Emiliano can feel Javier's affection for him in the gentle firmness of his voice. "You better go. It gets bad when people come home from the midnight shift. They usually stop for a few drinks before." He digs in his back pocket. "Take this for a taxi. It's going to take you two hours if you take a bus."

"I got money." Emiliano bumps fists with Javier. "We'll help each other." He wants to say something that will convey how like a brother Javier is to him, but men don't talk that way to each other. "So, I'll see you next Saturday. The over-night hike."

"I hope I can go. I think we'll need to take Marta to the hospital again. The doctor says it was this dust." Javier runs a finger on the hood of the car and shows Emiliano the white chalky substance that covers everything. "Can you come by this week? You can pick up Rosario's doll, and I might have some piñatas for you. Unstuffed."

"Sure. I'll come by on Tuesday. Later." Emiliano starts walking.

"See you," Javier calls after him.

He waves his hand in the air without looking back. He recognizes in his chest the same hollow sensation he felt last night, like something has been carved out of him, and now he feels the empty space.

He must learn to live with it. It is unavoidable.

CHAPTER 15
SARA

Sara sits in the back of a taxi, staring out the window, ignoring the driver's attempts at conversation. She feels something she has never felt before: like she will never again see what she is seeing. The man on the street selling mangoes on a stick, the woman in a pink dress walking and talking on her phone, the old man sitting on the sidewalk with one leg stretched out and one leg missing, begging for money. All the life around her she took for granted, before her life was threatened.

Now and again she sticks her hand in her backpack and touches the white envelope. It's true. Juana, her Juana, her mentor and supporter in her fight for the Desaparecidas, is corrupt. *Corrupt.* The word sounds like what is happening in Sara's heart: COR-RUPT. A ripping, a rupturing, a rending. How could Juana be a bad person? When did it happen? Was associating with bad people the only possible way to save *El Sol*? The bad times for *El Sol* started before Sara become a permanent employee. So she's been corrupt all the time Sara has known her? What about all those meetings with mothers of missing girls that they attended, all those articles denouncing government indifference and malfeasance—was that just a show on Juana's part? It all feels so personal, as if Juana's betrayal is a rejection of Sara specifically. She's okay with Sara being threatened, even killed. And that hurts.

"Everything okay, miss?"

She moves her head so the driver can't see her eyes in the rearview mirror.

"Things are never as bad as they seem," the man says when she doesn't answer.

No, actually, sometimes things are a lot worse than they seem. She glances at her cell phone. No text from Emiliano. It's irrational, she knows, but her fear now extends like a ripple in a pond out to Emiliano and Mami. She wants to be home with them, in the safety of the love they have for each other.

"You can drop me off at the next corner," Sara says. They are two blocks away from the bakery where Mami works. She'll wait until Mami's shift ends and then go home with her. Mami's friend Luisa will give them a ride.

She writes down the fare on the taxi voucher, signs it, and gives it to the driver. She adds a twenty-percent tip even though ten percent is the maximum *El Sol* employees are allowed to tip, per one of Felipe's memos. "Sorry, I don't have any cash," she says as he studies the voucher. "Your company always takes them."

"That's all right," he says. She has a feeling he's going to toss the voucher out the window as soon as he's out of sight.

"Thank you."

"Remember . . ."

"Things are never as bad as they seem." Sara fills in the blank for him.

"Correct."

Sara watches the driver make a U-turn and head in the opposite direction. He gives her a thumbs-up as he speeds away. There are so many people who are good in this country. Kind people like that taxi driver. She feels a guilty pang about Elias. Maybe he didn't deserve her mean thoughts about him today. She stops in front of a shoe store and stares without looking at the shoes in the window display. It is suddenly clear to her why, in the taxi, she was saying good-bye to everything. It is impossible to ever go back to *El Sol*. She cannot go back with Juana there. She has no job. She is no longer a reporter.

She is standing there, paralyzed by the thought, when her cell phone rings. Ernesto.

"We found the place," he says in his usual no-nonsense voice.

"You have?"

"You don't sound very excited."

"Something bad happened. I'll tell you in a minute. But first let me write down the address." She gets a pen from her backpack and then takes out the notepad she always uses for interviews. Her legs feel as if they are about to fold, so she leans against the display window for support. "Tell me."

"125 Calle Palacio de Mila. It's on the corner of Avenida Las Torres. Take Highway 45 past the airport and turn on Boulevard Camandari. That will take you to Las Torres. We only got a satellite view of the place, but it looks like a large lot with a three-story building protected by high walls. The third floor is something like an enclosed patio that probably serves as a lookout. It reminds me of the compound where they captured Bin Laden."

"How did you find it?" Sara suddenly feels exhausted.

"La Vaquita picks up and delivers linen there every Thursday. It's almost directly in the path of the east-west runway of the airport. All their other pickups and deliveries are closer to town. The place is listed as a residence belonging to 'Jacinto Vargas,' who doesn't exist as far as we can tell. It's the right place. No doubt."

Sara writes down the directions, her hand trembling. Linda is in this place. She's there now. Sara puts the notepad and pen in her backpack and notices that the battery icon on her cell phone is red. "Ernesto, my phone may go dead at any moment, so let me talk."

"Talk."

"I went back to the office to look for you, and when you weren't there, I went to Juana's office, and she wasn't in. I guess it was a good thing because I really needed to talk to someone and I was ready to tell her everything we've discovered. Then I decided to go home. Lupita told me where Juana keeps the taxi vouchers." Sara swallows. "In the drawer with the vouchers, I found the white envelope with the cell phone."

"Juana? No way!"

"It was inside another, bigger envelope with an *H* on it, in Juana's handwriting. Hinojosa probably already got a new phone. She must be holding it until it's safe to give it to him personally."

"Damn. I didn't see that coming." They are both silent for a moment. "Why? Why would she do that?"

"I don't know. Maybe she's being threatened as well. Or maybe she's doing it for the money. She told me at the quinceañera she would do whatever it took to save her job. Maybe she aligned herself with Hinojosa to keep *El Sol* from going under."

"That sort of makes sense. One day we were all getting laid off and the next we were back in business. But who knows? I've stopped trying to figure out why people do things. I'll stick to computers. So, what do we do now?"

"I found someone I can trust, someone from the FBI in El Paso. I want to talk to my brother and mother, because what I do will affect them, but if they agree, I'm going to give him the address you gave me."

"Mmm." She can almost hear Ernesto thinking. "Juana's going to be in that budget meeting for another two hours at least. I know because they called me in there a little while ago to drill me about why we needed four extra computers, and Felipe was ordering tacos from across the street. But when Juana comes out, if she sees that the phone is missing, she'll know immediately that either you or I took it, and she'll tell Hinojosa. We need to get ready."

"You?"

"Think about it. You told Juana I was helping with the threatening e-mail."

"Ernesto, you told me you have places to hide."

"Yeah. Don't worry about me. Call your FBI friend soon. We only have a couple of hours before all hell breaks loose. Have you looked at the cell phone?"

"No. It's still in the envelope."

"Where are you now?"

"I'm in the street, a couple of blocks from where Mami works. I better go. I want to have enough battery to call my brother. Make sure he's okay."

"Okay, okay. I'll be quick. Open the envelope and take the phone out carefully by the edges. Don't touch the screen or the back of the phone."

Sara follows his instructions. "I got it."

"What is it?"

"It's an Android. It has a stylus."

"Okay, it's got fingerprint ID recognition. That's good news."

"That's good news why?"

"María, one of our Jaqueros, was able to open one just like that by lifting a fingerprint of the owner from the screen and scanning it. We'll be able to break in."

"Ernesto . . ." Sara doesn't want him to be in any more danger.

"Look, I know what you're going to say, but we're deep in this mess already. Might as well take it as far as we can. Even if your FBI friend rescues the girls, the bald colonel bastard and his associates are still out there. Let's get as many of the sons of bitches as we can. We can do that with the information on that phone. Are you going home?"

"In a little while, after I pick up Mami."

"I'll drop by your house and pick up the phone. Just make sure you don't touch the back or the screen. And don't think about it too much. The only way to fight these people is by not thinking about the danger. I'll get the phone from you and take it from there. You need to disappear too. I'm leaving now."

Sara leans her forehead against the glass of the display window. "This is all happening so fast. I need to think."

"What did you think about when you saw the envelope in Juana's drawer?"

"I just grabbed it."

"Because doing what is right is in your bones. Just follow where your bones take you. Give me your address. I don't even know where you live."

Sara pauses. She never gives her address to anyone. Can she trust Ernesto? She trusted Juana and that trust was misplaced. Juana. Juana knows where she lives. Her image of being safe at home with Mami and Emiliano suddenly shatters.

"Sara, we're on the same side," Ernesto says.

What does trust feel like? Sara has no idea anymore. All she can feel is hope. She hopes that Ernesto is as good and brave as he seems, and she must listen to that hope, because without it, her world would be total darkness. She gives Ernesto her address. "You better come early," she says. "I think we'll need to find a place to spend the night."

"Be there as soon as I can. I'm going to go home and get a buddy to give me a ride to—"

The screen on her phone turns black. The battery is dead. Sara slides down and sits on the sidewalk beneath the display window. She thinks of the one-legged beggar she saw a few minutes before. Maybe she'll soon be homeless too.

She looks at the white envelope that held the phone. Folded inside is the note that Erica had written her family. The words are blurry and brown—written with eyeliner, she guesses—and it says almost exactly what Mr. Mirabiles recited over the phone. Then Sara reads the note that Mr. Rentería wrote to her.

Miss Sara. This was sent from our Erica. She's alive.
Help her. She wanted you to have this. You are the
only one she trusts and the only one we trust.

God bless you always,

Manuel Rentería

Sara folds the note, places it in the envelope, and stands.
There is still a little strength left in her bones.

CHAPTER 16
EMILIANO

SATURDAY, MARCH 25
2:03 P.M.

Emiliano tells the taxi driver to stop in front of Armando's house. He pays with the money Armando gave him yesterday. It feels like such a waste to pay fifty pesos for something that would have cost him five if he had taken a bus. He had to take a taxi to school after he dropped the Mercedes at Armando's house early this morning, so that's eighty pesos gone on taxis.

Through the iron bars of the front gate, he can see Armando's black Jeep. Someone is moving behind a window upstairs. When there's a lull in the street traffic, he hears the deep beat of a bass guitar. There, just inside the black gate, he sees his bicycle and trailer. Armando must have had someone bring it over from Taurus.

He pushes the button on the intercom outside the gate. The intercom and the camera on the brick fence are identical to the ones at Alfredo Reyes's home. Emiliano is surprised to hear Armando answer. "Hello?"

"It's Emiliano," he says, his mouth nearly touching the intercom.

"Come in."

There's a click and the gate swings forward at Emiliano's touch. He's halfway down a stone path when the front door of the house opens and Armando steps out. He's wearing jeans, a white T-shirt, and pink flip-flops. His black hair is wet and slicked up. "Emiliano! I was hoping I'd hear from you."

The warmth and apparent sincerity in Armando's words soothe the jagged edges that have been poking at Emiliano since he left Javier. "Did you get the box that Mr. Reyes sent you?" he asks. "I made sure the man who opened the gate for me this morning brought it inside the house. You were asleep."

"Yeah, yeah. Of course. Thank you. I hope that wasn't too much trouble. I had no idea Mr. Reyes was sending anything with you."

It's probably not a good idea to tell Armando that he didn't sleep a wink last night because of, among other things, that damn box.

"Hey." Armando puts his arm around Emiliano's shoulders and turns him toward the side of the house. "I'm glad you came in person instead of just calling. I want to show you something."

Emiliano manages to step out of Armando's hold without Armando noticing. Or maybe Armando does notice, but who cares. If he's going to do business with these people, it will be on his own terms, and friendship is not one of them.

"I don't know what you said or did, but Alfredo Reyes was really impressed with you, and he's not easily impressed. I knew he would be, that's why I sent you to see him. By the way, I took the liberty of asking my father to call Mr. Esmeralda yesterday after you met with Ernesto Reyes. I told you Jorge Esmeralda was my father's lawyer, right? Mr. Esmeralda called my father this morning and said some very good things about you. You're in, my friend. You're in!"

The full implication of what Armando means by "in" is unmistakable, but Emiliano does not want to talk about Perla Rubi with Armando. "I wanted to talk to you about what Mr. Reyes proposed," he says.

"Sure. But first you need to see this." Armando pushes a button on a wall and a garage door rolls up. In front of Emiliano is a black sports car that looks fast just sitting there. Next to it is a white BMW motorcycle. Armando walks up to it and touches the seat. "I got this for my birthday last week. Beautiful, isn't it?"

Emiliano nods. The motorcycle that he plans to buy from Joel Cardenas seems shabby by comparison. "Ninety horses?" he asks.

"Yeah? You know bikes?"

"A little." He's been doing some reading since Joel agreed to sell his bike to him.

"Good." Armando pulls a green plastic cover from another, smaller motorcycle. Emiliano takes a step closer. "It's no BMW, but . . . My father got it for me for my fourteenth birthday. It's a nice little scooter, one of the best Vespa makes. Primavera Touring. Single-cylinder four-stroke engine with catalytic converter and electronic fuel injection. Maximum speed is about 96 kilometers per hour, but I've gotten it to go faster than that. And look, it has front and rear luggage racks where you can carry your folk art things."

"What are you talking about?"

Armando fishes in his pocket and tosses Emiliano two keys attached to a rabbit's foot. "This will make you more efficient. You can't be riding around on that old bike of yours. It would take you half a day to get to the place where Mr. Reyes keeps the product. And I have other means of transportation, as you can see." Armando pats the BMW. "It's good as new. I had someone siphon out the old gas and put new in."

"I can't," Emiliano says.

"Sure you can. If it makes you uncomfortable to accept it as a gift, then think of it as a loan. When you buy a car or a better motorcycle, you can give it back." Armando turns the motor scooter around and slowly pushes it outside. He closes the garage doors. "You should get one of those thick chains and a lock if you're going to take it to school. Hey, you need a helmet? I got an old one you can have."

"That's all right." Emiliano is at a loss for words. He came over to tell Armando that he will work with Mr. Reyes under certain conditions, but he can't remember what they are now. "You knew I was going to say yes."

"I was hoping."

"Why? What do you get out of all this?"

Armando laughs. "Alfredo Reyes is an associate of my father's. I thought I'd do him a favor by sending him someone like you. Good people are incredibly hard to find."

Mr. Esmeralda said something to that effect. Emiliano tries to recollect his exact words. *Cortázar and Reyes are good businessmen. The success of an organization depends on the quality of the people who work there.*

"But what about you? The business that I'll be doing is so small. Whatever cut you want from it can't possibly make a difference to you."

"I'm not looking for a cut of your business," Armando says, smiling.

"Then . . ."

"The way this world works, my little friend, is that today I scratch your back and tomorrow you'll scratch mine. Hell, that didn't sound right. Look, connections are the only way to make it in this town. I don't have a head for business, as much as my father wishes I did. He wants me to help him develop malls and office buildings. And to be honest with you, I'd rather be flying on that baby in the garage than do the boring stuff he wants me to do. So, if you must know, my hidden motive is that someday you'll work with me and take care of all the business junk that comes naturally to you . . . and I hate." Armando pauses and studies Emiliano's face. "Relax. We're not monsters. We're businesspeople. Okay? Don't worry. You're doing the right thing for yourself and your family." He smiles and adds, "And you're doing the right thing for Perla Rubi."

Emiliano smiles as well. He touches the right handle of the motor scooter. "How do I get in touch with Mr. Reyes? To tell him I want to do business with him."

"I'll call him. You're all set. He'll get in touch with you."

He remembers his conditions. "I need to be in control of the volume and the type of product. And I'm the only one who has contact with the kids who make the crafts. No one else."

Armando laughs. "Do I have an eye for talent or do I have an eye for talent. You're going to go places, Emiliano. You're a born CEO. One day I'll say, 'I knew Emiliano Zapata when he was a nobody.' Come on, get on the bike. I'll open the gate for you."

"My bicycle," Emiliano says as they walk by it.

"I had Tony put it on the truck and bring it here. Thought it would be easier for you. And to be honest, it didn't quite go with the image of Taurus we're trying to convey."

"Can I take the trailer with me? I need it for my deliveries."

"Sure. Hold on." Armando goes back into the garage and comes out with a roll of electrical wire and a pair of pliers. "I think this will work. You know, Vespa makes these boxes you can attach to the racks. Optics are important, my friend."

"It's only temporary," Emiliano says as he latches the trailer to the back rack of the Vespa. "I'll look into that box for the luggage rack."

Armando walks toward the gate. "Thank you," Emiliano says as he opens it.

Armando responds by giving him a thumbs-up.

Emiliano climbs on the scooter and starts it. The scooter makes a soft sound, a smooth and steady purr. It's not a powerful sound, but to him, it's just right.

CHAPTER 17
SARA

SATURDAY, MARCH 25
3:17 P.M.

"What happened?" Mami asks Sara when they're inside their house.

Mami knew something was wrong as soon as Sara entered the bakery. She tilted her head as if to see Sara's face from a different angle, and they were both quiet on the car ride home. Sara had decided that she would wait until Emiliano got home to tell them both the news at the same time, but the moment Mami asks her what's wrong, the tears start to flow.

Mami hugs Sara and leads her to the sofa, holding her until she is able to speak. Sara tells her everything that happened from the time Felipe read the threatening e-mail until her last conversation with Ernesto an hour before. After she finishes speaking, Mami pulls Sara's head to her chest and they sit there quietly. Sara can hear her heart racing.

"We're not safe here anymore, Mami."

"I know."

"We can go to a motel. I can ask Joel to take us."

"We'll wait for Emiliano to get home. We have a little time, no?"

"A couple of hours. I need to wait for Ernesto to come for the cell phone. Where's Emiliano? Have you heard from him today?"

"No." A shadow comes over Mami's face.

"What?"

"I'm worried. Mrs. Cardenas called me at work today. Emiliano parked a fancy car in their backyard last night and drove it out very early this morning."

"Oh." Sara doesn't want to tell Mami about her late-night conversation with Emiliano, as it would only worry her more, but this confirms something is happening with her brother. "It's probably related to his business. You know Emiliano."

"Yes." But Sara can tell she is still worried. Mami makes a move to stand, but Sara holds her arm.

"I'm sorry for all this, Mami."

She hugs her. "If you were Linda or that girl Erica or any of those other girls in that horrible place, and if I was the mother of any one of them, I would want you to do what you did. Call that policeman in El Paso as soon as possible. Tell him the address. Maybe it's not too late to help Linda."

"I wanted to talk to Emiliano and you . . ."

"I know what Emiliano will say."

Emiliano. Sara's straight-arrow brother. Her Jipari. Sara also knows what he would want her to do.

She goes to her room to charge her phone and retrieve Agent Durand's phone number. Mami goes into her room as well and closes the door. As Sara changes into a pair of jeans and a T-shirt, she hears the murmur of her mother's prayers.

Agent Durand answers on the first ring, as if he was waiting for Sara's call. She reads him the address and directions that Ernesto gave her.

"I know the area. I'll set it up," Agent Durand says. "There's a special commando unit within the Mexican army that we work with. The commander will want to do some initial surveillance to see what he's up against, but then they will move quickly, maybe as soon as daybreak tomorrow."

Tomorrow. Linda might be free tomorrow. That thought alone makes all the sadness of the day seem worth it.

"There's something else," Sara says. "After we talked last time, I went back to the office and found the envelope with Hinojosa's cell phone."

"What? Where?"

"In my boss's office. She had it in a desk drawer."

"Juana Martínez? The woman you introduced me to when I visited *El Sol*?"

"Yes."

"Does she know you have it?"

"She was in a meeting when I took it and probably will be there for another couple of hours. Did I make a mistake in taking the envelope?"

"Oh, goodness. You're asking me that? No, that phone will be very helpful to law enforcement. I can only imagine all the connections it will reveal between Hinojosa and other corrupt officials and the cartels. So no, I don't think it was a mistake. But . . . as far as your own personal safety, you have to move fast and find a safe place. They'll be coming for the phone as soon as they figure out you have it."

Sara sees the goose bumps on her arms. She never imagined that fear could make a person cold. She forces herself to speak. "Ernesto, my friend from IT who's been helping me, is coming to pick it up. He thinks one of the Jaqueros can open it."

"I think that's a good plan. Let the Jaqueros deal with the phone. They can do things we can't legally do, and they'll know what to do with the information. It's also safer for everyone if the Jaqueros have the phone. No one will ever find them. Except your friend Ernesto is—"

"In danger. He knows. He'll disappear as soon as he gets the phone."

"Good. I'm going to put you in touch with Estela Gómez, a friend of mine. She's in the State Police, but not in Hinojosa's division. There are a lot of good people in the State Police and Estela is one of them. You can trust her. She'll find a place for you to stay. I'll call her now and then you call her soon, okay?"

"Okay. Thank you, Agent Durand. You . . . you're the only the person I could think of . . . to help me."

"Thank you, Sara. Be careful. Follow Estela's instructions. Good-bye."

"Good-bye."

Sara tears a page from a magazine on her desk, writes down the name and number that Agent Durand gave her, and sticks the paper in the pocket of her jeans.

She hears a noise outside her window, like a motorcycle, only not as loud. She opens the curtain, expecting to see Ernesto, and instead sees Emiliano on one of those scooters that she's seen in movies about Rome, only this one has his rusty trailer attached. What is he up to? She watches him dismount and take the scooter to the backyard, looking at it admiringly as he walks. She runs to the kitchen and gives him a huge hug as soon as he opens the back door.

"Whoa, whoa, what's gotten into you?" Emiliano gives her a couple of little pats on the back. Then, when he manages to pull away, he asks, "Why have you been crying?"

"Who's been crying?"

"You. Those purple puffy circles under your eyes." Mami comes out of her bedroom, and Emiliano walks past Sara to give her his usual kiss on her forehead. "You've been crying too. What happened?"

"Do we have time to eat?" Mami asks Sara.

"Not much. We need to leave as soon as Ernesto comes."

"I'll make something. We can take it with us if we need to. Sit down with your brother and tell him everything." Mami points at the kitchen table and then walks to the refrigerator.

"Tell me what? Where do we have to go?"

Sara pulls out a chair for Emiliano and waits for him to sit. Then she sits in the chair next to him. Emiliano's face hardly ever reveals what he is feeling, but as she speaks, she can see the blood in his face slowly ebb away. She doesn't know how long she talks. It could be five minutes or an hour. She reports all events and all conversations without any editorial comments or conclusions. When Mami puts two plates with eggs and beans in front of them, Emiliano ignores it and continues to listen without asking a single question. Now and then Sara can see his Adam's apple move quickly, as if he's having trouble swallowing the significance of her words.

"I'm sorry," Sara says. "I'm so sorry for doing this to your life." She puts her hand on Emiliano's arm. He stares at the untouched food on his plate.

After a few moments of frozen silence, Mami speaks. "There is nothing to be sorry about. What you did had to be done. Do you agree, Emiliano?"

Emiliano pushes his plate away and exhales. He speaks with a sadness Sara has not heard in his voice since the day

Papá's divorce papers arrived at their house. "Do you think *all* of our lives are in danger?"

Sara answers as gently as she can. "I think we should all lay low for a couple of days. We'll see what happens. All I know for sure is that it's not safe for you and Mami to be in this house right now."

She waits for him to reply, but Emiliano only stares at the plate of cold food.

"We'll figure something out," she says, trying to console him. "We should all go pack for a couple of days. I'll call the woman that Alejandro Durand told me to call."

He snaps his head upright and looks at her with a burning intensity she hasn't seen before. He starts to say something and then stops himself.

"What?" Sara says.

Emiliano's eyes are slowly turning red and his nose begins to run. Sara reaches for a napkin and hands it to him.

"Tell us," Mami says softly.

He puts his elbows on the table and grabs his head. "What's there to figure out? We can't stay here anymore. You can't work at *El Sol*. Mami can't work at the bakery. Where are we going to live? What about my school?"

Sara wants to reach out and touch him, to tell him somehow that she understands all he's losing, but there's nothing she can say. She looks at Mami, hoping she might have words that can help her brother.

"Emiliano." Mami's voice is firm and strong. Whenever she uses that voice, Sara and Emiliano know that whatever she says is the final word on the subject. "What your sister did was right. Do you understand? I'm talking to you." He lifts his head and looks at her. "What Sara did was what God wanted her to do. It's what God would want you to do, or me if we were in her place. Whatever sacrifice we need to make, we make as one. Now we all need to go pack some things."

Mami lifts herself slowly from the table. Emiliano and Sara stand as well. Sara gives Mami her arm and together they walk to Mami's bedroom. Sara does not look at Emiliano. She's afraid of the heartbreak she will see in his face.

At the door to her bedroom, Mami asks if Sara will lend her her phone. "I want to call my sister Tencha. She's closer to God than anyone I know. She needs to pray for us."

Sara brings her the phone and shows her Aunt Tencha's number. "Just press that," she tells her.

"Sara," Mami says, grabbing her arm and pulling her back. "I'm proud of you."

"Yes, Mami." Sara kisses her mother's forehead and closes the door. She takes a deep breath and returns to the kitchen, where Emiliano is standing over the sink, deep in thought. Sara puts her arm around his shoulders.

"We're in this together, Emiliano, don't forget. The one thing we have to do through all this is stay together. Right?"

"Right," he says, not looking at her.

"Sit for a second." She sits at the table, hoping he'll do the same.

He rubs his eyes but stays standing. "I don't want to lose all I have," he says, exhaling.

Sara supposes that by "all," he mostly means Perla Rubi. "Call her," she says gently. "Tell her you won't be in school for a couple of days, that you need to help your stupid sister who got some threats for something she wrote. Buy a little time. We need to figure out a way so all this doesn't mean the end of your life as you know it." He nods and smiles—a very small smile, but it's something. Sara changes the subject. "What's with the new transportation?" She points at the backyard.

"I'm expanding my folk art business. A friend loaned me the scooter."

"Is this related to the fancy car you were driving last night?"

He turns to look at her with a *how did you know* expression.

"Mrs. Cardenas called Mami."

"Kind of," he says.

Sara has a bad feeling that his "kind of" is more complicated than he's letting on. "Emiliano, maybe what's happening is good for all of us, for you too, in a way that we can't see at the moment."

He reflects on her words for a few seconds. Finally, he says, "What's Mami doing?"

"She's calling Aunt Tencha, getting the prayers started. You know, of course, that the reason all this is happening to us is because you turned agnostic." She smiles. The agnosticism is an old battle in their house.

"I'm about to start believing again," Emiliano says, another small smile on his face. He stands. "I think I better call Perla Rubi."

"And pack some things."

"And pack some things. We'll figure it out," he says,

touching the top of her head. She knows that's Emiliano's way of letting her know he still loves her. He walks into his room and closes the door behind him.

We'll figure it out, we'll figure it out, Sara repeats to herself.

What exactly they need to figure out, other than where and how to live the rest of their lives, she has no idea.

CHAPTER 18

EMILIANO

Emiliano closes the door to his room, leans back against a wall, and slides down to the floor. He feels as if someone snatched something precious from his grasp just as he was about to grab it.

Would he do what Sara did? It's the right thing to do; it is. It's just, why him? Why now? He spent hours last night thinking about the choice he had to make. He made the choice that was best for everyone, and he was at peace with it. Javier was on board. He sealed the deal with Armando not more than an hour ago. He rode the Vespa home, pushing it to 110 kilometers per hour, the wind whipping his face and the future open before him. And now? Why does he feel like the whole damn thing is unfair?

Emiliano, think of Linda. What if she's still alive? Think of the danger your sister is in. This is no time to be selfish, son.

"You have no right to preach to me about selfishness."

Emiliano doesn't mean to speak out loud, but he does. He reaches for his fake Bible, opens it, looks at the money, and then closes it. Linda gave the Bible to him for his fourteenth birthday. But her best present was the one she gave him last year, a week before she disappeared.

Emiliano gets on his knees, opens the left-hand drawer of his desk, and takes out his Swiss Army knife. How did Linda know he wanted the one with the small compass on the handle? He sits against the wall again and moves the compass around until the needle points north. She gave it to him at the very end of a surprise party that Sara orchestrated with Paco's help. He remembers the delight on Linda's face after he opened the box and looked up at her. It was perfect. Another perfect gift. How long did she save before she could afford to buy him the knife?

You see how Linda thought about you, Emiliano. Shouldn't you think about her now?

Emiliano tucks the knife in his pocket. There must be a way to make sure that Sara is safe and still salvage the life opening up in front of him. Sara says that Mami is calling Aunt Tencha in León, which means that Mami is asking Aunt Tencha if they can go live with her. But Sara and Mami won't have jobs, and what his father sends is not enough, so they'll need him to work. He will have to convince them that the money he brings in from his folk art business is the only way to survive, which means he will need to stay in Juárez. He won't tell them about Alfredo Reyes.

Why, Emiliano? Think about why you won't tell them. There's a reason why you're ashamed of your association with Mr. Reyes.

Emiliano goes out to the kitchen, where he dropped his backpack when Sara hugged him. He gets his cell phone, comes back to his room, and sits on the floor again. There is comfort down here that cannot be found higher up. He places the cell phone next to him and closes his eyes. He has to make this conversation count. He goes over in his mind what he is going to say. *My sister is in trouble. Someone is threatening her life on account of something she wrote about the Desaparecidas. I need to be with her, make sure she's safe.* Something like that.

He taps Perla Rubi's name on his phone.

Perla Rubi picks up on the first ring. "Emiliano! I was hoping it was you. Are you home?"

The sound of her voice, her concern for him, rips his heart. "I'm home."

"How was your day?"

"Good. Very good." Up until a few minutes ago.

"You never told me what you were going to do after you left me. How did you spend the afternoon?"

"No? I thought I did when I saw you this morning. I was following up on the business with your father's friend. And you? How was the game?"

"We lost."

"You lost? To Sacred Heart? How did that happen?"

"I missed four serves. Two went into the net and two out of bounds. The girls blamed you."

"Me?"

"For showing up before the game and rattling me."

"I'm sorry."

"I'm not. I think I spent most of the day thinking about you, about us." Her voice is almost shy.

That right there, that joy he just felt, is what is being taken away from him. There is no avoiding it. "Perla Rubi, something's come up. With my sister, Sara."

"What? You're scaring me. Is she okay?"

He's not going to be able to hold it together for too long. This has to be a short conversation.

"I can't talk right now. My sister's life has been threatened because of her work at *El Sol*. We're trying to figure out what to do . . . so that she's safe. I'm not sure I'll be in school on Monday. I might be out for a few days."

"Oh, Emiliano. What will you do?"

"We'll be all right. I'll call you as soon as I can."

"Okay. But where will you be?"

"I don't know right now."

"I can talk to my father. He can help."

"I think it's better if he's not involved. The people who are threatening Sara are bad people. Tell your father I talked to Armando Cortázar, the son of his client, and that I'm going to follow his advice."

"Be careful," she says with tenderness.

"I will."

"Good-bye, Emiliano Zapata."

"Good-bye, Perla Rubi Esmeralda."

Emiliano places the cell phone on his lap. He reaches up, turns off the light to his room, and then curls up on the floor, his hands over his ears.

CHAPTER 19
SARA

SATURDAY, MARCH 25
4:55 P.M.

Sara goes around her room opening drawers, staring at the contents, closing them. Does she pack for two days or for a lifetime? On the other side of the thin wall that separates their rooms, she can hear Mami's voice. She can't make out what she's saying, but the urgent tone tells her that the conversation with Aunt Tencha is more than just a request for prayers.

Three years ago, when it became certain that Papá was not going to return, Aunt Tencha pleaded with Mami to move to León, where they could all live with her. Aunt Tencha is a widow. Her daughter, Gracia, lives in Mexico City and her older son in Monterrey. Mami could get a job in one of the many shoe factories of Léon, and there was a three-bedroom apartment for rent in Aunt Tencha's building. But Mami said no. Emiliano had his school, and the Jiparis were just bringing him back to life. Sara had her internship at *El Sol*, which they hoped would become a permanent job after she graduated. They have never regretted the decision, but it looks like they might end up in León anyway. Sara tries to remember what the city is like. She was twelve the last time she visited with Mami.

Suddenly, the door opens and Mami rushes in. She holds out Sara's cell phone. "It started ringing as soon as I hung up. I

201

hit the little green phone and heard a voice. It's Ernesto from work. He says he needs to speak to you right away."

Sara takes the phone from Mami, who stands next to her, an anxious look on her face.

"Ernesto?"

"Sara, you and your family have to get out of your house right now!"

"What?"

Ernesto is breathing hard, as if he's running. "I checked Juana's activity on her computer from my terminal just as I was leaving. She sent an e-mail to that 'jeremias' address—you know, the one on the threatening e-mail. She told them you took the phone and gave them your address. Lupita must have told her you opened the drawer. I don't know. It doesn't matter. What matters is that people are on their way to kill you. Go. Run! I have to hide too."

Sara has the sensation of falling, as if an unknown trap-door has suddenly opened beneath her feet. "Ernesto . . ." she manages to say.

"I don't think I can make it to your house to pick up the phone. I'm going to give you a secure e-mail address where you can contact me. Find a way to e-mail me there at three p.m. tomorrow. Do you have pen and paper?"

She writes the e-mail address that he gives her on the white envelope with the phone.

"Bye, Sara. Be safe. Don't use your cell phone anymore. They can track your calls." He hangs up.

Sara stands there, the phone dangling in her hand.

"Sara, what is it? Speak. What's the matter?" Mami's face reflects the panic Sara feels.

"We need to get out of the house," Sara says. "The people who threatened me are on their way. Go put your shoes on! Grab your purse!"

"But where are we going?"

"I don't know. We'll go out the back door."

Mami shuffles away as fast as she can while Sara puts on her sneakers. She runs to Emiliano's room. He's lying on the floor in total darkness. He looks up, shielding his eyes, when she turns on the light.

"We have to get out of the house! I just got word that the people who threatened me are on their way here."

"What? Are you sure?" He jumps to his feet.

"Yes. Put your shoes on. We can go to the Cardenases'."

"We'll go the back way. How much time do we have?"

"None."

"Joel's house is too far for Mami to walk fast. You two can ride in my trailer. It's already hitched to the scooter."

Before she can say anything, Emiliano is out the back door. Sara goes back to her room, grabs the envelope with the cell phone, and puts it in her backpack. At the back door, she and Mami look dubiously at the trailer attached to the back of the Vespa.

"It's the only way," Emiliano says. "If we walk, we might run into them."

"Maybe we can just go next door to Mrs. Lozano," Mami suggests.

"It's too close. They might look there when they don't find us home. Come on, we'll go out through the alley."

Emiliano holds the trailer while Mami and Sara climb in. They sit on some old cushions that Emiliano has thrown in there. He pushes the Vespa and the trailer out the back, into the unpaved alleyway. Then he climbs on, starts the scooter, and pulls out.

They hear the *crack crack crack* of automatic weapons just as they reach the Cardenases' house.

CHAPTER 20
EMILIANO

Paco opens the door after Emiliano's second knock. His face lights up when he sees Emiliano and then darkens when he sees Sara and Mami behind him. Emiliano grabs his arm and pulls him outside before Paco can speak. In the distance they hear what sounds like harmless firecrackers.

"They're shooting up our house," Emiliano says. "We need to stay with you."

Paco steps to the side and holds the door open for Sara and his mother. Mr. Cardenas and Joel are sitting on a quilt-covered sofa, watching TV. Mrs. Cardenas appears from a back room, wearing a pink bathrobe.

"My God, what happened?" Mrs. Cardenas rushes to hug Mami, who is trembling.

"I'm going to put the scooter in the backyard," Emiliano tells the group.

"I'll go with you," Paco says.

Emiliano can feel his arms and legs shake as he leads the Vespa and trailer around Mrs. Cardenas's gardens.

"A Vespa now? What are you doing? Is this shooting related to the Mercedes you parked here the other night?" Paco opens the gate to the backyard. "Are you going to tell me or what?"

"It's about Sara. Her job at *El Sol*. They want to kill her because she found out where they're holding Linda."

"Linda Fuentes. Your first love? Should have been your only one, if you had any sense."

Emiliano shoots Paco a look.

"I'm sorry, I can't help myself. That's terrible about Sara." They listen. The shooting has stopped. "They spray the house with a million bullets before they go in. That's what they did at that party where they killed all those kids. Remember?"

"Yeah."

"It turned out they had the wrong address."

Emiliano shakes his head. "I should go back, see who it is. Get their license plate."

"You crazy?"

"I can hide. They won't see me."

"Don't be stupid. Think of your mom and sister. You're safe here. You can stay as long as you want."

"I'm going to go." Some kind of scalding liquid that obliterates all thought fills his head. He starts toward the street, but Paco holds him, putting his strong arms around Emiliano's shoulders.

"Easy, boy, easy. We'll go when it's safe, I promise you. Joel will take us. We'll park at the corner and then drive by, make sure nobody's there. What good will it do to get their license plate? Who's going to go after them? The police?"

Emiliano feels the heat inside his head slowly subside. Once there's some space for thought, Paco's words find their way in. He nods.

"What about the Vespa?"

"It's nothing. It's a loan."

"A loan." Paco shakes his head. "I hope you know what you're doing."

"Whatever it is I was doing doesn't matter now," Emiliano says.

"It's all about Perla Rubi, isn't it?"

"Let it go. Now's not the time to give me crap."

"Okay. Come on, let's go inside."

Back in the house, Sara tells the Cardenases a very condensed version of events. Emiliano notices that she leaves out all the particulars related to the cell phone in the white envelope. Paco goes to the kitchen and brings in two chairs. Emiliano looks out the door for a few moments. He sits only after Paco tugs his arm several times.

"But how did they find out where you live? You've been so careful to not let anyone know," Mr. Cardenas says, looking at Sara and then at Emiliano. "We've all been so careful, ever since you told us about the threats."

"Someone at *El Sol* told them. The only person who knows where I live. Someone I trusted," Sara says quietly.

"Have you told Mrs. Fuentes? About Linda, that she may be alive?" Mrs. Cardenas asks.

"I was waiting until I knew more. They've gone through so much. I didn't want to get their hopes up. It's possible that . . . she was alive on Thursday and she's not anymore." Sara looks at her hands.

"You need to call Mrs. Fuentes," Mami says with authority. "Carmela is right. Her mother needs to know. Even if the worst happens, a mother would want to know so she can pray."

"Okay," Sara says. "Is there a phone I can use? I'm not supposed to use my cell phone."

"You can use the one in the kitchen."

"What will you do now?" Mrs. Cardenas asks before Sara moves. The question is directed at Mami, so Emiliano and Sara both turn to her.

"We will go to León with my sister Tencha."

Emiliano freezes at the words. León? No, that can't happen.

"You can stay with us in the meantime," Mr. Cardenas tells them.

"Thank you," Sara says. "It's better if we're not with anyone we know. My friend from the FBI gave me the name of a woman in the State Police. She'll take us to a safe place." Then, looking at Mrs. Cardenas, she says, "I'm going to make those calls."

Emiliano watches Sara make her way down the hall toward the kitchen. She takes a piece of paper out of the front pocket of her jeans as she walks.

"León Guanajuato is a nice city. Not so much violence there," Mr. Cardenas says.

"The Pumas will lose every game without you," Paco tells Emiliano.

"Excuse me," Emiliano says abruptly. He stands and walks out the front door. Paco follows him.

Emiliano and Paco stand in the front yard next to the statue of the Virgen de Guadalupe. Emiliano takes the key to the Vespa out of his pocket and hands it to Paco. "Take care of it. It's not mine, so don't wreck it. I'll be back for it soon."

They both look up when they hear the sound of a helicopter flying overhead. After a while, Paco says, "Remember when they caught you stealing that camera and they were going to put you in jail? They let you make one phone call and you called me. How come?"

"How come what?"

"Why did you call me? You knew I was going to call Brother Patricio. Why not just call him?"

Emiliano plucks a leaf from a nearby rosebush. He rolls it and throws it away. "I was too embarrassed to call anyone else."

"So why are you embarrassed to tell me about what you're into now?"

Emiliano thinks. It would be so helpful to tell Paco about Mr. Reyes, about Perla Rubi, about Javier, but there's no way that Paco would understand or approve.

Paco waits for Emiliano's answer. When it is clear that there will not be one, he says, with kindness, "Maybe going to León and leaving whatever it is you're into is for the best."

A wave of anger rises in Emiliano's chest. "Why do you assume that whatever I'm into is bad?"

Paco only smiles. It's as if the anger behind Emiliano's words is all the proof he needs. "Let's go back in," he says. "I'll put the scooter in the shed, where it will be safe. It'll be waiting for you. Or write me a letter and tell me where to take it."

"Sorry, man." *It's not you,* he wants to tell him. It's what he's losing.

"Just be careful. I hate funerals."

Inside the house, Sara and Joel are standing by the door. Mr. Cardenas is on the sofa while Mami sits in a chair. The television is off. "It's okay that she was upset. A mother needs to know," Mami tells Sara.

"I hope so," Sara responds, but she doesn't sound too sure. Then to Emiliano: "The woman from the State Police is on her way. She's taking us to a safe house until we can go to Léon."

"I just called Felita Lozano," Mrs. Cardenas says, walking into the living room, agitated. "She was washing dishes, looking out her kitchen window, when she saw a brown car park in front of your house. Four men jumped out with machine guns. They opened fire for about a minute. In broad daylight! They didn't care who saw them! Chuy Lozano saw them go in the house and fire dozens and dozens more shots. They were in there about ten minutes. The Lozanos thought they had killed all of you. Anyway, they're gone. Chuy saw them get in the car and drive away. He even got their license plate and called the police. Lots of good that's going to do."

"Do you think they'll be back? I would like my rosary and maybe some things to wear," Mami says.

"I can go," Emiliano says.

"I'm coming with you," Sara adds.

"I'll drive you," Joel tells them. "We'll make sure they're really gone first. I'll get the keys to the car."

"Where are *you* going?" Mrs. Cardenas says to Paco, who is following his brother down the hall.

"For my shoes. I'm going with them."

Emiliano and Sara walk outside and stand by Joel's car. Sara puts her arm around Emiliano's dejected shoulders. "I'm sorry."

"I don't want to go to Léon."

"I know. I'm not crazy about the idea either. I still have nightmares about that parrot that lives in Aunt Tencha's bathroom."

"Bartolomeo."

"Yeah, that guy. He gives me the creeps, the way he turns his head and looks at me with one eye while I do my business."

Emiliano shakes his head. "What do we do? We can't go live there."

"We do whatever Mami asks us to do. It's as simple as that. Don't even question what she says or struggle against it in your mind. We owe it to her to go where she wants us to go. At least for a while." She looks down. "I know you're losing a lot. Your Perla Rubi. Your friends. Your school. I'm losing what I love the most—my job. Going to wherever Mami wants us to go is a sacrifice that we will make for her. A sacrifice. There's no other word for it."

Emiliano sighs. Sacrifice. That's what you call doing something even though you don't feel like it. That's the thing his father didn't do.

"Come on, let's go see what we can rescue from our home."

"Our ex-home," Emiliano corrects his sister.

CHAPTER 21

SARA

They drive the two blocks to their house in Joel's car. He parks in the alleyway in back. If the bad people return, they can run out the back and jump in the car. They get out and walk to the front, where a group of neighbors is standing.

No one speaks. There are no words to describe what they see. It is as if they are seeing what the house would look like if left unattended for a hundred years. Sara always imagined that bullets made small holes, but the cinder blocks of the house have cavities the size of baseballs. Every piece of glass from the two windows that faced the street has been blown out. Behind one of those windows is Mami's bedroom. If Ernesto hadn't called, she'd be dead.

Neighbors come up to them and offer their help. Oásis Revolución was a quiet neighborhood of working-class people. It had survived unscathed through even the worst of the cartel wars. Sara feels as if she just poisoned the existence of all these good people who have worked so hard to live unnoticed by the violence that surrounds them. She wants to tell them all not to worry, that she's not coming back. Their family will disappear and children can play on the street again.

Emiliano is the first to go in. Sara follows with Joel and Paco behind her. She stands in the hallway for a few seconds, looking at the devastation in the kitchen and the living room. The shooters opened up their machine guns inside the house. Mami's china blasted to pieces. The rocking chair, the TV, pictures on the wall, all shattered. As the tears fill her eyes, she sees Emiliano turn around quickly and dash into his room. She knows he needs a private place to rage.

"We shouldn't stay long," Joel says. "They could come back."

Sara goes to Mami's bedroom and searches for her rosary but can't find it. Through her teary vision, she sees the bed, Mami's dresser, the nightstand, all full of white dust and pieces of plaster and glass, and she knows she hadn't fully understood the reality of Hinojosa's threat until this moment. It had all been words, an abstraction. But here it is, palpable, shown through bullets meant for her and her family. Sara had never realized fear could be so *physical*, how it invades all of your body, from the top of your head to the tips of your toes. She can even taste it. It tastes like metal.

"We better hurry," Joel says from the doorway.

Sara takes Mami's old cardboard suitcase from the top of her closet and packs a few clothes for her. Then she goes into her room. It's clear that they were looking for the cell phone. All the drawers and books are on the floor. The mattress is upright against a wall. Every container that can hold something is broken. If she had left the cell phone in the room so it could be found, would Hinojosa and his people leave her family alone?

But right then, seeing what the shooters did to their house and would have done to them if they had been there, Sara is glad she had the cell phone with her. She never thought she could hate, but she hates Hinojosa and his evil. She packs her laptop and some personal things in a small suitcase. Just as she's leaving, she sees her journal in a corner, facedown with its pages open. She throws that in. When she steps out, Joel and Paco are at the back door, waiting anxiously.

"Where's Emiliano?" Sara asks.

"Still in his room," Paco says.

Sara moves quickly back to Emiliano's bedroom. He's standing, his hands limp by his side, looking down at his bed.

"They urinated on my bed," he says listlessly when she comes up next to him. "Why would anybody do that?"

"They're animals," she says. "We have to go." Sara sees his backpack next to his desk and hands it to him. He looks at it as if he has never seen such a thing before. "Emiliano, I need you to focus. Don't check out on me. Mami and I need you to be a Jipari right now."

It is the right thing to say. Emiliano snaps out of wherever he was and starts to look around his room. He pushes away the backpack Sara offers and instead grabs the larger one with an aluminum frame that he used on his Jipari outings. He opens the fake Bible, which miraculously was not touched, and takes out the wad of money in there. Sara helps him find a shirt and a pair of pants, underwear and socks. Then, as if remembering something, he opens the door to his closet and gets the hiking boots he treasured so much.

"Do you want to take the letters?" Sara points to the shoe box next to the bed.

"No," Emiliano responds immediately without looking at the box.

On their way out, Sara goes into Mami's room for one last look and finds her rosary under the dresser.

When they get back to Paco's house, a black SUV sits in the driveway with a woman in a blue T-shirt and jeans standing outside it. Joel slows down when he sees her.

"That's Estela Gómez," Sara says.

"Are you sure you can trust her?" Joel says.

"My FBI friend gave me her name."

"A State Police woman?" Paco asks skeptically.

"Yes," Sara answers with as much certainty as she can find inside herself. Although it's hard to have faith in anyone at that moment, there's no way that Alejandro Durand would give her the name of someone who could not be trusted.

When they get out of the car, Estela walks straight to Sara. She's a handsome woman in her mid-thirties, with short black hair and a slim body that makes her look more like a model in a fitness magazine than a policewoman. The grasp of her hand in Sara's is firm and confident.

"You ready?" she asks.

"Yes. Our mother's inside. You got here fast."

Estela stares at Joel and Paco until they get the message and walk away.

"Alejandro called me earlier this evening. I was getting ready to come see you when you called," Estela says.

"We just got back from the house. They destroyed it."

"Yup, that's what they do. You're lucky. You're safe now. But there's no time to waste. Get your mother and your brother."

Her words and the strength behind them make Sara smile.

She sounds like what Sara tries to sound like when she's on a mission to get the truth. "I'm so glad to meet a good police person."

"There's more of us than people think," Estela says, cracking a smile for the first time.

They say good-bye to the Cardenas family, knowing they put them in harm's way just by showing up at their house. They're tainted now, Sara thinks, contaminated by the virus of violence that she carries. She is so, so grateful to them. They all are.

"I need a favor from you," Sara whispers to Joel when it is her turn to hug him.

"Tell me."

"Go see Mr. and Mrs. Fuentes. They shouldn't be alone tonight."

"All right."

"And . . . if Linda . . . is alive, will you watch over her?"

He hugs her again, and Sara knows he understands what she is asking.

CHAPTER 22

EMILIANO

Emiliano climbs into the backseat of Estela Gómez's SUV, next to his mother. Sara is sitting up front. Estela asks all of them, "Do you have any cell phones?" Emiliano and Sara give her their cell phones and she drops them in a small bag made from a metallic weave. "We can't take the chance of someone tracking you through the GPS in your phones." Then she opens the glove compartment and takes out a plastic bag with a flip phone and a charger. "You can use this to call me and make the calls you absolutely need to make. Don't tell anyone where you are."

"I have another cell phone in my backpack," Sara says. "Did Agent Durand tell you about it? Should I give that to you too?"

"Alejandro told me," Estela responds. She takes another metallic bag from the console next to her seat. "Put it in here and keep it there. It's better if you hold on to that phone." Sara tugs an envelope out of her backpack. She pulls a cell phone out of the envelope by its edges and places it in the bag.

The safe house is across town near the Benito Juárez Olympic Stadium. The first time Emiliano saw the stadium, he was six years old, when his father took him to watch an exhibition game between América and Cruz Azul. After that game, his father began to teach him soccer skills. Every day they practiced ball control, kicking, passing. His father set up Coke bottles a short distance apart from one another and Emiliano dribbled around them. He closes his eyes when he sees the stadium. He doesn't want these memories in the midst of everything else going on.

Estela parks the SUV in front of a two-story upholstery shop. On one side of the building is a garage door. She pushes a remote control on the sun visor and the door rolls up. She drives the SUV in and closes the door behind her. Steps at the back of the loading dock lead to a second floor.

"Mr. Otero and his family run the upholstery shop," Estela Gómez explains as she helps Mami up the stairs. "You can trust them completely. One of his sons was a policeman who was killed by the Sinaloan cartel. He lets us use the apartment. He'll get you anything you need."

The apartment is a one-floor loft with a bathroom. In one corner of the room is a sink, stove, refrigerator, and pantry. Two sets of bunk beds line another wall. A sofa and two easy chairs stand in the middle of the room.

"Thank you," Mami says to Estela. "You're very kind."

"I wouldn't recommend going out, but if you do, wait until Mr. Otero opens his shop and walk out the front door as if you were a customer. What are your plans?"

Emiliano walks over to the window and peeks through the blinds.

"I have a sister in León. We'll be going there," Mami says.

"I suggest you do it soon. Day after tomorrow at the latest.

The people who are after you are relentless, and not even this place is safe for more than a day or two."

"So . . . do you know if something will be done about the house where Linda . . ."

Sara's voice sounds different to Emiliano—older, somehow. He can only imagine everything that's gone through her mind today.

"Yes, the house is being watched right now. Something will be done. You have my word," Estela says.

"Is there a place where I can send an e-mail?" Sara asks.

Emiliano listens closely. He too needs a place to communicate with Perla Rubi, Brother Patricio, Armando.

"There's a café near the stadium a few blocks from here. Café Rojos. They have terminals. Tell Daniel, the owner, that I sent you. He'll take care of you."

"Thank you," Sara says.

"We're indebted to you, Sara. What you're doing takes a lot of courage. Be careful now."

Sara watches Estela walk out the door.

"The only place we get a signal is over here by the kitchen window," Emiliano says, holding the cell phone Estela gave them.

"Is it okay if I take one of the lower bunks? I hate heights," Sara says.

"Okay," Emiliano responds, barely hearing her. What is he going to tell Armando? He'll say he's going to León with his mother and sister and will find a way to come back.

"Are you tired, Mami? Let's get some sleep." Sara takes Mami to the sofa and sits her down.

"I want to talk to you two. Emiliano, please come here."

Emiliano sits on the chair in front of Sara and his mother. Mami clears her throat and straightens herself up. She digs her rosary out of her purse and holds it tight in her hands.

Emiliano and Sara look at each other. They recognize the signs, the solemn look. Mami's about to tell them something so difficult for her that she needs God's help to say it.

"I have thought about what I am going to say since long before all of this business with the threat. I had always thought this was best, but could not bring myself to do it." Mami speaks with calm and conviction, fixing her eyes first on Sara and then on Emiliano. "I told you back at Carmela's house that we were going to León, but that is not what we're going to do." She takes a deep breath. Emiliano tenses. "I am going to León alone. You two are going to your father in the United States."

"What?" Emiliano jumps out of the chair.

"We're not going to leave you," Sara objects.

Mami motions for Emiliano to sit down and then waits until he does. "I lied to you. I'm sorry. I didn't call Tencha. I called your father. He has an extra room in his basement. You can live with him until you get a place of your own."

Emiliano feels his face burn. He does all he can not to blow up, but he knows that his efforts at containing himself are not going to work for much longer. Sara looks at him and speaks quickly, as if to divert the explosion that's about to take place. "But, Mami, how are we going to get there?"

"It doesn't matter! No! I'm not going to live with that man!" Emiliano shouts. It's the first time he has ever used a defiant tone with Mami.

Mami smiles at him, a loving smile, as if she knows and even sympathizes with the emotion behind his outburst. She speaks softly to him. "I want you to find someone trustworthy who will take you across the border. We'll pull all our money together so we can pay someone. Ask Brother Patricio to help you. He knows a lot of people. Roberto will drive down from Chicago and meet you when you're safely in the United States."

"Mami, he left us! He doesn't want us! He said no to us. He rejected us. Am I the only one here who understands that? No. I can't go live with someone who hurt you—us. Don't ask me to do that."

"I'm not asking you." There is no anger in Mami's words.

Emiliano can feel two powerful forces fighting inside him: his love and unquestioning obedience to his mother and the resentment he feels toward his father. Maybe three forces, when you count his anger at losing all that he loves in Juárez. He sees Sara shaking her head at him and pleading with her eyes not to lose it completely, not to say or do anything that he will regret later. But the idea of living with the man who broke his promise is too much to bear. "This is not the right solution to this mess. What am I going to do in the United States?" He remembers the soccer game, the chants. "They think we're all ignorant, rapists, narcos. This is my home. Here." Emiliano stands, realizes there's no place to go. Sits down again. Mami and Sara seem to be waiting for him to get it all out. But there are no more words coming out of him, only something hot traveling from his stomach to his throat.

What Sara says next, Emiliano knows is for his benefit. "We can't leave you, Mami. We're a family. What will you do in León all alone? And even if we make it to Chicago, it will be impossible to see you for a long time. We'll go to León with you."

"I will be all right with Tencha. But León is not the right place for either of you." She pauses, lowers her eyes. "Your father . . . he's made a good, safe life in America. It will be a good place for you. He's been asking for you to visit for a long time."

"It's not right for you to be alone," Sara insists. "We'll be safe in Léon."

"It's not just about being safe. Sara, you won't be able to do the work you love to do in León. The minute you write something in a newspaper, the people who are trying to kill you will come after you. And Emiliano, son, here in Mexico it is too hard for you to be the person God wants you to be."

Emiliano sits on the edge of the sofa, looking at his feet, shaking his head. Then he stands up and looks around the room. He wants to bolt out of there. Take off running through the streets. But there is no escape. Sara stands and tries to put her arm around him, but he shakes it off. "You can't do this to me," he says to Mami, pleading.

Mami looks at him steadily. Her eyes are full of silent love, but there is also an unshakeable strength in them.

Emiliano starts to say something and then stops. He turns and walks out the door.

CHAPTER 23

SARA

Sara finds Emiliano at the bottom of the stairs, sitting on an old couch. She sits next to him and waits silently for him to cool off. Mami's decision that they should go to Chicago surprised her until she understood her mother's reasoning. She loves reporting, and it would be very hard for her to continue to be a reporter in Mexico. And Emiliano, if he ever stops hating Papá, would eventually thrive in the United States. She tries to imagine what life would be like in Chicago. Living with their father and his new family will be uncomfortable but bearable. She'll find a job and eventually get a place for Emiliano and herself. Sara has always been optimistic, and as she thinks about the idea, it becomes more and more the best solution. What's painful for her is what they're leaving behind. Mami and her job have been her life these past few years; Mexico is in her blood, part of her, where she belongs. But perhaps she can belong in the United States as well.

Sara doesn't know how long they stay on that ratty couch with its insides spilling out. Emiliano's eyes stare straight ahead, his jaw clenched, his hands in fists. She keeps thinking about Estela Gómez's answer when she asked about Linda. *Something will be done. You have my word.* It gives her comfort to repeat those words, to hope with all her soul that Linda is still alive. But she knows Emiliano does not have that kind of life-giving hope—a meaning that makes the sacrifice worth it. If only there was a way to see the trip to the United States as an adventure. Maybe it can be an adventure that requires all of his Jipari skills. *The male ego. Challenge the male ego*, she thinks. It never fails.

She waits patiently for the right opening. There's got to be a way to reach the Jipari in Emiliano, her fearless little brother who loves challenges. When at last he breathes out a long, pent-up breath, Sara says: "Maybe we can convince Mami about the dangers in crossing over to the U.S. I don't think she knows how expensive it is to pay a coyote to take us across or how dangerous that is. I mean, so many people die at the hands of the coyotes. Maybe we could make it across the river without one, but through the desert? I don't think she realizes the impossibility."

"It can be done," Emiliano says.

She makes an effort not to smile. "Where? Arizona?"

"Texas."

"Really?"

"There's places."

"But how?" she says. "The Border Patrol is everywhere. How many days would we have to walk before we can get to a place where Papá can come get us?"

"Two, three days."

"Three days! What about water? It must be one hundred degrees out there even now."

"Stop it," he says. "I know what you're trying to do. I'm not as stupid as you think I am."

Sara laughs, and he smiles despite himself. "You know, little brother, I've never once in my whole life thought you were stupid," she says. He acts as if he doesn't hear her, so she quickly adds, "Do you really think your Jipari training is good enough to get us across?"

"Yeah, I can get us across . . . if I wanted to."

Sara nods thoughtfully. Her strategy is working. "Look, for me, the U.S. means a future I could get used to eventually, maybe, if I can learn to live away from the dirt and crime and packed buses full of sweaty, groping men—you know, all the things I love about Mexico." She checks to see if she's elicited a smile, but she hasn't. "For you, I know, it would be leaving a future you love. You don't know how sorry I am that you're so affected by something I did. But here we are."

"You did the right thing. You had to do what you could to save Linda."

The way he says this, as if he would have done the same thing, makes her happy. "I have a solution. To you not wanting to go."

"Oh, yeah?"

"Take me across. Once I'm safe with Papá, you can come back. If you can travel north, you should be able to travel south."

He looks into her eyes for a few moments. "And you really think Mami will go for that?"

"After I got my first death threat—you know, for the article about the joint task force—I said something to Mami about how I wished I was a journalist in the U.S., where I wouldn't have to worry about what I wrote. Later that night, when we were watching TV, she said out of nowhere that if I wanted to, she could contact Papá. I could go live with him."

"She said that?"

"I know, right? I couldn't believe it either. Can you imagine what it took for her to suggest that?"

"She actually thought our dear father would take you?"

"He's always wanted us to come. Besides, you don't know Mami if you think she'd give him a choice."

Emiliano chuckles. "You lost me. What does all this have to do with me coming back?"

"The only reason she wants you to go to the U.S. is because she believes in your abilities to get me there." Sara knows that's only partially true. Mami wouldn't have said something about Emiliano becoming the person God wanted him to be if she didn't have a good reason for it. "If you come back in a couple of weeks and tell her I'm safely on my way to Chicago, I think she'll be okay . . . eventually."

"And I would live with her and Aunt Tencha in León?"

"Isn't Aunt Tencha better than living with Papá?"

"Any place is better than that," Emiliano says without missing a beat.

"After you live in León for a while, maybe Brother Patricio can find you a place to live here like he's done for other kids. Or you can live with Paco. I think Mami would be okay with you returning to Juárez if you're back in school and living in a decent place. She may not say so right away, but deep inside she'll be happy that she'll have you close enough to visit. If we're both in the U.S., she won't see us for a long, long time."

"If ever."

Those two words stop Sara cold. She hadn't yet processed the fact that she might not see Mami again, maybe ever. Should she fight Mami and insist on going to León with her? What will life be without her? And what about the loss Mami would feel? Maybe she should go back and tell Mami there's no way she will leave her.

Then Emiliano speaks. "Mami's right. At least about you. León, or any place in Mexico, is not the place for you. These guys who are after you will eventually find you, and you'll never be able to be a reporter. I'll get you across."

"And you'll come back?"

"Yeah. I'll come back."

"But maybe Mami is also right about you, about you not being able to be the person God wants you to be here in Mexico."

Sara expects him to dismiss this idea immediately, but instead he seems to reflect deeply on it. Finally, he says, "A person is not *meant* to be anyone. Each person chooses who they want to be."

"I think we are all meant to be the best person we are capable of being. You're right that we need to choose to be that person. But sometimes, circumstances make it hard for us to make the right choice," Sara says. "Do you really want to be the sort of person who hides expensive cars in the neighbors' backyard and brings home fancy scooters? Is that who you want to be?"

He glares at her briefly and then looks away. "We'll have to lie to her. She can't know that I'm planning to come back."

This is such an unusual thing for Emiliano to say that Sara

is struck silent. There's something like fatigue and maybe even self-disgust in his tone, as if he's been lying already and now has to pile one more on top of the stinking bunch. But she has to admit he's right: It would not work to tell Mami the truth. She would never agree to his return. Her comfort, if there is any comfort in losing her children, lies in the fact that Sara and Emiliano will be together. Sara makes a mental note to think more about his attitude later.

"Okay," she says. "Let's get some sleep."

CHAPTER 24
EMILIANO

Emiliano, on the top bunk, is unable to sleep. He can hear Sara tossing and turning in the bed below, and now and then he hears a deep sigh coming from his mother. The whole family is awake. What are his mother and Sara thinking about? His mother got very nervous and worried when Sara told her they would cross the border by themselves without the help of a coyote. She calmed down a little when Emiliano explained he had a plan that was a lot safer than putting their lives in the hands of a stranger. His mother did not want to show sadness, but he could tell she was already feeling what it will be like to be separated from her daughter and son. He knows they are her life. How can she be so willing to let them go? And Sara—surely Sara is awake because she's hoping that Linda will be found alive, wishing she could be there when she comes home.

Emiliano tries to order his thoughts, but they keep jumping around. He will take Sara across the border. What will he say to Perla Rubi? In a few hours he will call Brother Patricio and together they will start planning the journey. He'll get Sara across and return. Thank goodness he had enough sense to grab his Jipari backpack. He's got his compass, knife, first aid kit, sunglasses, hat, flashlight, lighter, and other desert survival tools. He remembered to get his boots. That was fortunate.

Brother Patricio will get the other things they'll need to make the trip: hiking shoes for Sara, two-gallon water bags, and, of course, maps. Sara's shoes have to be a perfect fit, otherwise she'll get blisters. There won't be any time to break them in slowly.

He makes an effort to slow down his thoughts, to point them all in one direction. What will he do when he comes back? He must find a way to live in Juárez. The decision to work with Alfredo Reyes has been made, and there's no need to question it yet again. Maybe he can live with Armando. No, that's probably not a good idea. Nothing has changed. He needs to keep his association with Armando and Reyes at a minimum, and he and Javier will keep the whole criminal enterprise under control. Criminal enterprise. Is that what it is? It's a business. He'll make it work somehow. *Do what is best for everyone,* Perla Rubi says. That's what he will do. Just because he doesn't know the details doesn't mean he can't make it happen. One step at a time. When you're walking in the desert, the step in front of you is the only one that demands your attention.

He'll take Sara across and then come back. That's the plan. With any luck he won't have to see his father. What would he say to him if he saw him? Maybe he'll remind him of the promises he made before he left for the United States—the food truck, their working together, his return.

"You promised," Emiliano says to himself.

"Emiliano, go to sleep," Sara tells him from the bunk below.

Sleep finally subdues Emiliano's churning mind just as daylight filters through the blinds. When he wakes up, the apartment is hot and his mother and Sara are at the small table by the stove, drinking coffee and quietly conversing. Emiliano strains to hear what they are saying.

"Do you need to call Luisa to tell her you're not coming to work?" Sara asks her mother.

"I'm sure she's found out what happened. I know Felita Lozano, and I'm pretty sure she's called everyone by now. The person I want to talk to is Mrs. Rivera. The house was destroyed, from what you tell me. She's been good to us. Waiting for us when we couldn't pay the rent. I have to tell her I will pay her back for the damages. She'll have to move out all our furniture, and that will be an expense as well."

Emiliano gets up, crosses the room, and kisses his mother on the top of her head. It's his way of apologizing for yelling at her yesterday. "I need to call Brother Patricio," he says.

"I'll call Estela and ask her if he can come over. I need to find out about Linda. You might want to take a shower in the meantime." Sara pinches her nose.

"Sara took a shower this morning," Mamá says before Emiliano can respond. "She says there's hot water and little bottles of shampoo like in a hotel. We're all lucky to be alive, even if we're smelly."

"It's Sunday. Brother Patricio is busy with Mass. Maybe I can see him this afternoon."

"We can meet him at Café Rojos. Remember, Estela told us about it."

"Sara, say the rosary with me while Emiliano calls Brother Patricio. If we can't go to Mass today, at least we can pray here," Mamá says.

Emiliano waits until he hears Sara and his mother praying. Then he stands in front of the kitchen window, with his back to his sister and mother, and calls Brother Patricio.

"Emiliano! I'm so glad you called." Emiliano appreciates the warmth in the brother's voice. "Paco told me about the attack on your house last night. Are you all right? Is your sister all right? Your mother?"

"We're all fine. We're hiding in a safe place. Brother, this is important. No one must know what I'm about to tell you. You're the only person other than my mother, my sister, and me who will know this. My mother is going to León to live with her sister, but she wants Sara and me to go to Chicago."

"Chicago? That's where—"

"Yup, you got it. There's no changing her mind. She's set on us going."

"But how—"

"We need to find a way across the Rio Grande and through the desert to a place where he can meet up with us. I was thinking of that park next to the Rio Grande. The one we thought of visiting with the Jiparis, before we found out how difficult it was to get visas."

"Big Bend National Park."

"Sara and I could follow one of those abandoned trails like regular visitors. Then . . . he could meet us somewhere in the park."

"It's okay to call him Papá. He *is* your father."

"Not right now, Brother, please."

"Okay. I'm sure there are Border Patrol checkpoints on the roads leading in and out of the park. Your father would need to

meet you somewhere beyond those checkpoints. You're looking at some hard walking. Many immigrants have perished
making that kind of long-distance crossing."

"Yeah, but it will be different for us. We'll be prepared. It
was August when we took that plane ride. It's not so hot now.
But we need to move fast. Every day the temperature goes up.
We should leave tomorrow." Emiliano thinks for a minute. "I
need maps and as much information as you can get me about
the location of those Border Patrol checkpoints. We need to
find a good place for . . . my father to meet us. Sara and I need
clothes and desert supplies. I'll make a list, but you'll know better than I do. I'm going to go to a café that rents computers and
do as much research as I can, but we can't do this without you.
Can you meet me later today?" He pauses. "What? Why are
you laughing?"

"I'm sorry. I'm not laughing at what you and your family
must be going through. It's just that after all the years of my
urging you to reconcile with your father, God's found a way for
it to happen. You have to admit it is ironic, to say the least."

"There's nothing ironic about this, whatever that means.
And there won't be any reconciling. You going to help us
or not?"

Brother Patricio sighs. "Of course I will help you. But there
must be some other way out of this predicament. You know the
politics in the United States right now. People are talking about
walls and electric fences with enough voltage to fry a human
being. The Border Patrol has sensors on the ground that can
detect movement. An illegal crossing is not the best option.
Surely, your sister would qualify for asylum. She's being

persecuted by the government of her country, for goodness sake. If that's not what asylum is for, then I don't know
what is. One of my brothers in El Paso helps people with
immigration . . ."

"No. You can't tell anyone."

"I will ask about the asylum process without mentioning
any names."

"Can you meet at us Café Rojos this afternoon? It's near
the Estadio Olímpico."

"I need to help out with the eleven o'clock Mass and I'll
need a couple of hours to get the maps and make some discreet
inquiries about Border Patrol checkpoints. Is two o'clock okay?"

"Yes." Emiliano pauses. "Brother, does Perla Rubi
know . . ."

"About last night's violence? She knows. The whole school
knows. Paco called everyone on the team, and I'm sure word
got to her. Emiliano, we're starting a collection for you. We
know your family lost everything."

"My mother is worried about the damages to the house.
She feels bad for the landlady. We have some money but not
enough to rebuild a house."

"You're welcome to the money in the Jiparis' rainy-day
fund."

"Thank you. It would be a loan. I'll pay it back."

"There are Salesian brothers in Chicago. I'll get you some
names and phone numbers." Brother Patricio says, his voice
faltering, "I will miss you."

Should Emiliano tell him about his plans to return? A gut
feeling says no.

"Emiliano, are you still there?"

"Oh, oh, Brother, there's one more thing. Can you let Javier know? Tell him to take any new piñatas to Lalo. He has a shop near the bridge on Avenida Juárez called La Azucena. Lalo will buy them from him. But tell him not to accept the first price that Lalo offers."

"Yes. I know he'll want to know how you are. You're like his big brother."

"Yeah." *Some big brother.* "See you soon, then."

He stands by the window with the phone in his hand. The street below him is busy with families on the way to church. He should probably call Armando so he can tell Mr. Reyes that the answer is yes, he wants to do business with him, but he'll be away for a week or so. Armando's number was in his cell phone, but he doesn't have that anymore. He'll call Doña Pepa at Taurus. She must know how to get in touch with Armando.

He sits on the bottom bunk where Sara slept and puts on his shoes. When he looks up, his mother and sister are looking at him expectantly. How much of his conversation with Brother Patricio did they hear?

"Everything okay?" Sara asks.

"I'm going to meet Brother Patricio later today at Café Rojos."

"I'll go with you. I need to e-mail Ernesto, and I can help with the research for our trip too. My middle name is *research*. Mami, will you be okay alone?"

"Yes, go with your brother. Can you leave me the phone? I need to call Roberto again. How long will it take you to get to a place where he can pick you up? Maybe it would be better if you talked to him so you can explain."

"No!" Emiliano snaps. Then, softening his tone: "I don't

have enough information. I'll know more after I talk to Brother Patricio. It will take us a day to get to the place on the Rio Grande where we will cross, then two or three days to reach a point where he can meet us. Tell him that tonight you'll let him know the date and place."

Following Estela Gómez's instructions, they go out through the front door of the upholstery shop. A gray-haired man kneeling on the ground, his mouth full of tacks, looks up and waves at them as they pass by. Emiliano and Sara step out on the street. Sara takes a deep breath and smiles. "It's good to be alive, isn't it?" Then a bus drives by, spewing black exhaust, and she begins to cough.

"This way," Emiliano says. "Focus. You can't be daydreaming when we're in the desert. You'll step on a snake."

"Sorry. I was thinking about Linda. I wish I knew when they were going to raid that place."

"That police woman, Estela. She looked determined and tough. She'll call you. But . . ."

"I know. But I refuse to believe it will be bad news. It doesn't help to think that way."

Emiliano nods. Of all the people he could have with him in the desert, he could do worse than Sara.

He takes long, fast strides and Sara runs after him. On the corner, the smell of grease from a taco cart reminds him that he's hungry. He looks up and sees the pale blue sky. It will be a hot day today. Not a good sign. It will be even hotter in the desert.

"Slow down," Sara says, out of breath. "You're so nervous. You need to calm down. Conserve energy, like you always tell me."

Sara's right. He needs to act with calm and purpose. Three days ago nothing rattled him, unless you consider obsessing about making enough money to buy Joel's motorcycle a kind of rattling. Now there's an unpleasant disturbance in his brain, in his very soul, making him uncomfortable with an itch that is not physical.

"We need to build up your lung power," Emiliano says. "Look at you. We've walked half a block and you're huffing and puffing." He speeds up a bit more.

"I'm going to kill you before this is over," Sara says.

When they walk by a bakery, his stomach growls. He needs to put something in there, after he talks to Perla Rubi. He looks around to make sure no one is following them, then speeds up again.

Sara looks back as well. "So what should I research at the Internet café?"

"You need to research the asylum process. If you have time, research the detection methods used by the Border Patrol."

"Asylum?"

They hurry across a street when there's a gap in traffic. When they reach the opposite sidewalk, Emiliano continues speaking without stopping or looking at Sara. "If we get caught, you need to request asylum. It was something Brother Patricio said this morning when I called him. He said you have a good case because you're being persecuted by the Mexican State Police. Find out what you need to do and say, what documents you need, where will they take you, all of that. Find out all you can."

"You think we'll get caught?"

"If I think the route we're taking is a good one, you can be sure others have thought so too. If others have thought about it, the Border Patrol knows about it as well. Going through this park isn't popular with immigrants because it's hard to get there from other places in Mexico, but enough have tried."

"Wait, what about you? If we get caught, you need to ask for asylum too."

"Not me. If we get caught, they'll put me on a bus and send me back home. I'll try not to look too happy."

Café Rojos is only a little bigger than Mr. Esmeralda's office. It has a red Formica bar, behind which there is an espresso machine, an electric grill, a microwave oven, and a toaster. Four tin tables press one against the other. A few high-school-age kids sit with their laptops and iced coffees. Emiliano stays back while Sara talks to the owner, a young man named Daniel who's about Sara's age, and, it turns out, Estela Gómez's cousin. Emiliano searches for a phone he can use to call Doña Pepa but there's none. Then Sara waves to him and he follows her and Daniel into a small room in the back. Two computer terminals sit on a bench, occupied by boys playing video games. Daniel says something to them and they immediately log off, pick up their backpacks from the floor, and leave the room.

"They have to go to soccer practice anyway," Daniel says.

"Is there a public phone around here?" Emiliano asks.

"There's one in front of the stadium." Daniel digs into his pocket and takes out a phone card. "You'll need this. There's about ten minutes left on it." Then he says to Sara, "Let me log you on."

"Be careful," Sara tells Emiliano as he walks away.

The Benito Juárez Olympic Stadium reminds Emiliano of

238

the time the Pumas beat the Aguilas for the city championship
and the right to represent Ciudad Juárez in the state championship games. The stadium seats twenty thousand people, and it
was almost full on that scorching June night. He remembers
walking out of the dressing room tunnel, holding the hand of a
little boy as if he were playing in a World Cup game. The little
boy's name was Beto, and his hand was small and fragile, and
holding it almost made Emiliano cry.

He spends one valuable card minute getting Taurus's phone
number from directory assistance. He'll have to keep the conversation short if he wants to call Perla Rubi.

The phone at Taurus rings three, four, five times. Emiliano
is sure that Doña Pepa works on Sunday.

"Hello."

It's Armando. A little bit of luck is always welcome. Now
he will have more minutes for Perla Rubi.

"Hello? Who's this? Hello."

"It's me. Emiliano."

"Emiliano!" Armando shouts into the phone. "You all
right?"

"Yeah. Why wouldn't I be?"

"I heard about your house."

"Really? How?"

"Juárez is a like a big spiderweb. Nothing happens in one
end that the other end doesn't know."

But exactly how did Armando find out? Who told him? He
wants to ask more, but stops himself. "Look, I'll be away for a
couple of weeks. I wanted you and Mr. Reyes to know. But I'll
be back. Your scooter's safe."

"I'm not worried about the scooter. Where you going?"

Emiliano hesitates. "Away from here."

"I understand. Emiliano, if there's anything my father or me or Mr. Reyes can do to help with your situation . . ."

"Thank you." What exactly does Armando know about his situation?

"You'll be away two weeks, you say?"

"Maybe less." A female voice says there are five minutes left on the card. "I have to go now. I need to make one more call on this card."

"Okay, Emiliano. Hey, one more thing. Whatever is happening with your sister doesn't affect you. Do you understand?"

There's a hollowness in the pit of Emiliano's stomach. "My sister?" he says. "What do you know about my sister?"

"Everything. I know everything. What she did and why people are coming after her right now. All I'm saying is you yourself don't need to worry. You're protected. That's one of the benefits of our friendship, of your association with Mr. Reyes and with me and my father. When you come back, you'll be okay. You know what I'm saying?"

"Yes . . . I think so. I'll call you in two weeks, then. I have to go now."

Emiliano stands back, staring at the phone. He doesn't know whether to feel relieved or afraid. Relieved that Armando is so helpful and understanding. Relieved that "Sara's situation" does not affect him—he's protected. Afraid that Armando knows about the shooting of his house, that he knows about Sara's work, that he knows people are pursuing her. How does Armando know so much so soon? That spiderweb he talks about—didn't Mr. Esmeralda mention a spiderweb as well?

He calls Perla Rubi. On the sixth ring, he hears her voice. "Hello?"

"It's me."

"Oh, my God, Emiliano. Are you all right?"

Her concern reassures him, reminds him of one thing he can trust. "I'm okay," he says. "I'm in a phone booth so I don't have much time. We're in a safe place. Hiding. They're still after Sara. I wanted to hear your voice."

"Emiliano, I talked to my father. He wants you to call him. He can help you. Do you have a pen? I can give you his number."

"I don't have a pen. But—"

"Call him at his office. Licenciado Jorge Esmeralda. He's in the phone book."

"Perla Rubi—"

"Do you need money? We can help."

"We're okay. I'm going to take Sara to the United States."

"But how? Do you have visas?"

"I know a place in Texas where it will be safe to cross. It's a big national park with hiking trails and old roads. We'll be okay. Someone will meet us at the other end of the park. The important thing is that I'll be back."

"When? When will you be back?"

"Eight days maybe."

"*The time remaining on this card is ten seconds,*" a voice says in his ear.

"I better go now."

"Call my father, okay? Promise?"

Emiliano closes his eyes, exhales. "Perla Rubi Esmeralda . . ." He falters.

"I know. I love you, Emiliano Zapata."

He hears a dial tone.

His time is up.

CHAPTER 25

SARA

It is almost two when Emiliano returns to Café Rojos. Sara jumps off the stool where she's been sitting and hugs him. "I've been worried to death about you. Where have you been?"

He lets her keep her arms around him for longer than she expected and then he pulls gently away. "I talked to Perla Rubi. Then I went for a walk."

"Okay," she says. She can see in his face that the conversation was difficult. Did he not tell her he was coming back? He sits down on a stool next to the terminal where she was working and stares at a sandwich on a paper plate.

"Daniel made it for us. It's good. You should eat."

He nods, but he doesn't touch it. Instead, he rips a blank page from Sara's notebook. "I'm going to make a list of what we need. We have to plan this trip carefully. Preparation is everything." There's a quiet firmness in his voice, as if he's determined to erase from his mind whatever he's been thinking for the past two hours.

Sara sits on the stool next to him. "I got a lot done, you want to hear? It might affect what we talk about with Brother Patricio."

Emiliano stops writing and looks at her expectantly.

"It turns out that about ninety percent of asylum requests

from Mexican citizens are denied. In order to be granted asylum, you need to show 'credible fear of persecution on account of race, religion, nationality, and/or membership in a particular group or political opinion.'"

"'Credible fear of persecution'? You got more than that. You got actual persecution. They can come take a look at our house if they want."

Sara goes on, "Most of the asylum applications from Mexicans are denied because the U.S. doesn't see persecution from the cartels as persecution for political opinion or against one of those protected groups. Even if you show that the Mexican police cannot protect you, that's not enough."

"What if it's the Mexican State Police who are after you?"

"U.S. courts say that persecution by government officials in cahoots with the cartels is still persecution by the cartels. It's not the same as persecution by a government."

"And you still want to live there?"

She continues reading her notes. "If we get caught, and we plead asylum, we'll be sent to a detention center while we wait for a hearing in front of an immigration judge. That can take months and even years."

"What are the detention centers like?"

"Well, they're kind of crowded and not all that pleasant from what I can tell, but some people get released if they have someone in the U.S. who can vouch for them. People even get work permits while they wait for their hearing." She puts the notebook down. "That's how Papá will get a chance to make himself useful: He can vouch for us."

"You get released if someone can vouch for you?" Emiliano asks skeptically.

"Sometimes a bond is required. And not everyone gets released. It looks kind of arbitrary, who gets released, who gets deported, and who can stay, but the main thing is that it's a chance. Even if we make it to Chicago, we can still apply for asylum later."

Sara expects him to correct her and say that it would be her and not "we" who would be applying, but he doesn't mention it. "So," he says, thinking, "we need to ask Brother Patricio to take pictures of our house full of bullet holes, and maybe get some statements from the neighbors, and you need to get ahold of your threatening e-mails, and have all that with you so you can give it to the Border Patrol if we're caught."

"I was thinking that I would leave all that with Brother Patricio. They'll let us make a phone call if we're caught, won't they?"

"Put everything on a flash drive and bring it with you, *and* leave a copy with Brother Patricio. I wouldn't count on the Americans letting you make any calls. Now let me go back to my list."

"What about my friend at the FBI? I could call him if we get caught. He would help us with an asylum request and tes-tify on our behalf. He knows who's after us."

"Listen," Emiliano says, looking straight into her eyes. "The key to survival is to assume the worst and prepare for it. We're going to a place where we're not wanted. Not only are we not wanted, we are hated by many. Get that through your head."

Then he lowers his head and continues working on his list.

By the time Brother Patricio shows up, Sara has transferred all the threatening e-mails from her account as well as all her articles about the Desaparecidas onto a flash drive. Emiliano perks up when Brother Patricio arrives. They close the door to the back room, and after Sara and Emiliano recount again the details of the threat and the events of the previous night, the three of them look at the map of Big Bend National Park that Brother Patricio brought. He's marked the proposed route in red.

"The best place to cross is here," Brother Patricio says, pointing to a red dot in the Rio Grande.

"Boquillas," Emiliano says, peering at the map. "How do we get there?"

"Getting there might be even harder than crossing through the park," the brother says. "There's no direct road from Juárez. We need to go south to Chihuahua and then take the highway north."

"We?" Emiliano beats Sara to the question.

"I'm going to drive you," Brother Patricio says firmly. "Tomorrow morning if that's okay. I already got Mr. Salas to take my classes."

"But . . ."

"I'm afraid that's not up for discussion. Your mother can travel with us to Chihuahua and take a bus to León from there. You get to spend a few more hours with her and we bypass the bus terminal in Juárez, which may be under observation by the very same people who are keen on exterminating you."

"Thank you," Sara says. Emiliano silently bites his lip. Sara remembers that even as a child, Emiliano bit his lip when someone did something nice for him. It's as if he doesn't hold himself worthy of the kindness offered to him.

Brother Patricio carefully folds the map of Mexico. "Now, let's talk about the route."

The route that Brother Patricio has marked will take them from Boquillas to a dirt road on the eastern boundary of the park. The road ends about ten miles from the north entrance to the park. That's where the hardest part of the trip will begin. They need to head east past the boundary of the park, on open desert and mountainous terrain, to a place beyond the last Border Patrol checkpoint.

"So," Brother Patricio says, a worried look on his face, "you're looking at maybe forty miles of hiking within the park and another forty to get to Sanderson, Texas. I recommend going all the way to Sanderson and having your father meet you there. You can stay at the Catholic church there until he arrives. I already talked to one of the deacons. Going all the way to Sanderson instead of getting picked up somewhere close to the Border Patrol checkpoint will mean another half day of walking, but it's better than trying to coordinate a meeting point and a precise meeting time with your father."

Emiliano studies the map with unconcerned concentration. "What's here?" He points to the place where Brother Patricio's red line ends.

"That's the place that I've confirmed is beyond the Border Patrol checkpoint. Sanderson is only twenty miles east of that." Brother Patricio takes something that looks like an old-fashioned cell phone out of the backpack he carried in.

"I can't take that," Emiliano says instantly. "The Jiparis need that. You know how much we had to save to buy it."

"What is it?" Sara asks.

"It's a handheld GPS device. And yes, of course you are taking it. If you wish, you can mail it to me from Chicago."

Sara turns to look at Emiliano. He has not told Brother Patricio that he's coming back? Why? It gives her hope that maybe he has changed his mind—until Emiliano dashes it with an almost imperceptible shake of his head.

Emiliano and Brother Patricio go over every minute detail of the equipment and the route over and over again. They are engineers carefully constructing a delicate, complicated bridge, accounting for every nut and bolt. Sara has never seen Emiliano like this, protractor and compass in hand, calculating distances and directions.

At three p.m. she excuses herself, goes to one of the terminals, and writes an e-mail to Ernesto on a newly created e-mail account. In the subject line she writes: *Grateful*.

It's me. Are you there?

She hits SEND and waits.

I'm here. Are you safe?

Yes. Thanks to you. That was a close call yesterday. I still can't believe Juana would give them my address.

That was a surprise even for a cynic like me.

Ernesto, what should I do about the phone?

Hold on to it for a while. I'm being watched. You won't believe how many people are looking for you. For me too, but mostly for you. What are your plans?

I'm going to the U.S. with my brother, Emiliano. The undocumented way, as they say.

Oh. That's good. That's very good, actually.

Why?

The Jaqueros have connections in the U.S. who can help with the phone. They're even better than us. I know, hard to believe, huh? They have more resources than us, anyway, and it will be easy for them to get inside the phone.

Sara has to wait for a few minutes for the next message.

E-mail Yoya at crazyfreeyoya@gmail.com when you get to the U.S. She'll give you an address where you can send the phone or she'll find someone in her organization to pick it up. She'll be able to retrieve the information in the phone and send it to us. We'll know what to do with it. I want to nail Hinojosa and his cronies for good. I wish you didn't have to carry the phone around. But even if they knew you didn't have the phone, these people would still want to find you—revenge for turning them in. Be careful. Don't tell anyone where you're going!

Sara writes down the e-mail address. *Got it. Thank you, Ernesto. What will you do?*

I'm going to Mexico City. There's tons of Jaqueros there. I'll be okay. I almost forgot to tell you. I've been digging in Juana's computer from here. I found statements in her files from a bank in Panama which in turn made some big loans to El Sol. I always wondered where El Sol got the money to stay afloat. Hinojosa uses that same bank.

Sara remembers the conversation with Juana at the quinceañera.

Does that mean Felipe is bad too?

No evidence of that. I think Juana got the loans and didn't tell Felipe how. I also found correspondence between Juana and Elias. Something was going on between them at some point. Sara, I have to go. It was an honor knowing you.

It was an honor knowing you, Ernesto. Good-bye.

Sara stares at the screen, smiling to herself as she remembers Ernesto's conversation with Guillermo about the quinceañera. She will miss Ernesto so much.

"Excuse me, Sara?" She turns quickly to see Daniel holding a cell phone. "For you. Estela."

"Estela?" Sara says weakly. There's no saliva anywhere in her mouth. Brother Patricio and Emiliano stop talking.

"I thought I'd find you there. Hold on. I want to put someone on the phone." Estela's voice is upbeat, happy.

There is a long silence and then Sara hears a voice as familiar as her own. "Sara. It's me."

Sara shuts her eyes tightly, but the tears rush out nevertheless. "Linda. Linda. You're alive!"

"I am. Barely, but I am."

"Oh, my God. Are you okay?"

"Yes, yes. This morning, these grenade things go off. Then there was smoke. Doors bursting open with people in bulletproof vests. All I could think of was *Sara did it. My friend Sara saved us.*"

"Thank God, thank God."

"But . . . Officer Gómez said you were in danger. Will you be all right?"

"Yes. Don't worry. We're going away for a while. Have you been home yet?"

"They don't want me to go home. My mom and dad and my sisters. They're on their way here. Then we'll go to a safe place. I . . . need to be myself again. That place, Sara . . ."

"It's okay. You stayed alive. That's what you had to do."

"I'm so full of hate right now. Pray for me, okay?"

"I will. I will. Don't worry. Time will heal you."

"I hope so. I wish you were with me. That would be a big help. Officer Gómez is making a sign for one more minute. I don't know how to thank you, Sarita. I messed up your life really bad, didn't I?"

"No, no. You made it much better."

"Sara, my friend Erica . . . she took Hinojosa's phone . . ."

"Yes?"

"She . . . They killed her."

"Oh, Linda."

"They were going to kill me too. They waited . . . for some reason."

"It's okay, don't cry. It's okay that you're alive. God wanted you to live."

"Sara, I have to let you go." There's a pause. "You're my best friend."

"And you're mine."

Then Sara and Linda say at the same time:

"Forever and ever."

Part II

United States

CHAPTER 26

EMILIANO AND SARA

They cross the Rio Grande with the sun still hidden behind the Sierra del Carmen mountain range to the east. Emiliano steps in the river barefoot, his arms slightly outstretched for balance against the tug of the current. When he reaches the center, he turns to look at Sara behind him. She is surprised by the glacial cold of the water and by the soft silt of the river bottom that seeks to swallow her feet. Maybe it is just Mexico not wanting to let go of her. Emiliano waits until he sees her take a second careful step and then continues. When he reaches the other side, he helps Sara to the muddy bank. They climb a rocky slope and then stop to look back at the small town of Boquillas. Brother Patricio, on the other side of the Rio Grande, raises his hand in the gesture of a blessing and Emiliano and Sara wave.

They arrived at Boquillas the evening before, when the few adobe houses in the village were dark and silent. They followed a dirt road that ran parallel to the river and parked the car in a grove of cottonwoods. Then they waited for dawn.

At some point during the night, Sara walked a few yards away, spread a blanket on the grass, and tried to sleep. Now and then, when the ruckus of the frogs quieted down for a few moments, she could hear the murmur of Emiliano and Brother Patricio's voices. She wondered whether Emiliano had finally decided to tell Brother Patricio that he planned to return. All through the trip, Emiliano had acted as if he was leaving Mexico forever. After they put their mother on the bus to León, Emiliano could have told Brother Patricio that his absence would only be temporary, but he didn't. Why?

Then again, Sara could count on her two hands the words spoken during the trip. She sat in the backseat with her mother on the way to Chihuahua, holding her hand, listening to her Hail Marys. Now and then she fixed her eyes on the profile of Emiliano's pensive face staring out the window. What was he thinking? Was his heart breaking like hers? The thought that they might never see their mother again kept coming back to her, no matter how many times she tried to shoo it away.

On top of the rock, Emiliano watches Brother Patricio's car turn into the village's main street. He sticks his hand in his pocket and feels his mother's rosary. She should have given it to Sara and not to him. Sara sat with his mother and prayed in unison with her, two voices forming one single prayer. He doesn't believe that their prayers were heard or had any power other than a calming effect. So why did his mother cup his hand and drop the rosary in it just before she boarded the bus to León? And why didn't he tell her he didn't deserve it? When Sara isn't looking, he slips the rosary over his head and tucks it under his shirt.

The only sound this early in the morning comes from the river. Sara thinks that if time could make a sound, it would be like the gentle but constant rush of water. In the distance, to the west, from where the river flows, she can see the limestone canyons carved by the river's patient march. During the eight-hour ride, she read the books on Big Bend National Park that

Brother Patricio brought for them. It took millions of years for the river to carve those canyons. She feels so small compared to that immensity of time. And yet, here she is.

Emiliano begins to make his way through the thick cane growing on the banks of the river. The flutter of a gray dove startles him momentarily. He points at the ground so Sara will see the dove's nest with the miniature eggs, and they step carefully around it. He stops when they emerge from the band of greenery that borders the river. In front of them rises an embankment. On his right, Emiliano sees a well-worn footpath up the cliff. Many, many other Mexicans have come this way before. He climbs it carefully so that Sara can see where he plants his feet and do the same. He is tempted a few times to offer his hand when she begins to slip but decides against it. Instead, when he senses her struggling, he simply waits for her to find a way up. She's carrying two gallons of water, weighing about eighteen pounds, plus another fifteen pounds of food, clothing, and other equipment. He made the load as light as possible, aware that after a few hours of walking, thirty-three pounds is going to feel like eighty. He smiles when he remembers the trouble he had convincing her that carrying her six-pound laptop was not possible.

Sara's forehead is moist when she reaches the top of the cliff. The morning is cool enough to wear a sweater and she's already sweating. That is probably not a good sign for things to come. The river, a brownish amber color when they crossed, has a dark emerald tint when seen from above. She takes off her floppy canvas hat and wipes her brow with the red bandanna Emiliano insisted she carry in the back pocket of her white chino pants. In addition to the two-gallon bag of water, she carries another water bottle in an outside pocket of her backpack, as does Emiliano. Is it too early to take a drink? The indigo dawn is slowly transforming itself into cobalt blue. She hears the chirping of birds and something like the tick of a clock. She scampers up the rock where Emiliano is standing.

"Don't worry," Emiliano says. "The rattlesnakes are down in that cane we walked through."

"What's that noise, then?"

"A grasshopper waking up."

"So, we're past all the snakes?"

"There's more where we're going. But the ones that can kill you for sure are by the river."

Emiliano and Sara stand on the rock, looking across the river at the mountains of Mexico. They remind Sara of a picture of an old man that Emiliano showed her after he came back from a trip to the Sierra Tarahumara. The old man stood next to a wooden hut, holding a crooked walking stick, his face wrinkled and weathered by age and hardship. It was the eyes that caught Sara's attention. It was as if they had been looking at what mankind had done to the world since the beginning of time.

Someday I will remember this moment, Sara says to herself. *Will I ever see you again, my Mexico?*

The image of her mother climbing into the silver-and-blue bus comes to her. The bus driver helping Mami up the steps. Then she imagines her mother looking out the window as the bus pulls into the León terminal. She sees Aunt Tencha hugging her mother—two women who know loss comforting each other. They will embrace and cry a little, and then they will take a bus to the tiny apartment, where Mami will have a cup of coffee and then maybe go lie down in the bedroom filled with pictures of Tencha's grandchildren.

Sara sighs. "I miss Mami."

Emiliano nods. "She's happy knowing you're safe," he tells her.

He jumps off the rock, and after a few moments Sara does as well. Now both of them face north. There in front of them is a vastness of reddish dirt, cacti, and creosote bushes that goes on forever, it seems. Way in the distance there's a barely perceptible line where the sky and the earth touch. It's as far as the eye can see. A series of hills and peaks gradually rises to mountains to the west. The proximity of the emptiness of the desert and the massive reality of the mountains takes Emiliano's breath away. It's as if someone deliberately mixed beauty and immensity to elicit awe.

"Is that the end of the park?" Sara points at the horizon.

Emiliano smiles. "That's where we'll end up late tonight if we hurry." He turns Sara's shoulder slightly and points to the left. "That pile of wood over there is the ruin of the old tramway that Brother Patricio told us about. A little way from there is the abandoned dirt road. You see it? It's a thin white line like a thread."

"How far is that, you think?"

"Maybe three miles."

Sara gulps. "That's only three miles?"

Emiliano takes his compass from his right pocket. He moves his hand until the needle trembles on true north. Then he points in the direction they will walk. Navigation, once they get to the dirt road, will be easy. There's no need for the GPS as long as they stay on the dirt road. The map of the park describes the road as "rough" and recommends travel only with a four-wheel-drive vehicle. They should be able to pass through it undetected. They will see the dust of an oncoming vehicle long before it reaches them. If someone does come, they'll get off the road and lie flat on the ground behind a bush. Emiliano reminds himself to listen for the mosquito-like drone of an approaching plane as well.

"Okay," he says, tightening the strap that connects his backpack to his waist. "I'm going to start walking at a pace that covers four miles per hour while the sun is still low. Then when the sun gets a little stronger, I'll slow down to three miles an hour. Around noon, we'll stop and wait for the sun to go down. We'll go slowly the first day while your legs get used to walking and your back adapts to the weight of the backpack. Then maybe tomorrow we can go faster. Drink some water. You need to drink a gallon of water each day. We're carrying enough water for three days, and later today we'll reach a place where there's water, so there's no need to be stingy with it. Have some of the raisins and dried figs. From now on, don't take your hat off."

Emiliano starts walking. Sara sees that there is no way to walk next to him. There is not a set path, so they must weave their way through cacti and creosote bushes, and the space between the plants is not wide enough for two persons. She expected to have a hard time keeping up with him, but his pace is measured, comfortable. If they went a little bit faster, maybe they could make five miles an hour. The night before they left for Chihuahua, Emiliano and Sara went over the map one more time, Emiliano pointing out the wavy lines that denoted the hills, mountains, and canyons: The tighter a circle, the higher the elevation of the mountain. Emiliano said then that on the earlier part of the trip, where the terrain was flatter, they might be able to walk as much as six hours a day.

"Six hours doesn't seem like much," she remembers saying.

"You'll see," Emiliano answered.

Now as they walk, she feels she could definitely do at least eight hours—four in the morning and four in the evening. She does the math. If they walk at the leisurely pace of four miles an hour like they're doing, and they do that for eight hours, then they could cover thirty-two miles a day. Emiliano and Brother Patricio calculated that the distance from the river to Sanderson was around eighty miles. Once they get within twenty miles of Sanderson, they will also be within range of a cell tower, and they could communicate with the deacon of the Catholic church at Sanderson, who could come pick them up if need be.

"Watch out for those," Emiliano says, tapping his boot on a round, flat cactus studded with long, pointed thorns. "It's called a 'horse crippler' for a reason. The thorns pierce through the hooves of horses and soles of shoes."

Sara steps over it, making a point to remember that the cactus has deceivingly innocent, pale pink flowers. What was it she was thinking? She was doing some math in her head. Eighty miles divided by thirty-two is two days plus a little more. But if they walked a little faster, say, five miles an hour, and they did that for eight hours, they'd get there in two days. She feels strong enough to go five miles an hour. Yet Emiliano wants to slow down to three miles an hour for six hours. At that speed, it will take a week to get to Sanderson.

"Stop it," Emiliano says without looking back.

"What?"

"Thinking that we can walk faster or farther."

"How . . . ?"

"That's what everyone thinks their first time out in the desert. It doesn't work that way."

"If you're slowing down because of me, you don't have to. I'm fine."

Emiliano stops to check his compass. He looks to his right and locates the sun. They have maybe four hours before the temperature reaches somewhere in the eighties. The eighties of March are not the one hundred and change of August, but it's still hot enough to kill you. He takes off his hat, runs a hand through his hair, and feels the moisture in his scalp. He reaches back, takes the bottle of water from the side of his backpack, and drinks. He gestures for Sara to do the same. When she finishes drinking, he looks at her feet. "How are the shoes?"

"They're bored from going so slow. We're never going to get there at this rate."

"Are you hungry?"

"A little. You must be too. We haven't eaten since yesterday afternoon."

Emiliano takes two protein bars from the same pocket where he keeps his water bottle. He hands one to Sara and starts to unwrap the other.

"We didn't pack much food," Sara says. The slight alteration in direction that Emiliano made after he checked his compass has given them enough space to walk side by side.

Emiliano waits until he finishes chewing. "Food's not that important. The important thing is water. Food requires digestion and digestion uses water needed by your muscles."

"And your brain. That needs water too."

"No, not your brain. The less you use your brain, the better."

Sara speeds up but Emiliano maintains the same pace. "You don't need to baby me," she says. "I'm in pretty good shape."

"I'm not babying you."

"Would you be doing anything different right now if I wasn't here?"

"Yes."

"What?"

"I wouldn't be talking."

"No, seriously. Would you be walking any faster?"

"No."

"Really. You wouldn't be walking faster?"

"No. If I were alone, I might go a little farther today than I will with you, but not that much."

"Somehow I don't believe you."

"Believe me."

The path they're on narrows again and Emiliano pulls ahead.

Sara reflects after a few minutes of walking: Maybe it's not such a good idea to push Emiliano to go faster. The more time she's out here with him, the more time he'll have to realize that living with Papá may be what is best for him at this moment in his life. *In the United States, you can be the Emiliano God wants you to be.* What did Mami see or sense in him to make her say that? Why was Emiliano reading Papá's letters the night after the party? All that Sara can think of is that he was seeking guidance for some grave decision he needed to make.

Emiliano motions for Sara to stop. He looks up, tilts his head. After a few moments, he kneels beneath the outstretched arms of a tall cactus. Sara does the same.

"What is it?" Sara whispers.

"A car," Emiliano answers in a normal voice. He lies on the ground behind a small mound of red dirt and brush. He motions for Sara to lie down as well. They see the dust of a vehicle traveling south on the dirt road they want to take north. "That's strange."

"What?"

"Brother Patricio said no one uses this road anymore."

"Looks like a sports car," Sara says, squinting. They watch in silence as the black car reaches the southern end of the road and then stops. No one gets out. "What are they doing? Just sitting there? There's nothing to see."

Emiliano points to a small rectangle of shade under a cactus. They crawl there and sit. "We'll have to wait until they leave."

"Is it the Border Patrol?"

"In a Corvette?"

"You can see what kind of car it is?"

"It's easy to make out the shape of a Corvette," Emiliano says. He looks concerned. It's the first time on this trip that Sara has seen fear on his face. "It's not the kind of car that someone visiting the park would drive on that road."

"Then who?" Sara asks, now afraid herself. "Maybe they're smugglers and they're waiting for a shipment of drugs."

Emiliano remembers the fast-looking car parked in Armando's garage. That was a black car as well. But Armando's car was smaller, a Porsche maybe.

"They're getting out," Sara whispers.

In the distance, Emiliano sees a man with a black cowboy hat emerge from the driver's side and a man with a brown hat from the other side. The man with the black hat is wearing black pants, a white shirt, and a black jacket. The man with the brown hat has a beige jacket. Who wears jackets in the desert? They stand in front of the car, looking toward the river. Then the man with the black hat turns and looks in their direction. Emiliano presses his face against the dirt and pushes Sara's head down as well.

"Are they coming over here?" Sara asks.

"Shhh." The men are a good quarter of a mile away, but sound travels far in the desert. Emiliano looks behind them. Other than the small mound of dirt they're on, there's no place to hide until you get to the cliffs near the river. He raises his head slowly. Now both men are looking straight at them. One of them reaches into the car and takes out a pair of sunglasses. "I think they saw us," Emiliano whispers. "If they start walking this way, we run back to the river. Leave the backpacks and run."

"Who are they? Do you think they're looking for us?"

Emiliano can hear the same fear in Sara's voice that he feels in his chest. He needs to calm down so he can think clearly. People wear those kinds of light jackets to hide the pistols on their hips. Maybe they're undercover Border Patrol agents, but why would the Border Patrol need to hide their identity? And why would they risk ruining the suspension on an expensive car? It's impossible that the men are looking for them. Who knew where they were going to cross? No one. They didn't tell anyone their plans. Did they?

"Are they still there?" Sara asks, her face pressed to the dirt.

Emiliano takes off his hat and sunglasses and raises his head slowly. The men are conferring with each other. He notices a pair of binoculars hanging from the neck of the man with the brown hat. With binoculars, it would have been easy to see Sara and him make their way from the cliffs above the river.

The good news is, there is no way that they can use the car to catch them on this path, and if they come on foot, he's sure they can outrun them. He'll let Sara run ahead, and if they catch up to him, he'll do whatever needs to be done so she's not caught.

"Remember that place where I showed you the dove's eggs?" he says. "If we need to run, head back to that spot and crouch in the cane."

"What about you?"

Emiliano doesn't answer. He watches the men approach the edge of the road. They seem to be contemplating the distance they would need to cover to get to Emiliano and Sara, and they're not the type of men who like to get their shoes dirty, he thinks.

He's right. The two men get back into the car. They turn it around and drive slowly away.

"Are they gone?"

Emiliano kneels on the ground and Sara lifts herself up to sit. They watch the car until it is a dot in the distance.

"They're after us, aren't they?" Sara asks. "Hinojosa's men?"

"It sure looks that way."

"But how? The only people who knew where we were crossing were Brother Patricio and Mami."

"And our dear father."

"Emiliano, come on. Even *you* can't possibly believe that."

"Did you tell Ernesto maybe?"

"No. I told him we were coming to the United States, but I didn't tell him how or where."

"We need to figure out what we do now."

"We can't go back, can we?"

"I don't think so. If we return to Boquillas and try to make it back to Chihuahua, someone will find us on those long, straight roads. At least here it's hard to get to us. We need to keep on going, only we won't travel on the road like we were planning. We'll go that way." Emiliano points to the ridge of mountains to the east.

"Can we do that?"

Emiliano clears a few rocks from the ground and sits so that he can still see the car in the distance. Then he opens his backpack and spreads a map of the park in the space between him and Sara. "The road the car is on was the one we were going to take north, up to this east-west road here." Emiliano points to a line at the northern edge of the park. "Instead of going straight north, we'll go northeast, up here to the beginning of the east-west road. From there we travel through these canyons and ridges toward Sanderson."

"Is that longer?"

"Longer and harder. I was counting on the flat surface of the road and on the places in the park where we could get water. But it's doable. And there's no way those guys can get to us in that car."

"Okay."

"Let's go, then." Emiliano stands. The car is a black dot on the long straight road, but it has stopped again. If he can see the car, the two men can see them with binoculars. "We'll head back the way we came, and then when they can't see us, we'll turn around. They'll think we went back to Mexico."

"I don't understand," Sara says, picking up her backpack. "I don't understand how they could find us."

They move on, first in the direction of the river and then, when they reach the cliffs and the car is no longer visible, north toward the mountains. The early morning warmth is transforming slowly into heat. They walk in silence, full of a dark foreboding.

"Do you have that flash drive with all the asylum evidence?" Emiliano asks Sara.

"Yes, I have it right in this little secret pocket inside the backpack."

"Take it out and put it in your pocket."

"Really? Why?"

"Because if we have to run, we'll need to leave the backpacks behind. You need to have that flash drive."

"Okay." Sara stops, takes off her backpack, opens it, and pockets the flash drive.

"What about Hinojosa's cell phone?"

"It's in the front pocket of my backpack."

Emiliano kneels down, takes the silver pouch with the cell phone from Sara's backpack, and sticks it in the left-hand pocket of his pants.

"Why you?" Sara asks.

"It's better if I carry it."

They put their backpacks on and continue. Sara lets Emiliano move ahead. She looks at his bulging backpack. She had a hard time lifting it off the ground when she tried before they crossed the river. He is carrying twice the load she is, and now he has the cell phone as well. It's as if he wished to take away all her heaviness, all danger, and put it on his shoulders.

There's so much love in her heart for her little brother at that moment that it hurts.

CHAPTER 27
EMILIANO AND SARA

TUESDAY, MARCH 28
9:14 A.M.

Emiliano picks up the pace and so does Sara. Now they're moving—only they don't seem to be making much ground. The terrain requires concentration, or else you step on one of those horse-crippling cacti. Sara is a few steps behind Emiliano, although there's enough room to travel side by side. She's thought about walking next to him and talking to him, but Emiliano seems to be weighed down by thoughts. Thoughts can be heavy. Sara knows because she's lugging a few herself. Juana told the bad people where Sara lived, knowing what they could do to her and to her family. That thought is so hard to carry. There must be something lighter she can think of as she walks down this endless road. Linda. Thinking about her gives Sara strength. What is Linda doing now? Surely she's with her family, her mother, maybe Joel. "That's nice," she says, imagining the scene.

"You say something?" Emiliano asks without looking back.

"Just talking to myself."

The mountains keep getting farther and farther away. They've been walking for how many hours? How can three hours seem like ten? She straightens when she notices herself slouching and thirty seconds later she's drooping again. She doesn't want to think about the men in the black car. Ernesto told her that Hinojosa would not give up. But how? How could they know where they were crossing? She goes back to the safe house and the time when Emiliano told her and Mami that he knew a place where they could cross. After that, who did they talk to? Mami called Papá, but they can both be trusted. Sara talked to Daniel at the Café Rojos and then to Ernesto, but she didn't tell them where the crossing was going to be. And Emiliano talked to Brother Patricio and to . . . Perla Rubi. When he came back to the café, he said he talked to Perla Rubi and then went for a long walk.

It must be Perla Rubi. Emiliano must know that. Perhaps her family has some connection to Hinojosa. Even if she didn't intend to betray Emiliano and Sara, she could have said something that would have given them away. Should she confront him or wait for him to tell her?

Sara decides to wait. It will be better for him to come to terms with that realization all by himself.

Emiliano forces himself to stay alert. Now and then he looks back in the direction of the road and the black car. He knows no car or vehicle can travel the terrain they are walking, but that hasn't stopped him from checking. The good thing about his vigilance is that it's a barrier against the pain he felt when Sara asked who knew where they were crossing. The realization that came to him at that moment was like an electric shock to his soul.

The conversation with Perla Rubi on that public phone by the Olympic Stadium. He's gone over what he said to her again and again. He told her they were crossing from Mexico into a national park in Texas. They were going to follow trails and old roads to the end of the park. Did he actually use the words "national park" or did he just say "Texas"? It's ridiculous to even imagine Perla Rubi doing anything that might hurt him.

But it is also irrefutable. If the men in the black car are looking for them and saw them—and he knows in his heart that they are and they did—the only explanation is Perla Rubi. It hurts to even think it, but there's no way around not thinking it. Perla Rubi must have told her father, possibly not knowing the consequences. Mr. Esmeralda, on the other hand, had to have known what that would mean for Sara—and he still told the bad guys.

This city is like a spiderweb. Every thread is connected directly or indirectly to every other thread.

"Damn," he says out loud.

"What did you say?" Sara says from behind him.

"I'm just talking to myself."

Sara skips a couple of steps ahead and joins Emiliano. She smiles when he looks at her apprehensively.

"What?" Emiliano asks.

"I need to talk periodically, otherwise I'll explode."

"You need to be very quiet. Sounds—"

"Travel far in the desert, I know. But I'm going batty listening to my thoughts, which are very loud out here. Do you ever get any happy thoughts in the desert? I'm still waiting for one to come."

"It's getting hot," Emiliano says, looking up. "In a couple of hours, we'll have to pull off the road for a while."

"A couple of hours?" Sara asks, deflated.

They march on side by side.

"I'm sorry I never got to write that article about the Jiparis. It would have been good for people to know about them."

Emiliano looks straight ahead and makes no sign that he is listening, but he doesn't tell her to stop talking either. Sara proceeds carefully. "I loved that pledge the Jiparis take. *I will be honest with myself and others.* That's so beautiful, that an explorer group would have its members make that pledge about honesty. I mean, what does it have to do with exploring, you know?"

Emiliano doesn't respond. He looks as if he's somewhere deep inside himself. Then, just before he pulls ahead of her, he speaks softly.

"It's not possible to live without some kind of lying. It can't be done. If you think it's possible, then you're fooling yourself."

Sara lets Emiliano move in front of her. His words don't jibe with the Emiliano she's always known—the brother who was lied to by a father and who, after that, despised lying more than anything. Emiliano's wrong. Maybe most people can't live without some kind of lying. But that doesn't apply to Emiliano. If there's one thing Sara knows without a doubt, it's that for her brother, it is not possible to live *with* lying.

The Emiliano who came back from Perla Rubi's party is different from the Emiliano who went there. Maybe he was reading Papá's letters to tell himself that people lie. Papá promised him he'd come back and didn't. If Papá could lie, so can he. Is that it? Something happened to him back home that made him say that it's not possible to live without lying. What lying did he have to do or feel he has to do?

CHAPTER 28

EMILIANO AND SARA

When the sun is directly in front of him, Emiliano slows down and waits for Sara to catch up. He can tell that she is tired because her feet barely lift off the ground. There were times during the past twelve miles when he thought about walking next to her and letting her do all the talking and questioning he knows she is itching to do. That will still come, but he decided it would be better if he let her talk when they were resting.

"You look exhausted," he tells her.

"A little. My legs feel heavy." She reaches down and touches her thighs. "Like they've got molasses circulating in there instead of blood."

Emiliano looks in the direction of the mountains. "There's a canyon about half a mile from here where we can find shade. Or we can put the tarp up over a couple of bushes and rest underneath it. It will be more comfortable in the canyon, but it means a mile or so of extra walking. It's up to you."

"Tarp sounds good, for some reason."

Emiliano finds two creosote bushes about ten feet apart from each other. He kneels in the space between them and takes off his backpack. He unlaces the tarp from the top of the aluminum frame and ties it to the two bushes with leather straps. The shade is enough for them to sit with their legs stretched out, their heads almost touching the tarp. They eat a chocolate bar in silence and then Emiliano arranges his backpack so he can use it as a pillow. He lies down but keeps his eyes open.

Sara takes off her shoes and socks. "How long will we rest?"

"Three or four hours, until the sun starts going down. Then we'll walk through the night until we get to the east-west road."

"How many miles per hour were we walking back there?"

"We started off at a good clip. Maybe three miles an hour. Then, after about a mile of that, we slowed down. You started falling back. All told, we walked about fifteen miles."

"That's all?"

"It's a good start."

"Whoever thought walking could be so painful?"

Emiliano turns on his side and watches Sara touch the blister on the big toe of her right foot. He sits up and finds the first aid kit. He hands her a tube of disinfectant and a small square of gauze. "Put a little bit of the ointment on so it won't get infected, and when we're ready to start again, wrap the toe in the gauze."

"This is not good, is it?" She examines the middle toe on her left foot. "I got another one coming over here." She lifts her foot so Emiliano can see the red spot.

"You should have told us the shoes were too tight."

"It's okay. They'll stretch out. Should I put my shoes back on?"

"You can leave them off."

"What about scorpions?"

"They're resting in a cool place. Under a rock somewhere."

Sara takes a notebook and pen from her backpack. She places her backpack against a bush and leans against it. She crosses her legs and begins to write in the open notebook in her lap.

"What are you doing?" Emiliano says with one eye open and one closed.

"Writing," Sara answers, not looking up. She bites the plastic pen thoughtfully.

"Writing?"

"I want to write down everything that happened since I got the threatening e-mail about Linda."

"Why?"

"I've been thinking that maybe asylum is our best option after all. We can do that after we get to Chicago. Writing it all down will help me remember all the details. What if the story of why we came to the United States was published in a newspaper? It would help us if we had the press behind us. When I was researching the asylum process, I found out that it was more likely to be granted to people who were well known—writers and poets from Mexico who were persecuted for their writings. So it will definitely be a help if our story gets known."

Emiliano smiles, shakes his head.

"What?"

"Why don't you go ahead and get it out of your system? Then we can get some rest."

"Get what out of my system?"

"You just said that asylum is *our* best option and something *we* can do when *we* get to Chicago. Look, let's do this. You can try to convince me to live with our dear father for the next hour. I promise I will listen to what you have to say, and you can give it your best shot. But after that hour, if you're not able to convince me, we won't talk about it anymore and you won't waste precious mental energy thinking about it. What do you say?"

"You really will listen? I mean really listen. You'll be honestly open to the possibility? Can you do that?"

"Hold on." Emiliano shuts his eyes. Ten seconds later, he opens them again. "Okay, my mind is honestly open to the possibility of living with the man who told Mami and us to go to hell."

"Emiliano, I know you're not serious. I know you don't really want to hear me try to convince you. But . . ."

"But?"

"I'll take the hour you give me. We'll talk about it for an hour and then that will be it. I won't mention it again during our trip."

"But?"

"But there's one condition."

"What?"

"If I ask you a question, you have to tell me the truth. You need to follow the Jipari code of honesty for one hour. Can you do that?"

Emiliano stares long and hard at Sara. Why would Sara ask him that? She's very clever, his sister. And when is he going to tell her that it's his fault the men in the black car are after them?

Sara holds Emiliano's gaze and restrains herself from saying anything. The fact that Emiliano is taking so long and thinking so hard about her request means she's hit a nerve. He's hiding something.

"Okay," Emiliano finally says. "I will answer truthfully, whatever you ask."

Sara closes her notebook. "Let me see, where do I start?" She needs to remember all she's learned about interviewing people at *El Sol*. "Tell me about the party last Friday at Perla Rubi's."

The question takes Emiliano by surprise. He anticipated the first question would be *Why do you hate Papá so much?* "What does the party have to do with anything?"

"Something happened at that party. You were one Emiliano before and a different one after."

"Nothing happened."

"Emiliano. Remember. The truth."

Emiliano reaches out and breaks a twig from the bush next to him. The shadow of gloom that passes over his face tells Sara that her instinct to start with the party was the right one. "Emiliano, not answering a question that needs to be answered is the same as not telling the truth. What happened at that party?"

"Does it really matter?"

"Yes."

"Why?"

"Because whatever happened at that party is what you'll be going back to when you return. I know your conscience is bothering you about something that happened to you that night. You wouldn't have been up all night reading Papá's letters otherwise. What's the real story behind the Mercedes and the Vespa? What kind of life is waiting for you in Juárez? How did the men in the black car find us?"

Emiliano exhales, shakes his head. He's got to hand it to

Sara. She's good. Why did he ever think he could hide the truth from her? A force inside him is pushing him to speak, if only to avoid the agonizing loneliness of the truth. And what is the truth? The truth seems so complicated and difficult to untangle. Or else the truth is so very simple: *I told Perla Rubi where we were going to cross. She told her father and he told Hinojosa. Oh, and when I go back, I'll be stuffing drugs in Javier's piñatas.*

That's it. That's all he has to say to Sara. A few words. Is it so hard?

"Tell me."

"I can't."

"Something's tearing you up inside. I can tell."

He wants to speak. He wants to let his sister in. But if he does, if he tells her, then she will be burdened by worry and concern.

"You want to know what I think?" Sara says. "I think you're torn between being who you really are and who Perla Rubi and her family want you to be. It doesn't seem like the two are the same. You know, it's possible to be in love with someone and realize that you can't be happy with them."

"You're really going to give me advice on love?"

Sara blushes. It's true. Her credentials in this area are not stellar. "I know a little."

"Joel."

"Yes, Joel. He and I were not meant to be more than good friends. We found that out pretty soon after we started dating and we were both grateful we did. But most of what I know about love and relationships, I learned from Mami."

"Mami?"

"And Papá too, I guess."

"Papá?" Emiliano chuckles.

"The two of them. They gradually came to understand and accept that even though they loved each other, neither one of them was happy with the other. Not truly and deeply happy, the way a man and wife should be. They saw life so differently. He wanted things she didn't want and vice versa."

"And he didn't want things he should have wanted," Emiliano says pointedly.

Sara ignores his remark. "They admired each other. I mean, they liked the qualities the other person had. Mami liked Papá's energy, his drive and ambition, and his never wanting to be bored in a job, and Papá liked how solid and steadfast and calm Mami was. But the reality was that it was hard for them to be together day by day. I mean, it was hard for each of them to be themselves with each other. When they were together, they each had to pretend to be what they thought the other person wanted them to be."

Sara stops to look at a neon lizard that crawled from a bush nearby. The lizard twists his neck for a better look at Emiliano. When the lizard scampers away, he says, "I heard Mami cry in her room the day the divorce papers came."

"Yes," Sara responds. She remembers Mami's tears too. "Letting go of a person you love, even one who is not right for you, still hurts."

What Emiliano is thinking but doesn't say is this: *A father doesn't abandon his son . . . or his daughter. He has an obligation to make a marriage work, to keep the promises of a father, even if keeping the promises of a husband make him unhappy.*

"It wasn't just Papá who ended the marriage," Sara continues. "They ended it together. Papá took the first step, yes, but Mami came to accept the decision as correct. At that point, the divorce became mutual. Mami now believes that what they felt for each other, as beautiful as it was, was not enough. She loved him so much. But she wanted him to be happy, so she let him go. And I think the same goes for how Papá feels about Mami." She waits a few moments, then continues, "And you're wrong about Papá not wanting the things he should have wanted. He loves you and wants to be with you. He always has. Someday you'll need to find a way to forgive him for wanting to be happy. You would prefer he'd stay in Mexico and be some kind of martyr. So, anyway, that's what I learned from Mami and Papá about loving someone. Whoever you love also has to be the right person for you."

Emiliano has to keep his eyes away from Sara for a few seconds. He looks down toward the roots of the bush, searching for the lizard. Finally, he turns back to his sister. The look of anguish on her face reflects exactly what he's feeling.

"It's not just Perla Rubi," he says. "It's the world she lives in. It's the world I wanted for all of us. I wanted Mami to not have to work anymore and for you not to take those stupid buses everyday. I don't know if I can let go of that."

Sara wishes she could find words of comfort. But there aren't any words that will make Emiliano feel better. The only words he needs to hear are ones that will increase the hurt. But she must say them, because he is her brother, and telling him the truth is how she loves him.

"But there are conditions to living in that world, aren't

there?" she says softly. "It's those conditions that are bothering you. It's like it says in the Bible, 'What use is it to gain the whole world if you lose your soul?'"

Silence is Emiliano's only response. But that's enough for Sara. She waits for his eyes to meet hers again, and then she tells him, "You know that you can never be the person those people want you to be. If you're honest with yourself, you know that."

Emiliano puts his arm over his eyes. Then he turns his back to Sara.

Sara watches him breathe. There's no need to say anything else.

CHAPTER 29
EMILIANO AND SARA

TUESDAY, MARCH 28
9:46 P.M.

There is something about walking in the silence of the night with only the stars to light your way. It's as if solitude finally feels right. Sara watches Emiliano ahead of her. His walk is different than before their afternoon rest stop. He seems fragile and vulnerable for the first time. She's held herself back from continuing the conversation they had under the tarp. It's clear that the words she spoke are working inside him like some kind of abrasive—eroding the old, she hopes, and making space for something new.

Emiliano stops. In front of him is the east-west road. They step on it and walk toward the place where it ends. His calculations took them to the exact spot they wanted to go. He lets Sara catch up with him. If they can walk a couple more hours, the trip tomorrow will be easier. But Sara is in pain. He can tell by the way she's been limping and dragging behind him for the past three hours.

"Let's find a place to sleep and rest your feet for a while," he says.

"I'm okay, really. Let's keep going."

"No. We'll stop. We've done more than what we planned on doing the first day. We need to find a place far enough from the road that no one driving on it will see us."

"I can keep going," Sara says again. But she's glad that Emiliano does not believe her.

Two hundred yards from the end of the road is a declivity on the ground made by some past torrential rainstorm. Emiliano spreads the tarp on the pebbly surface and hands Sara a thermal blanket. From here, they cannot be seen by anyone driving on the road when they are lying down or even sitting down. Emiliano gives Sara one of the six bean burritos he is carrying.

"Doesn't look all that appetizing, does it?" Sara says, looking for the edge of the cellophane wrapping. "What time is it?"

"Around ten," Emiliano says, glancing at the stars. "If we sleep for five hours, we can walk a few hours before it gets hot tomorrow."

"This has been one of the longest days of my life. It's gone on forever." Sara takes a bite of the burrito. "Is there anything worse than cold beans?"

When they finish eating, Sara fishes out the other long-sleeved shirt she's carrying and puts it on. She carefully spreads antibiotic ointment on her blisters. There are three of them now, a new one on the right heel. The two on her toes are red and raw. She puts her socks back on and looks over at Emiliano to see whether he plans to sleep with his boots on. He's taken them off.

"Should I sleep with my shoes on?"

"It would be better if you let your feet breathe."

"What about scorpions and tarantulas?"

Emiliano is lying face up with his backpack for a pillow. "If you feel something crawling on you, just keep still. Nothing's going to sting you if you don't panic." He sits up, turns around, and digs in one of his backpack's pockets. He gives Sara two small, thick rubber bands. "Put these over your pants, around your ankles, so nothing goes up your leg."

Sara looks at the rubber bands with horror, then grabs them and places them just above the hems of her pant legs. She pulls her socks up as far she can and puts her shoes back on. Her feet can go without breathing for a few nights, as far as she's concerned.

They lie there gazing at the sky without speaking. Every time Sara looks up, there are different stars. Are the stars moving or is the earth moving? Or both? The whole mess of creation is just one constant never-stopping dance. It's dizzying. For a moment it feels as if she's going to fall into the void above, and she grabs the edge of the tarp, but then she remembers the scorpions and folds her arms like Emiliano. It's cold.

"Settle down," Emiliano says. He sits up and puts his thermal blanket on her.

"What about you?"

"Shhh."

A few minutes later she hears him snore. She turns on her side and watches him. It's like when they were children and shared a bedroom. Whenever she felt afraid, all she had to do was remember that Emiliano was there. She knew that as the older sister, it was her responsibility to be brave, but it was his presence that took away her fear. A little while later she feels herself sinking into sleep.

In his dream, Emiliano is driving the Vespa with Perla Rubi holding tight to him. He feels the wind on his face and Perla Rubi's warmth on his back and he's happy, so happy. Then he hears a scream, and when he turns around, he sees Sara tumbling onto the road. The scream came from Sara. Then a heavy weight slams into his chest, and when he opens his eyes, he sees one of the men from the black car—the one with a brown hat. He has a boot on Emiliano's chest and is grinning. For a moment, Emiliano hopes that the man and the grin are part of the dream.

But they are not. Emiliano tries to writhe away from the pressure bearing down on him, but the man presses his foot harder into his chest. Next to him stands the man with the black hat, pointing a pistol at Sara's face. Emiliano sees a roll of gray duct tape in the hands of the brown hat. He struggles again to get himself free from the man's foot, but the man moves the sole of his shoe to Emiliano's face.

"Relax," the brown hat tells Emiliano.

It is early dawn. How could he have overslept? Ever since he can remember, he has been able to wake up without an alarm whenever he wanted. What a time for his internal clock to fail.

"It's okay, Emiliano," Sara tells him.

In one movement that seems almost too graceful for a man that big and heavy, the brown hat lowers himself to place one knee on Emiliano's face. Before he can recover from the shock of the pain on his ear and cheek, the man has grabbed Emiliano's hands. He wraps duct tape around the wrists first, then the ankles. Finally, he cuts a smaller strip and places it over Emiliano's mouth.

"Why are you doing that?" the man holding the gun on Sara asks. "Let's get what we came for and get it over with."

Emiliano understands that the man on top of him is in charge. Why *is* he getting tied up and not Sara? The brown hat pats Emiliano's pockets. He takes out the silver pouch with the cell phone and smiles gently at Emiliano, as if he had a bet with himself that Emiliano would be carrying the phone and he won. The man stands up and puts the cell phone in his pocket.

"Great," the man holding the pistol over Sara says. "Hey, Lester. Let's finish this and get out of here."

"What's your hurry?" the brown hat says, his eyes on Sara. He takes the pistol from the man with the black hat. "Go put the backpacks in the car."

For the first time, Emiliano sees their faces clearly. The man with the black hat is Mexican, but he speaks perfect English. The man who was on top of him, the one in charge, is white and American. Emiliano makes a mental note of his name: Lester. Lester is calm and steady and clearly comfortable with a pistol in his hand.

Sara sits up and rubs her throat. She looks at Emiliano next to her. She can tell he's trying to tell her something with his eyes. What? That quick flick of the eyebrows. What does that mean? Go away. Move away. Is that it?

"There's no need to hurt him," she says to the man with the brown hat.

"No?"

"You got what you were looking for. Just go."

"Actually, we're not done."

"Come on, Lester. Can we just get it over with?" the man with the black hat says, holding a backpack in each hand.

"Go ahead. Do what I told you. Put their backpacks in the back of the car. See if you can find any papers or pictures in there."

The man with the black hat heads to the car, shaking his head and mumbling to himself.

"I'll do whatever you want me to do if you let him live," Sara says to Lester.

Lester looks at her and then at Emiliano and back at Sara. He motions with the pistol for Sara to stand. She turns for one final look at Emiliano. *It's all right*, she tells him with her eyes.

As soon as Lester and Sara walk away, Emiliano pulls the rosary from under his shirt. The tape is wrapped around his wrists but his fingers are free. The cross on the rosary is made from some metal that is thin and sharp. Emiliano knows because the cross has stabbed him in the chest a few times while they've been walking. He grabs the cross with his thumbs and begins to rub the sharp corner against the tape. Slowly, the tape begins to tear.

Sara climbs out of the gully where she and Emiliano spent the night, Lester behind her. The man with the backpacks is ahead of them, walking toward the car.

"Where are you taking me?" Sara notices that Lester has lowered the pistol.

"Someplace."

"And my brother?"

"He'll find a rock and cut himself loose in a while. I'm going to let him live just like you wanted me to."

She turns to see the grin on the man's face. "I want you to leave my brother's backpack. He'll need water."

"He'll be okay if he heads back where he came from." Lester points with his chin in the direction of the Rio Grande.

"Lester, right?"

"You can call me Les if you want."

"I don't think you really want to do this. You don't need to do this."

288

He keeps smiling. "You like to talk, don't you?" He motions with the gun for her to keep walking. Sara sees the man with the black hat taking money from Emiliano's backpack.

"Please don't do this," Sara says. She stops and turns to face Lester. "If you let me live, I won't tell anyone. No one will know you let me live."

"Oh, they'll know."

Sara sees Emiliano climb slowly out of the gully. He puts his index finger on his lips and then motions with his hand. Sara turns around and walks. "Tell me what you want me to do."

"I'll tell you, all right. Don't you worry about that."

Emiliano is halfway between the gully and the man with the gun. The other man is behind the open trunk of the car with Sara's backpack. Lester is holding the pistol in his right hand. Nothing will work unless he drops the pistol. Emiliano sees the man by the car look in his direction. Now or never.

The man by the car shouts as Emiliano runs as fast as he can. He feels the thorns of a cactus rip through his foot but he doesn't stop. He jumps onto Lester's back just as the man begins to turn. He kicks Lester's hand with as much power as he can muster and the pistol flies toward Sara. Now Emiliano wraps his right arm around Lester's neck and uses his left hand to tighten the chokehold. Lester coughs, twists, turns, and bends like a wild horse.

"The gun. The gun!" Emiliano shouts at Sara.

The man with the black hat is running toward them, waving his own pistol. Lester pummels the side of Emiliano's face with his fist. Sara lunges for the pistol on the ground but the other man kicks it away. She falls to her knees, the pistol just out of reach.

"Shoot him!" Lester stammers, coughing and spitting. He turns so that Emiliano's back becomes a broad and easy target for the man holding the pistol. Lester is so tall that Emiliano's feet dangle in the air. Sara looks up and sees the man's hand tremble, trying to take aim, and just as he's about to press the trigger, she smashes her fist as hard as she can between his legs. The pistol goes off as the man drops it and folds over in pain.

Sara turns, still on her knees, afraid of what she will see. Lester is lying facedown with Emiliano on his back. She looks for the dark red of blood on the white of Emiliano's shirt but doesn't find anything. Lester's gun is lying next to her. The man who fired the shot is holding himself, grimacing. She picks up both pistols and walks toward Emiliano. Lester is not moving, but Emiliano still squeezes his neck harder and harder.

"It's okay," Sara tells Emiliano. "I have the guns. You can let go."

There's something like a growl coming from Emiliano's mouth. His eyes are tightly shut, his jaws clenched.

"Emiliano, let go. He's passed out. Emiliano, don't. Let go."

It takes a few moments for Sara's words to reach Emiliano's consciousness. The man underneath him is still breathing. He can feel a trickle of air on his forearm. If he lets go now, the man will live. This is the man who was taking his sister away, who told his partner to shoot Emiliano in the back. Why should he let go?

Sara looks to make sure that they are safe from the other man. He's running toward the car, maybe to get another gun.

"Emiliano, don't kill him, please. You don't kill people. You're a Jipari."

The words sound silly, but they work. Emiliano loosens his grip. He sits on the man's broad back, resting, panting.

The sound of a motor starting reaches them and they both look toward the road. The black car is heading west in a cloud of dust.

"Our backpacks" is all that Emiliano can think of saying.

"Is he . . ."

Emiliano flips Lester over on his back with difficulty, places two fingers on the side of his neck. "No," he says, standing up. "I cut the flow of blood to his brain so he fainted. He'll be up in a few minutes."

"Look." Sara points to a widening dark spot on the ground beneath Lester's right leg.

Emiliano kneels and tilts Lester on his side. He sees a small hole in his pants, stained with blood. He tears at the hole with two index fingers. Blood, almost black in color, is trickling slowly but steadily out of an orifice not much wider than a shirt button. The bottom half of Lester's leg falls loose, connected to his thigh only by skin and a couple of tendons. "The bullet blasted the whole knee. It went out the other side. There's no bone joint to hold the leg." Emiliano lifts the leg and lets the calf and foot dangle in the air for Sara to see. She turns her head away.

"Will he die?"

Lester starts coughing. Emiliano and Sara stand back. They wait for him to open his eyes and then for his eyes to focus. He grimaces as he tries to sit himself up, but the leg can't respond to his commands. He falls back on the ground, recognizing Emiliano first and then Sara.

"Where's Joe?" he asks through gritted teeth.

He hasn't felt the pain yet, Emiliano thinks.

"He took off in the car," Sara tells him.

Lester gives a little nod as if to say that was to be expected.

"We should go," Emiliano says to Sara in Spanish. "His friend will be back with help soon."

"He's not coming back." Lester's words are barely audible. The man apparently understands Spanish. He moans.

Now he's starting to feel the pain.

Lester's chest begins to heave and he covers his eyes with the crook of his arm. Sara and Emiliano let him feel miserable in private for a few moments. Then Sara pulls Emiliano a few paces away.

"Can you stop the bleeding?"

"He was going to kill you. God knows what else."

"Emiliano . . ."

"He told his friend to shoot me. That bullet has my name on it."

"Emiliano, we have to do something."

"Sometimes you sound just like Mami," he says grudgingly. He walks back to Lester, who is on his side, writhing and moaning softly. Emiliano taps him on his butt with his bare foot and realizes for the first time that he's also bleeding. There is pain deep inside his left foot. He looks at Sara's feet. She has her shoes on. Emiliano can't remember whether he put his boots inside his backpack last night, like he sometimes does to keep the critters out. If he did, he's as good as dead. He can't survive out here without shoes.

"You think you can walk on one leg?" Emiliano asks the man.

Lester shakes his head. "I can't even move it. The bullet busted my whole kneecap, didn't it? God, it hurts!"

Emiliano looks over at Sara. Does she really want to help this man? He steps over Lester's body and starts to walk toward the gully. He walks slow, planting both feet firmly on the ground. He doesn't want to limp in front of Sara.

"Emiliano . . ."

"I'm going to get the tarp," Emiliano snaps back. "We need to drag him to the gully, where there'll be some shade. We need to stop the bleeding somehow. See if we can keep his sorry ass living a little longer."

Sara can't keep herself from smiling. She walks over to Lester and kneels next to him. "I don't know that much about first aid, but the more you move the leg, the more the blood spurts out."

"We were using those . . . bullets that . . . burst on impact."

"Stay calm," she says. He opens his eyes for a second to look at her with something that resembles embarrassment, like a child who doesn't want to be seen crying by his playmates.

Sara remembers the disgust she felt toward him as they walked away from Emiliano, after she told him that she would do whatever he wanted. It was all that she could think of saying to save her brother's life and her own. It made her sick to imagine this man touching her. Now the disgust and anger come back to her, but she forces herself to touch his shoulder through a monumental effort of will.

Her touch quiets him. He stops moving. He shuts his eyes as if her kindness is too painful for him.

In the gully, Emiliano looks at what is left of their

equipment. Two thermal blankets. Sara's water bottle, half-full. And best of all, his boots. *Mami's prayers*, Sara would say. What else is left? The knife with a miniature compass that Linda gave him, and his and Sara's hats. Emiliano sits on the ground and looks at the bottom of his foot. He clears the blood away with a sock and finds the four places where the thorns pierced his sole. He puts on his socks and boots. A foot fortunately does not bleed much, and the pressure from standing and walking will help stop what little bleeding there is. As for the pain that is now shooting all the way to his ankle, all he can do is ignore it.

Emiliano and Sara roll Lester onto the tarp and drag him to where the gully levels out, then through the gully until they reach the deepest shadows, where they spent the night. They find two rocks, which they use to elevate the leg. The man's blood drips steadily to the ground. Sara takes the pouch with Hinojosa's cell phone out of Lester's jacket. She remembers Elias carried his cell phone in the same pocket of a similar jacket. That seems like ages ago. She places the cell phone pouch on top of a rock nearby.

"I'm not going to make it . . . am I?" Lester whimpers. He is pale and weak and has started to shiver. Sara covers him with a thermal blanket.

"Can you make a tourniquet to stop the blood?" Sara asks Emiliano.

"The bullet didn't hit an artery, otherwise the blood would be gushing. Tourniquets are for arteries."

"But the blood is coming out nonstop," Sara says. "The bleeding is worse at the back of the knee."

Emiliano kneels down and says to Lester, "You think you can lie on your stomach with your leg up on a rock?"

Emiliano and Sara take Lester's jacket off and then turn him on his stomach and prop up the leg. They put the part of the leg where the knee used to be on a flat rock and his lower leg on a higher rock. Emiliano takes out his knife and makes a long tear in Lester's pants. He motions for Sara to give him her bandanna and then sits next to Lester and presses down on the wound with the rolled-up cloth.

"Ohhh," Lester groans.

"I'm going to put pressure on the wound for a few minutes to see if the bleeding slows down."

"It's the bone. The flesh . . . don't hurt as much as the bone."

Sara sits on the gully wall opposite Lester's face. "Your friend will get help and come back, won't he?"

"No. He's gone for good. Oh, God."

"I wish you'd stop using God's name. You have no right to invoke his name after what you were thinking of doing," Sara tells him.

Emiliano smiles. Again, Sara sounds just like Mami.

Lester starts shaking.

"The blood is coming out harder. Get ahold of yourself or you'll die faster." Emiliano pauses. "On second thought, go ahead and move as much as you can."

"Emiliano!"

Lester takes a series of shallow breaths. It reminds Sara of a woman in labor trying to fight through the pain. "I . . . can't believe . . . you helping . . . me."

"Me neither," Emiliano says, staring at Sara.

"It's not possible that your friend won't come back with help, or call someone and tell them you're hurt. I can't believe he'd just leave you here." It suddenly occurs to Sara that Joe or whatever his name was probably doesn't know that Lester has been shot. She and Emiliano didn't know right away either. "What kind of a friend is that?"

"He's a . . . rookie. Scared. Shouldn't have . . . brought him."

"You're a very sick person, you know that?" Sara says. "And I'm not talking about the bullet wound. Your friend is sick too. You don't leave a friend behind, no matter what."

"I know it. I know I am."

Emiliano removes the bandanna from the wound. They both watch the small opening on the leg. The blood has stopped flowing. Then a moment later it begins to ooze out again. Emiliano shakes his head, stands up, and motions for Sara to follow him.

Emiliano moves far enough away that Lester won't hear them. He looks at the sun, well above the rim of the mountains. Today will be hotter than yesterday, he can tell already. "We should be going."

Sara glances at Lester. "How bad is it?"

"He's going to bleed out in a couple of hours. With pressure on the wound, maybe he'll last an hour or two longer."

"We can't leave him."

Emiliano shakes his head. "Our trip is over, then. If you want to save him, the only way to do that is for one of us to go get help while the other one tries to stem the bleeding. The main road is about four miles west of here. You can flag a car, call for help."

"Me?"

"Sara, listen to me. If we want to save that man's life, you won't make it to Chicago. Do you still have the thumb drive with all your asylum documents?"

Sara pats the pocket of her leg. "Yes." Emiliano never ceases to amaze her. It was so smart of him to have her keep the thumb drive in her pocket rather than her backpack.

"Get help and then turn yourself over to the Border Patrol. Tell them you're seeking asylum."

"And you?" The idea of leaving Emiliano scares her more than anything that's happened that morning.

"I'll wait with the guy, putting pressure on his wound. I'll be able to tell when a car is coming before it gets here. When I see the dust, I'll run and hide behind those rocks on that hill over there. Then after everyone is gone, I'll head back down that road, the way we came."

"Ahhh!"

They both turn in the direction of Lester's cry.

"We should leave him for the buzzards," Emiliano says. "That man is no different than the people who shot up our house or the man who owns that cell phone back there. He works for them."

Sara notices pain flashing across Emiliano's face. "You're hurt."

"It's nothing. I stepped on a cactus. I'll be all right." The pain in his foot is nothing, nothing, compared to the pain in his heart. There's no more denying the truth. Perla Rubi is the reason they were found. His sister was almost raped and killed because of Perla Rubi or her father, or both.

Strength ebbs from his legs. He lowers himself to the ground. Sara kneels and then sits next to him.

"You told Perla Rubi where we were crossing, didn't you?"

Emiliano nods. He closes his eyes and speaks. "She probably mentioned it to her father. Her father . . ."

"Knows Hinojosa."

He opens his eyes and looks straight ahead. "Or knows people that know him. It's like a spiderweb. Every thread is connected."

Sara holds her head in her hands. It will take a long time for her to figure it all out, but she understands enough. She sees clearly what has been tearing Emiliano apart and the life that awaits him.

"Emiliano, do you really want to go back?"

You're protected. That's one of the benefits of our friendship . . . When you come back, you'll be okay.

The men were taking Sara. They were going to leave him behind, knowing that he would free himself in a short time. They were letting him go because he is protected. The thought that it was Sara they were after and not him sickens him.

And yet even now, despite all he knows, he still wants to return to Perla Rubi. Even after her father told Hinojosa where they were going to cross, he still wants to be a part of her world. He doesn't understand how this can be. It doesn't make sense. Yet there it is. All he knows is that he feels a powerful pull toward Perla Rubi and Armando and Mr. and Mrs. Esmeralda and even Alfredo Reyes. Those people accepted him, welcomed him, treasured him even. They never abandoned him or broke any promises to him. And if they are dirty, well, so is he.

His silence is the answer to Sara's question.

She stares at him until the unrelenting sorrow in her eyes makes him stand. She stands as well. "All right. I'll go because

I don't want that man to die. I still have a conscience." She pauses long enough for him to understand the implied accusation. What the hell has happened to her brother? Emiliano, whose compass always pointed toward goodness. When he looks up, she says, her voice quivering, "If you want to return and be part of that spiderweb, as you call it, then go ahead. But first you're going to take Hinojosa's cell phone to Sanderson. When you get there, you're going to e-mail Yoya—her e-mail's in the pouch—and then you're going to send the phone wherever she tells you. I put all of our lives in danger for that cell phone. I gave up my home, my job, my mami, to save some poor girls. I sacrificed everything. Mami sacrificed being with the two people she loves the most. I don't want my sacrifice and Mami's to be for nothing.

"And when you get to Sanderson, you're going to tell Papá that I asked for asylum, and you're going to make sure he finds out where I'm being detained so he can vouch for me. You're going to do all that, Emiliano, because otherwise this is all for nothing, and if it's for nothing, it's because of you. Because of *you*. Do you understand? And you can't let all I've done be lost."

Emiliano watches the tears make wet tracks on Sara's dusty face. He doesn't know what to say. He wants to tell her how sorry he is, but he's no longer sure that any words coming out of his mouth will be true. Whatever comes out has a good chance of being a lie and he doesn't want to lie to her.

"I'll go to Sanderson. I'll take care of the cell phone. I'll tell our father where you are before I return to Mexico."

He can give her that.

CHAPTER 30

EMILIANO

WEDNESDAY, MARCH 29
8:16 A.M.

Emiliano watches Sara return to the place where they slept, pick her hat up from the ground, climb out of the gully, and walk away. He waits and waits, hoping that she will turn around and say good-bye, and when she doesn't, something wants to break in him.

When she is small in the distance, he looks around. There are rocky hills about three hundred yards to the east where he will run when he sees a car coming. It will take Sara an hour or so to reach the main highway, so there's no need to worry about a vehicle just yet. If only they had spent the night up in those craggy hills. How did the men find them?

He looks down and sees the footprints made by Sara's shoes. The men must have stopped their car at the end of the dirt road and simply followed his and Sara's footprints. How stupid on his part not to anticipate that. *Hope for the best, prepare for the worst,* as Brother Patricio liked to say.

The wounded man is making little whiny sounds like a baby who's tired himself out from bawling. Emiliano takes a deep breath. An agave cactus with red flowers blooms nearby. He kneels next to it and carefully cuts one of the pads from the joint. He grabs the pad with his thumb and index finger, taking care not to touch any of the protruding thorns.

When he gets back to Lester, Emiliano digs his knife from his pocket and opens the blade. He uses the knife to tear away the man's pants up to his thigh. The leg is now uncovered from the upper thigh to the edge of his cowboy boots. Emiliano considers taking the boots off the man but decides to leave them on. The tight boot with its skinny point is probably slowing down the flow of blood.

Emiliano cuts the cactus pad in half and shaves off the edge so that the pulp of the plant begins to ooze. Then he rubs the viscous pulp on the wound. The gooey substance will ease the pain and slow the bleeding. He rubs gently around the edges first and finally presses the edge of the cactus hard into the bullet hole.

There's a long, muffled scream from Lester.

Emiliano can feel small pieces of shattered bone under the skin. The patella—he remembers the name from his first aid books—is mush. He folds Lester's jacket and places it on top of the rock supporting the middle of the leg. There is white spittle coming out of the man's mouth, snot from his nose, and tears from his eyes. Emiliano takes his knife and makes a hole in the sleeve of the man's denim shirt. From that hole, he rips out a large swath of the shirt and uses it as a bandage to press on the wound. The blood is flowing slower now, but still flowing. The man's got maybe one hour before he goes into shock and then a coma. Two hours, if Emiliano keeps pressing on the wound. Emiliano sits on the ground and pushes down on the bandage.

Lester opens his eyes, looks at Emiliano's legs stretched out next to him, and says weakly, "Your sister . . ."

Lester's words, his face, everything about the man reminds

Emiliano of his own ugliness. He has no intention of speaking, but the words come out of him. "Went for help."

"Why?"

"She wanted you to live."

Lester sticks out his tongue to moisten his lips. Emiliano reaches for the bottle of water and pours a few drops into the man's mouth.

"Guy I work for. He said . . . get the cell phone. Finish the girl. Let the boy go."

"Someone hired you."

"No. A favor to . . . some big shot in Juárez. I follow orders. He said to take his nephew . . . Joe. That guy. Back there. Ran away. He's a coward."

"And you are?"

"No. Not a coward. Worse. Your sister . . . she's so pretty."

"Shut up."

"I'm sorry. Couldn't kill her. So pretty. That . . . saved her. When you think about it."

Emiliano watches Lester. It's confusing. It's like seeing evil and some kind of goodness and innocence all rolled into one, inseparable. Lester opens his mouth to take in more oxygen. Any moment now Emiliano expects him to stop breathing. Instead, he sees the man swallow hard. He's trying to speak.

"Don't talk," Emiliano says to him.

"Wall . . . wallet."

Emiliano reaches in the man's back pocket and takes out a bulging brown leather wallet. He shows it to the man. The man is dying. Emiliano is keeping him alive and he's worried about his money.

"Open."

Emiliano opens the wallet and shows him the bills. "All still there," he says bitterly.

Lester shakes his head. "Yours. Take it."

Emiliano closes the wallet and puts it next to the man's shoulder. "No want your money," he says with the best Mexican accent he can come up with.

"Please," Lester says. He speaks clearly for the first time. "Thousand dollars. For you. To get away. Please."

"No."

Emiliano lifts his hand and removes the wet bandage from the wound. He waits a few moments. There's no blood flowing. Then out it comes again, with more force. Emiliano rips another piece of cloth from Lester's shirt. He balls it and presses down again.

"I'm gonna die."

"Probably. Sooner if you talk."

"Just before I came. I went and got . . . these copper-tip bullets." Lester tries to laugh, coughs a few times. "My wallet. Please." Lester takes the wallet with one hand and opens it. He gestures for Emiliano to hold it while he lifts a picture out of one of the wallet's compartments. "My son."

The boy in the picture is about seven. The smile has a gap where a tooth is missing and the face is full of freckles. Lester struggles to speak. "Lives with his mom. Over in Odessa. His mom and me divorced . . . when he was four. She doesn't let me see him. Can't say I blame her." He shuts his eyes and then opens them. "I don't mind . . . dying. Hell, I been killing myself. I only mind for . . . him. Jimmy." Lester closes his hand around the picture. Then he closes the wallet and gives it to Emiliano. "If there was a way for you . . . to tell him. His daddy loves him.

There's a paper in there . . . with his momma's phone." He grabs Emiliano's hand. There's a desperate, wild look on his face. "I know I have . . . no right to ask. In my wallet, his mother's phone. Can you call her? Tell her Les wanted you to give a . . . a message for Jimmy. Tell him his daddy loves him."

Emiliano can feel in Lester's grip all the force remaining in the man. The grip is as insistent as his eyes. He notices the scars on the inside of the man's arm. Five or six old needle marks run along the contours of the veins. He thinks about Javier's piñatas.

"Please. Will you call him?"

Emiliano nods. Lester lets go of Emiliano's hand. Then he asks softly, "You still got your father?"

Emiliano shakes his head. The man will keep on talking until his last breath. "Yeah," Emiliano says, pressing hard on the wound.

Lester winces. "It wasn't supposed . . . to turn out like this. I wanted to be a real father to my Jimmy again. He needs to know . . . how much I love him. I don't want to die with him not knowing . . . You tell him. You promise. Promise me."

"I promise."

Lester thanks Emiliano silently and then closes his eyes. Emiliano stares at him. This dying man's last wish is for his son to know that he was loved by his father. He remembers the letter he read in his bedroom the night after the party. *You don't know how much it hurts me that you may think I don't love you,* his father wrote. He didn't believe his father's hurt was real when he read the letter, but maybe he was wrong.

Emiliano checks Lester's wrist and waits until he feels the almost imperceptible pulse. In one of the wallet's compartments, he finds a piece of paper with a telephone number. He takes it and puts in his pocket. He pours a small amount of water on the last piece of torn shirt and touches Lester's lips and forehead with it. He is about to cut another piece of cloth from Lester's other sleeve when he hears a sound. He stands.

Far away there is a white cloud on the east-west road.

Quickly, he bends down and wraps the wound as tightly as he can with the wet bandanna. Then he grabs his hat, the water bottle, and Hinojosa's cell phone and climbs out of the gully.

CHAPTER 31

EMILIANO

Emiliano kneels behind the rust-colored boulders and watches the white truck park on the side of the road. Sara gets out from the passenger side, and then the driver steps out—a woman, blond hair in a ponytail, olive-green uniform, not much older than Sara. Sara leads the way toward the gully, her eyes searching the rocks where he's hiding.

Emiliano sinks to the ground, relieved. Of all the people whom Sara could have flagged down, a park ranger is not bad.

A few minutes later the park ranger climbs out of the gully and runs to the white truck. She opens a tin box in the bed of the truck and takes out a green canvas bag. Emiliano watches her run back to Lester. Now and then the top of her head bobs above the gully edge as she ministers to Lester. Then he hears a hollow, throbbing sound, and when he looks up, he sees a helicopter approaching from the west. Emiliano climbs up a few yards and crawls under a rock overhang.

There, lying on his stomach, he watches the red-and-white helicopter touch down in a swirl of pink dust. The woman with the ponytail waves at the three men in the helicopter. Before the blades have stopped turning, two men carrying a stretcher with an aluminum suitcase on top jump out of the helicopter and run toward Sara and the park ranger.

How long does it take to lift a man onto a stretcher? Hours go by, or so it seems, before Emiliano sees the group make their way to the shallow end of the gully. Lester is covered with a gray blanket, a clear plastic mask on his face and an IV bag on his chest. He must still be alive. They walk, slowly, deliberately, in single file: the men carrying the stretcher, the park ranger, and finally Sara. Just before they emerge from the gully, he sees Sara take something from her back pocket and place it quickly under a rock.

The helicopter lifts up from the ground, rotates slightly in place, and disappears with a roar. Sara and the park ranger shield their eyes from the dust. When the helicopter is in the distance, they get into the truck. The ranger makes a U-turn and the vehicle moves slowly away. Emiliano crawls out from under the overhang and stands so that he can follow the truck until it's out of sight.

"Good-bye, Sara," he whispers.

Emiliano climbs down the hill and walks to the rock where Sara placed the object from her pocket. He kneels down and picks it up. It's a map of Big Bend National Park, which she must have found in the park ranger's truck. He checks both sides, and at the bottom, he sees Sara's scribble.

Ranger Sandy Morgan. Going to sheriff in Alpine,
Texas. Then Border Patrol for asylum. Be good.

He has been holding back tears since the first time Sara walked out of the gully, but now he lets them flow. Who is there to see or hear him? A buzzard circles above him. It smelled Lester's blood and came hoping for a meal. It is so quiet out here. The ground is warm.

Since when did he become such a crybaby? Tears are valuable liquid he will need.

Emiliano wipes his eyes and nose with the sleeve of his shirt and spreads the map on the ground. He can follow the original plan, the one they had before they saw the black car, and walk parallel to the main road until he runs into the hiking trail clearly marked on the map. Or he could take a shortcut through the mountains behind him and save maybe five hours of walking. That is, if he can walk in a straight line. But there is no such thing as a straight line where there are mountains and canyons.

He takes out his knife, finds north on the miniature compass, and then finds a mountain east of that point to use as a landmark. If he walks in the canyons, there's no way he can get lost as long as he walks east. Even assuming the compass is off by a degree or two, he will still reach the highway that leads to Sanderson at a point beyond the Border Patrol checkpoint. Walking in the canyons will provide shade, and then he can walk farther and need less water than he will walking out in the open under the sun. The soft silt of a canyon's floor will be easier on his aching foot.

Another option flits through his mind: He can go back to Mexico the way he came. The road they traveled yesterday is right there in front of him. He can be in Mexico by nightfall, find a place to sleep in Boquillas, and then hitch a ride somehow to Chihuahua. From there he could take a bus to Juárez and mail the phone to Yoya. He is protected. Armando told him so and Lester confirmed it.

He stands, folds the map carefully, and sticks it in his back pocket. He looks in the direction where he last saw the white truck.

He made promises. To Sara—he taps Hinojosa's cell phone in his pocket—and to Lester, God only knows why. Of course, he's made promises before that he didn't keep. The Jipari pledge comes to mind. When he thought about the pledge, the night after the party when he was deciding what to do, he figured the pledge was a promise made to God, and thus meaningless if you didn't believe in God. But it comes to him here, as he watches the dust from the white truck, that all promises are promises you make to yourself. What happens when you don't keep a promise? Something in you begins to die. He'll send the cell phone and make the call for Lester, and then he'll go back to Mexico, where he belongs.

He turns toward the mountains and starts walking.

The fever starts two hours later. He knows it is a fever because the heat comes from inside him, and the heat continues even when he sits under the shade of a rock. The pain in the sole of his left foot is also getting worse and worse. When he takes off his boot, he sees a clear liquid coming out of two small punctures in the middle of a red welt. He presses on the swelling and the pain almost makes him scream. The liquid on his finger smells like the street where Javier lives. The fever, the swelling, the tenderness, the pus, the smell—all are signs of an infection. He pours water on his foot and cleans it with a strip of cloth he tears from his shirt. He wraps another piece of cloth around the foot, puts his sock and boot on, and keeps on going.

The next indication that things are terribly wrong comes after the sun sets. He has difficulty urinating. The color of the urine is a dark yellow and the liquid burns him. That's not good. He's losing more water through sweat than he is putting in. He knows that in addition to the infection—maybe because of it—dehydration has started, and unless he drinks more water it will continue. He unfastens the water bottle and examines it. Five or six very small swallows are left. His mouth would salivate in anticipation of taking that last drink, except his mouth has no saliva. Thirst is a painful, empty wanting. The thought of it expands in your brain until you can't think of anything else. As much as he wants a drink of that water, just a sip, a tiny sip to moisten his lips, he decides against it. He needs that water for tomorrow. What he has to do now is rest. Rest will not stop the process of dehydration, but it will slow it down. Nothing, except maybe an injection of penicillin, will stop the infection.

He sits and leans against the western wall of the arroyo with his swollen foot elevated on a rock. He takes out the piece of agave cactus that he cut before descending the arroyo and rubs the gooey side on the wound. He remembers telling the man Lester not to talk, but he wishes he could talk to someone now. Anyone.

The bottom of the arroyo has fine white sand. Water flowed through here sometime last century. There were times during his walk where the abundant plant life in the dry creeks gave him hope of finding a spring nearby. He stands on one leg and hobbles to the opposite edge of the arroyo. He picks up a piece of wood about a foot long. The stick smells like mesquite. Maybe it's the root of a tree that was carried by a flood. He goes back to his spot and begins to whittle the edge of the stick with his knife. When the end is finally pointed, he uses the stick to dig a small hole next to him. One time, the Jiparis camped in an arroyo similar to the one where he is now, and

Brother Patricio found water only a couple of feet beneath the surface. Emiliano digs and digs but does not find water. He has only succeeded in perspiring more of the precious and limited liquid in his body.

The fever is making him dizzy. He tells himself to be smart and be calm and simply rest. He lies down and watches the sky slowly darken. The first stars appear—all at once, it seems, as if someone realized it was time to turn a switch on. He is so thirsty. He is burning up inside and outside and someone is skewering his foot with a hot iron. Where is Sara now? Did Perla Rubi know what would happen to his sister when she told her father where they planned to cross? What is Perla Rubi's father's name? He can't remember. That's not good. He can go back to Juárez because he is protected. Armando told him as much. Today was a humid day. It shouldn't be so humid in the desert. Humidity prevents the body's sweat from evaporating, so your body makes more sweat. That never made any sense to him, but it's in all his survival books. There are lots of things that don't make sense. When dehydration gets really bad, a person can't even cry. Or rather, they can cry but tears don't come out. Crying without tears, what's that like? He cried this morning. Stars can make a person want to cry for some reason. It's probably because you feel so small out here, so forsaken. The light from that star, one of the stars that makes up Orion's belt, took more than a thousand years to reach him. What is the name of Perla Rubi's father? He can't remember. That's not good.

Better close his eyes and sleep for a couple of hours. The only way he'll make it at this rate is to walk in the cool of the night. He's sleepy and the stars in Orion's belt are trembling. It feels as if he's going to fall into the sky. Is it dizziness he feels? Nausea? He wants to vomit, but what is there to vomit? That's not good. He shuts his eyes. A coyote barks four times and then lets out a lonely howl. Another one responds. Emiliano wraps his hand around the sharpened stick. He's so sleepy. Just two hours and then he walks. Find Polaris. Follow it. He won't get lost if he follows the North Star.

A raindrop falls on his forehead and then another lands on his lips and his tongue licks the sweet moisture. When you are very thirsty you can taste the otherwise unnoticed flavor of water. It is sweet but not too sweet, bitter but not too bitter, like the perfect ratio of lemon and honey. It is a flavor that is both indescribable and absolutely right. Emiliano opens his mouth to receive the raindrops that are now falling one after another, like pearls in a necklace that has come undone. The drops soon turn into a torrent and Emiliano begins to gag with the water entering his mouth and throat and lungs. He tries to rise, but the water pushes him down. He hears muffled thunder, and then a rushing current crashing through the arroyo sweeps him up as if he were no more than a twig and slams him against protruding boulders. A crooked mesquite tree has somehow found a way to grow sideways from the walls of the canyon and Emiliano reaches for it and manages to hold on to a branch. He pulls himself up and hugs the slim trunk of the tree. But he can feel the water rising and soon it is up to his chin and Emiliano will drown unless he somehow makes his way to one of the top branches. He pulls himself up as high as the tree will bear his weight, and when he looks down, he sees a hand rise from the water and grab a lower branch. Then another hand reaches up and latches on to Emiliano's ankle. Javier's head bobs up from the water, gasping. How did Javier get here? The tree is not strong enough to support the weight of two people and it is bending and cracking as Javier manages to get a grip on Emiliano's arm. Emiliano pulls his arm loose, but Javier grabs Emiliano's leg again. Emiliano tries to shake his leg, shake him off, because what else can he do? They both will die if Javier doesn't let go. Isn't it better for one person to die than two? Javier holds on tighter, pleading, but Emiliano has no choice but to kick Lester in the face. Lester? Where did Javier go? It doesn't matter, he's got to kick himself free. He kicks Lester once and then again harder and then the branch Emiliano's holding snaps and Emiliano falls into the roaring water and now it is his father holding him. It is his father's hand that is keeping him from being swept away by the powerful current. His father is holding on to him with one hand and holding on to Lester with the other and Lester is holding on to Javier, who is holding on to what remains of the mesquite tree. It is Javier's grip on the tree and Lester's grip on Javier and his father's grip on Lester that is keeping him from drowning.

Emiliano opens his eyes. Where is he? The sun is shining on his face. He sits up and looks around. There on the opposite wall of the canyon is the exact mesquite tree that appeared in his dream. It must be almost noon if sunlight is reaching the west side of the canyon. Emiliano tries to stand but his legs are weak. He crawls over to the east wall, where there is shade. He unfastens the water bottle from his belt, unscrews the top, and drinks the last gulp of warm water. His forehead is moist with perspiration. The damn dream made him sweat. Great! That's just what he needed: to lose his precious sweat on a dream.

Emiliano places his hand over his heart, puts two fingers

over the aorta in his neck, and counts to ten. His pulse rate is about a hundred beats per minute, about forty beats faster than normal for his athlete's heart. That's not good. And the fever is worse. The only good news is that the pain in his foot is gone. He bends his leg to look. The skin surrounding the place where the cactus needles entered has blanched and has a leathery texture. It feels dead. He presses hard to make it come alive again. Finally, the pain returns, along with a dark green substance coming out of the wound that is thick as glue and smells like decomposed flesh. How could this have happened to him? He's stepped on cactus needles before. He has been on longer hikes in higher temperatures and never reached the same stage of dehydration that he's in now. Maybe it has something to do with the fight with Lester. The adrenaline that shot through his body when he saw Lester walk away with Sara, the sheer rage needed to choke the living daylights out of him, all of that weakened his system. How else to explain the exhaustion, the rag-doll condition of his body? Rosario's rag doll was so beautiful. Brother Patricio told Javier where to find Lalo so he could sell his piñatas, unstuffed, and also Rosario's doll. He closes his eyes and sleeps.

He is dying. This certitude comes to him as soon as he opens his eyes and sees the indigo sky. Somewhere out there, the sun is sinking into a horizon he cannot see. He is dying. It's a fact as solid as the rock he leans against. He knows the symptoms of dehydration and has ticked them off one by one as they came. If dehydration doesn't kill him first, the infection in his foot will. It's no longer an infection. The putrid smell coming from his foot can only be gangrene. There's a kind of gangrene that travels fast. Fast. Fast and quick like the days of his life.

He read somewhere that a great peace descends upon you during the last few minutes before death. He hopes that happens, because he doesn't want to die with this restless, prickly heaviness in his chest. It's not fear of dying. It's sadness and shame and something else he can't name. He knows where the sadness comes from: the sorrow that Mami and Sara will feel when they don't hear from him. He wishes he could prevent their suffering, but he is as powerless over that as he is over everything else. He's in a small canyon with walls only slightly taller than he is, but they might as well be the burning cliffs of hell for all that he can climb them. If only he could make it to the surface, where it's more likely someone will find his body. His mother and sister would prefer the closure of knowing he was dead to never knowing what happened to him. He remembers when the Jiparis went to the outskirts of Juárez with other groups to search for bodies of Desaparecidas—the wrenching sorrow on the mothers' faces when they were told that their daughters' remains were found, but also, something like gratitude.

He's not someone who likes to analyze himself, wondering why he feels this or that. It made Brother Patricio happy to tell him the real reasons behind his actions, and Emiliano let him do it, because what other sources of fun did the poor man have? But that kind of spinning of the mental wheels is not for him. Even on his long, silent hikes with the Jiparis, his thoughts dwelled on his handicraft business, the tasks that needed to be done when he got home. Strategizing about business and making money was where his mind found its best groove. The one exception was when images of Perla Rubi overwhelmed his brain and other things. But even that didn't stop his careful calculations on how to win her heart. Perla Rubi. He searches for the force that tied him to her every day, from the time he woke up until the moment he fell asleep, but it is gone. Where did that force go? He makes an effort to remember the kiss she gave him at her mother's party, but the memory is made of cardboard, has no flesh, no life.

Now, bereft of any tomorrow, he turns his gaze inward to the loud hurt in the middle of his chest. It began as a small bruise, now that he thinks about it, a discomfort he chose to ignore. When did it start? When Javier told him he would help him, if that's what he wanted. When he knew without a doubt that Perla Rubi was responsible for the men in the black Corvette. When Sara found out he was associated with bad people and he wanted to go back anyway. And now here it is, a wound so big it clamors to be healed. It's sadness and shame and something else he can't name. Like the time he threw his largest marble at Paco's face and the gash on his forehead was so big he had to be taken to a hospital. The remorse and then the desperate need for Paco to forgive him—that's what he feels now, only worse.

It is the wishing that hurts the most. He wishes he would have told Sara the conversation between him and Mr. Esmeralda that night in his room when she asked for details. He wishes he would have said no when he realized that he was asking Javier, an addict, to work with drugs. He wishes he'd never driven that Mercedes. He wishes he would have stuck to his humble but good dream: Joel's motorcycle, and eventually a shop where he sold folk art made by poor kids. He's suddenly overcome with an immense sense of waste: wasted time, wasted opportunity, wasted life. Lester back there wanted his son to know that he was loved. The time he could have spent loving but didn't, that's the waste that was killing Lester. The same waste that is killing him now. He is afraid for the first time. Not of dying but of dying like this. It can't be that he will die like he didn't get what life was about. He just didn't get it. He knew it once. How did he forget? When did it happen?

The image of the brown manila envelope comes to him. He sits next to Sara at the kitchen table and watches Mami open the envelope. She hands the papers over to Sara, her eyes clouded with tears. Sara reads in silence for a few moments and then hugs Mami. Emiliano picks up the document and reads the top line: PETITION FOR VOLUNTARY DIVORCE. The anger started then and there, and everyone assumed that in time it would go away, but he made sure it didn't. He kept it alive. That anger turned to wanting more, to be more and better than his father. But he was never better, was he? What did his father say in that letter? *I'm not perfect but at least I can say I'm not a criminal. I want to do well doing honest work.* The man, his father, a flawed human being like any other, chose to be and do good, as best he could.

"All right," he says. "All right. I got it."

How can the body produce tears when the only liquid left is blood? He feels the last drop of liquid in him streak down his cheek. He crawls on his stomach to the middle of the canyon, where there's more of a chance someone will see him, and when he gets there, he sees two flashes of orange-tinted light in the sky one right after the other.

He turns on his back. The North Star comes out first, even while the sky is still a dark blue. He manages to keep his eyes open long enough to see the Milky Way spread from one end of the universe to the other.

Then his eyes close.

CHAPTER 32
EMILIANO

FRIDAY, MARCH 31
11:45 A.M.

The first word he hears is in English.

"Hello."

Is English the language spoken in heaven? Or maybe he's in that other place where hearing English makes more sense. The fact that he's thinking and even cracking little jokes to himself must mean he's alive somewhere. He's afraid to open his eyes.

"He's coming to."

The face he sees is brown with black eyes, thick eyebrows, pretty. It reminds him of the clay nativity set with the Mexican-looking Baby Jesus that his mother takes out for Christmas. The woman in front of him looks like the Virgin Mary. Then another face appears. This face is worn out, deeply tanned, unshaven; the hair is sparse and white; the blue eyes are so light you can almost see through them. A Joseph of sorts?

"How you doing?" He recognizes kindness in the man's gruff voice.

There's a clear plastic bag with transparent liquid hanging from a wooden coat hanger on the wall and a plastic tube running to his arm.

"Glucose," the man explains. "And penicillin for the foot. Lupe here hooked you up."

Emiliano looks around the room. A noisy fan oscillates on a wooden table next to him. The walls are made of dark wood. There are pictures of people standing in front of adobe houses, some of them on horses. An old-looking rifle hangs on one of the walls. Someone shot at him with a pistol. Who? When was it? Not too long ago. He closes his eyes.

He feels a woman's soft touch on his arm. It must be the pretty woman—Lupe. Lupe is a nice name. It's short for Guadalupe. Still with his eyes closed, he feels his bare chest. His rosary is gone.

"Looking for this?" Lupe opens his hand and drops the rosary in there. Her smile reminds him of Linda Fuentes, his first crush. What about Perla Rubi? Her smile was not like that. It was more cautious, more controlled somehow.

"Pressure's going up," he hears her say a few moments later. "He'll be all right. Change the bag when that one's empty, just like I showed you. Don't let him drink too much water at once. I left some pills in the kitchen. One every four hours until they run out. Keep draining that foot. Call me if the fever goes up again."

"Thank you, Lupe. I'd like to pay you for this."

"I'll send you the bill." The way she says it, Emiliano knows she never will.

The last thing he thinks about before he falls asleep is the white truck with his sister in it disappearing down the long dirt road.

The old man's name is Gustaf, but Emiliano doesn't know whether that's his first name or his last name.

"My name is Gustaf," he says, the first time Emiliano is

fully conscious. Then the man shows him a one-gallon plastic milk bottle and tells him to pee in it until he can make it to the toilet down the hall. One good thing about the old man is that so far he isn't much of a talker. He comes in, puts a bowl of soup on the wooden chair next to Emiliano's bed, looks at him for a few seconds, and then leaves. Or he comes in, squeezes Emiliano's foot until he can barely endure it, and changes his bandage, all without uttering a word.

On the second day, the old man is sitting on the wooden chair, pulling the needle from his arm, when Emiliano decides to speak.

"I have to go."

Gustaf doesn't say anything. He's concentrating on the needle. After he pulls it out, he rips the adhesive tape from Emiliano's arm in one quick movement.

"You speak English," Gustaf says, not looking at Emiliano.

"I have to go," Emiliano repeats.

"Go where?"

"Number two."

"Ah! Get up, then."

Emiliano pulls the sheet back. He's wearing boxer shorts for the first time in his life. He's suddenly embarrassed that someone, this man or the woman named Lupe, must have seen him naked.

"You soiled the ones you had on," the man says, moving the wooden chair out of the way. "It happens with heatstroke. The body gets rid of what it don't need no more."

Emiliano sits at the edge of the bed and waits until he can feel his legs. He tries to stand but he has no strength. There's gauze around his left foot.

"Gotta keep draining that. We almost got all the yuck stuff out."

"Was it gangrene?"

"You know your first aid. Lupe said it was the start of something called wet gangrene. But we caught it before it took hold."

The man grabs his arm and pulls him up. Emiliano hops on his right foot. When he walks out of the bathroom, the man is no longer there. There's a wooden crutch leaning against the wall. Emiliano hobbles back to the room where he's been lying and looks out a small window. Gustaf stands in what looks like a corral. He's got a straw hat on and is trying to get a rope around the neck of a skinny horse. Emiliano can't help but laugh when he sees the horse wait for the man to get close before skittering out of the way. Then the man and the horse and the corral start spinning and Emiliano stumbles back to the bed.

When he wakes up again, it is dark outside. At the foot of his bed, he finds an undershirt, another pair of boxer shorts, a long-sleeved cowboy shirt with pearl buttons that snap on, a pair of denim pants, and white cotton socks. Beside the clothes is a towel, a bar of soap, and a toothbrush still inside a plastic package. A pair of flip-flops lie next to the bed. The message seems to be that he should take a shower, brush his teeth, and get dressed. He sits up and then stands carefully. He can walk without the crutch if he doesn't put too much pressure on his left foot.

After the shower, he finds Gustaf in what looks like a living room, sitting in a reclining chair, watching television. He has a TV tray in front of him and is eating something with a spoon out of a plastic bowl. Next to the bowl there's a glass of water and a bottle of hot sauce. Gustaf barely looks at Emiliano when he comes in. "Help yourself to some stew," he says with a movement of his head toward the kitchen.

Emiliano walks to the kitchen and ladles stew into a bowl next to the stove. He opens a cabinet and finds a glass, which he fills with water from the faucet in the kitchen sink. He finds a spoon and puts it in the stew, and then he stands still, not knowing where to go. There's a small round table with four chairs in the kitchen, and he begins to walk toward it when Gustaf shouts: "Over here."

In the living room, Gustaf motions to the TV tray by the sofa and Emiliano sits down. The old man doesn't say much, but it's not as if he's rude or unwelcoming. The TV is ancient a tiny round screen encased in a huge wooden cabinet. Emiliano studies the scene on the TV. A big bulldozer is pushing earth around. Then the face of a man who looks a lot like Gustaf appears, shouting, "No guts, no glory!"

"Damn fools!" Gustaf says. "They out in Alaska. More than one hundred thousand dollars they spent already getting themselves there and renting equipment and what have you, and all they got is a few nuggets of gold."

Emiliano finishes his stew and then, during a commercial, he asks, "How you find me?"

Gustaf digs in his chair until he finds a remote. He turns down the volume. "There's this one horse who I swear is out to end my days. I got him four summers ago at an auction over in Marfa. Cost me all of two hundred dollars. Every year he finds a hole in the fence and heads for those canyons. This year I was ready to let him be, let him get eaten by the coyotes, serves him right. Ornery creature. Never been able to put a saddle on him.

I was chasing him again like an idiot when I saw the buzzards circling the way they circle when they see a good meal. Figured the damn horse finally got what's coming to him. So I went to where the buzzards was to make sure. Instead I found you. The horse climbed down the canyon and was just standing there, a few yards from you, didn't even flinch when I lassoed him. I put you on his back and brought you here. Called Lupe, she's a nurse over in Sanderson, and she brought you back to life."

Emiliano waits a few moments. The gold-digging show comes back on but Gustaf doesn't turn the volume back up. "I came from Mexico," Emiliano says.

"You don't say."

The old man's mischievous grin makes Emiliano smile too. Gustaf turns up the volume and they watch in silence. When the show is over, Gustaf pushes the TV tray to one side and stands up. He tosses the remote on the sofa next to Emiliano. "Guess I'm going to turn in. Turn off the lights when you're done." Gustaf stops at the entrance of the hall that leads to the bedrooms, turns around, and walks back toward Emiliano. He sits on the edge of the reclining chair and folds his hands. "I went through your pockets. Hope you don't mind. I thought maybe I'd find an address or something. Found a funny-looking bag with a cell phone. It's in the desk drawer in your room. There was a map of the park in your back pocket with Sandy Morgan's name. I know Wes Morgan, Sandy's father, so I called him."

"My sister gave me the map."

"That must be Sara. Sandy picked her up?" Emiliano nods. "Wes is representing her asylum case. He's got her going to the West Texas Detention Facility in Sierra Blanca where he thinks she has a better shot. Wes is a fine lawyer. Your sister's in good hands."

Emiliano sits up, feels his heart knock against his chest.

"One other thing. Lupe called this morning. She says a man showed up at the clinic asking if they knew of any undocumented Mexicans that mighta been found out in the desert. Lupe didn't tell him nothing. He gave her his name anyway just in case she heard something. Bob Zapata. Been in Sanderson for a few days, I guess." Gustaf waits for a response from Emiliano. When he doesn't get one, he continues, "You know him?"

Emiliano waits. Then, softly: "My father."

"I know a little bit about a father not knowing where his son is, so I can tell you. That man's worried about you. He's hurting to see you."

Silence.

"Well, he's staying at the Desert Air Motel. There's a phone book in the drawer next to the forks and knives. If you want to call him, you can call him. If you want to stay, you can stay. I could use the help around here. Good old hard, honest work. Or go back to Mexico. It's up to you."

The old man stands up and limps slowly away.

"Do you know where I can send an e-mail?" Emiliano asks before he leaves the room.

Gustaf turns and nods. "I got a computer in my office. It don't move around, so if you need to use it, you gotta do it in there. Don't be looking at any naked people."

After he leaves, Emiliano stands, picks up his bowl, spoon, and glass, and cleans them in the kitchen sink. Then he goes to Gustaf's office. Gustaf's computer is even older looking than his television. Tomorrow he'll send an e-mail to Yoya and ask for an address where he can mail the cell phone. He examines the pictures on Gustaf's desk. In one of them, a much younger Gustaf and a boy about Javier's age are on top of a black horse. The boy's tan hat is too big for him so most of his face is covered. All you can see is that he's laughing. That reminds Emiliano, he promised to call Lester's wife. What was Lester's boy's name? Jimmy.

Emiliano makes his way outside through the kitchen door. He walks away from the house in the direction of the corral he saw out the window of his room. The dome of the universe is black and has more stars than Emiliano has ever seen before. There are so many stars up there that it looks as if someone carrying a tray tripped and spilled a few million. If Sara or Mami looked up at the sky now, they would see the same stars. Tomorrow, after he calls Lester's wife, he'll take care of the other promise he made to Sara. He'll call his father and tell him about Sara's asylum petition so he can vouch for her. Then what? *Good old hard, honest work. Or go back to Mexico.* Gustaf's words. That's the choice he needs to make.

Emiliano locates the Big Dipper and then traces an imaginary line until he gets to the five brightest stars in the constellation Cassiopeia. He's always liked that constellation. Brother Patricio taught him how to find it during their trip to the Sierra Tarahumara. But the night has to be dark for Cassiopeia to be seen.

Maybe there'll be a park in Chicago where the stars of Cassiopeia will shine.

ACKNOWLEDGMENTS

I would like to thank Marcos Paredes of Rio Aviation and Jen Peña of Jen Peña Photography for sharing with me their love, knowledge, and experience of Big Bend National Park; Ramon Santini for his company and friendship as we explored this most beautiful park; Joseph Borkowski for his general guidance on IT issues; and Sara Fajardo and Nuestras Hijas de Regreso a Casa for helping me to see with greater clarity the beauty and pain of Ciudad Juárez and its people. I am forever grateful to Faye Bender, my agent at the Book Group, for her unwavering faith in my work, and Cheryl Klein, my editor at Arthur A. Levine/Scholastic, who continuously makes me a better writer and person.

ABOUT THE AUTHOR

Francisco X. Stork is the author of six novels, including *Marcelo in the Real World*, which received five starred reviews and won the Schneider Family Book Award; *The Last Summer of the Death Warriors*, winner of the Amelia Elizabeth Walden Award from ALAN; *The Memory of Light*, which received four starred reviews; and *Irises*. He lives near Boston with his family. You can find him on the web at www.franciscostork.com and @StorkFrancisco.

THIS BOOK WAS EDITED BY CHERYL KLEIN
AND DESIGNED BY CHRISTOPHER STENGEL.
THE PRODUCTION WAS SUPERVISED BY
RACHEL GLUCKSTERN. THE TEXT WAS SET IN
SABON, WITH DISPLAY TYPE SET IN NEUTRA.
THE BOOK WAS PRINTED AND BOUND AT
R. R. DONNELLEY IN CRAWFORDSVILLE,
INDIANA. THE MANUFACTURING WAS
SUPERVISED BY ANGELIQUE BROWNE.